BAREFOOT IN THE PARKING LOT

VINEET VERMA

THE BODY

JANUARY 17

Andy stepped out of the restaurant with his buddies, Stephen and George, shuddering as the chilly winter air hit him. He already missed the previous week of uncharacteristically warm temperatures. Trying to ignore the numbing feeling, he reminisced instead about the scrumptious meal he had just enjoyed at his favorite joint. That was worth enduring a little cold weather. Plus, he couldn't have asked for better company. There had been plenty of laughter at the table as they had swapped stories, amusing anecdotes about coworkers and tall tales about which hot woman had eyed who, the kind of talk you would expect from twenty-somethings who had downed a few drinks.

Once he had located his car in the parking lot, Andy's attention was diverted towards a pair of long, shapely legs that made their way up into a short, pink skirt and an attractive rear. As he admired the view, his mind raced, wondering whether the rest of that body was just as mind-blowing. Wondering whether he should talk to her, if he would be lucky enough to get her number. Those thoughts were interrupted a few seconds later, when the woman turned to glance at him. In another split-second, she turned back and disappeared into the darkness. In that instant he had caught the terrified expression on her face. He couldn't figure out what had scared her so. It was not like he and his buddies were so hideous. In fact, judging from the attention he received from the ladies, he was quite confident it was just the opposite in his case.

There was something on the ground where she had been. Probably the reason she was there. Intrigued, he walked over, his friends by his side. A man lay motionless on his back with a serene look on his face. Next to him was an open wallet, various membership cards, and a syringe. At first, Andy thought the man was asleep. But then he recoiled in horror and receded a few steps. There was no movement in the chest. The man wasn't breathing. Andy was one of the lucky few who had never experienced death firsthand, and in this moment, he realized how different it was from seeing it on screen.

"Whoa, dude, is he ... dead?" asked Stephen in a trembling voice as Andy bumped into him. Now, Stephen did have experience with death, having attended his dear grandpa's funeral when he was nine. It was a memory that still spooked him to this day. Fearing the worst, he had moved behind Andy for protection, George right beside him.

"Sure seems like it," replied Andy. He stood there staring for a while before morbid curiosity took over, and he walked back to the body.

"You think he's a junkie?" he asked, pointing to the syringe.

"I don't think so. I mean, he looks clean and healthy. Besides, both his sleeves are buttoned up. He couldn't have been shooting himself up," added George.

By now, Stephen had mustered enough courage to join his friends.

"Hey, he reminds me of ... Is he really ...?" he said as he bent down to reach for the cards. Almost simultaneously, George went for the syringe.

"Guys! Wait! Don't touch anything!" commanded Andy, proud that years of watching crime shows was finally paying off. He was well aware they shouldn't be touching anything at a crime scene. "Let's call the cops."

Andy noticed the disappointment in his friends' faces but was relieved to see they were in agreement. He dialed 911 and calmly provided all the details – as calmly as he possibly could, considering that his heart was still beating a thousand times a second. Then they waited patiently in the quiet of the night. No one was in the mood for tales anymore.

———

MAYA TURNED INTO HER DRIVEWAY, noticing the empty garage as the door opened. That meant her husband, Jay, was not home yet. He routinely worked late but was usually back by 10:00 p.m. Tonight he had not responded to her texts and calls.

She eased the car into the garage and closed the door behind her. Once in the kitchen, she made one last call to Jay which went unanswered. A sense of unease was building up inside her. She called Anjali, her next-door neighbor and closest friend. Anjali didn't have any information about him. But talking to her, and hearing her reassuring voice gave Maya some comfort.

Jay didn't have any close friends. His entire social circle consisted of Maya's friends and a couple of his colleagues. She decided to call Robert next. She didn't know him well, but enough to know that he would remember her. They had chatted briefly when they had met at his party a few months ago. It was also because of that shindig that she had his number saved in her phone. She dialed and got to the point after a quick exchange of pleasantries.

"Jay is not home yet. Is he with you?"

"We were in a meeting earlier, but he left around seven p.m. Haven't seen him since."

"Oh. Did he say where he was going?"

"No. But he looked really chipper. I assumed he was going home. Don't worry, he'll turn up soon."

Maya downed a tall glass of water. It had been a long, tiring day. One of those days that had demanded a lot from her. Now that she was home, she felt the need to wind down. She went to her room to change and get ready for bed. But Jay had still not turned up by the time she was done. Weilin. She could ask Weilin. But was it too late? She peered out the window at her neighbor's house. The lights were still on. She took the chance. But the call was fruitless. Weilin had not seen or heard from him either.

Maya plopped on the couch and started browsing Netflix, something to keep her occupied while she waited. It didn't work. She was halfway through an episode of *Narcos* when she drifted into sleep.

A while later she was awakened by the doorbell. Through the fog of sleep, she stared at the screen for a few seconds before she remembered why she was there. She turned off the television and checked the time. 2:00 a.m. So late. She took a deep breath to calm her nerves as she got on her feet and walked over to the door.

SUNNYVALE HOMICIDE DETECTIVE Paul Conley was seated at his desk, trying to wrap up a case report with a giant bag of Doritos open by his side. It was almost 10:00 p.m. on a Wednesday night, and he was itching to get home. He pictured himself crashing into bed, wrapping himself in the fluffy comforter, and drowning in deep slumber. Little did he know that this blissful picture would remain just that. He would not be getting much sleep tonight.

"Still working?" asked his partner, Angela White, as she settled into the chair across from him.

"Just wrapping up the Hinkley report," he replied as he reached into the bag for the next handful.

Angela's face broke into a mischievous smile.

He turned to her and said, "What? I'm hungry," knowing full well why she was smiling. She never missed an opportunity to rib him about his appetite.

"Hungry? I saw you scarf down a double cheeseburger and a bunch of fries an hour ago."

"Well, work makes me hungry. I need my snack."

"Your belly says it all," joked Angela.

Paul's gaze moved to his gut, an unwelcome addition to his tall and once lithe body. He had let himself go in the last year, slipping into unhealthy habits. Handling heartbreak was not easy. Unlike him, Angela had maintained herself well. He envied her tall, slender figure, but he knew she had earned it with her healthy lifestyle.

"Hey, I thought you Californians weren't into body-shaming."

"Is that why you left Kansas? Too many jokes about your belly?" Angela continued, referring to his move from Wichita the previous year.

Angela's phone rang before he could respond to her jibe. She hung up after a couple of minutes and turned to him. "No rest for the weary, Paul. Homicide downtown. Gotta go."

Paul sighed. Someday he would make it home early and get some sleep. Too bad that day wasn't today. He picked up his jacket and walked out with Angela.

SUNNYVALE HAD A SMALL DOWNTOWN, anchored by Murphy Avenue, which was a short street with small businesses, primarily restaurants, on either side. It was a great place to hang out after work and on weekends. It had been a low-key area until a few years ago when the transformation had begun. The street was spruced up, and a bunch of commercial office buildings, housing, and additional retail had sprung up around the core. They drove past the "Historic Murphy Avenue" sign at the entrance and into the parking lot of the popular restaurant, Sha Sha Shawarma. The body had been found in a dimly lit alley adjacent to the lot.

By the time they got there, the yellow crime scene tapes were up, and a few people in the distance were trying to catch a glimpse of the action. Angela spotted a cop standing next to what she assumed was the corpse. She hadn't seen him before. Probably one of the new recruits. Shawna from Forensics stood next to him. Before she had a chance to walk over, Angela saw Officer Spencer coming towards her. He was one of the junior cops in the department, one of many that had been hired in recent months to replenish the depleted ranks of Sunnyvale DPS. In spite of those efforts, they were still severely understaffed.

"Good to see you, John. You in charge here?" she asked.

"You bet. As you can see, we sealed it off quick. Only the necessary folks are in here."

"Who's with Shawna?"

"Oh, that's Ashton. He started earlier this week. Quite an exciting welcome for him."

"Ah. You his FTO?"

New recruits were paired with the more experienced officers who played the role of Field Training Officer. Having a junior officer like Spencer performing FTO duty underscored the dire situation with staffing.

"Yep. Lucky me."

"Sergeant Drake didn't show?"

"Nah. Sarge is swamped."

Angela didn't like the sound of that. She had hoped at least one senior, competent officer would have made it to the scene.

"I see. Who found the body?"

"A group of three guys. They were returning from dinner at a nearby restaurant when they spotted him."

"Where are they now?"

"There," John pointed towards an area outside the yellow tape. Angela could see them leaning against a car, all of them glued to their phones.

"They're standing there all by themselves? No one watching them?" asked Paul, sounding agitated. "They could be discussing what they saw, influencing their stories. And what if they're already posting this stuff on Facebook and Twitter?"

John threw up his hands. "Hey, I know, I know. But this is all I've got, okay? It's only Ashton and me. We did tell them to not talk about it or post anything on social media."

"Like they'll listen. Anyway, Ashton there doesn't look very busy, does he?" said Angela.

Spencer took the hint and motioned to Ashton, who trundled over to the witnesses to keep them in check while Angela and Paul walked over to the body.

Angela took a few moments to observe the corpse. The dead man lay flat, face up, and looked peaceful. She would not have suspected foul play based on this image. She recognized the face, and for a fleeting moment the thought that he was gone made her sad. Her gaze moved from his face to the full-sleeved button-down shirt and jeans he was wearing. She noticed some stains on his shirt but nothing that indicated blood. She couldn't see any sign of a blow to the body either. In fact, the only thing that jumped out at her was his bare feet. Now, why would someone like him be barefoot outdoors on such a cold evening, she wondered. She moved on to the syringe that lay next to his head. It seemed empty. Next to it was an open wallet with his driver's license on top. The license confirmed her initial observation. It was Jay Sharma, the CEO of Intelligent Systems.

Shawna turned to Angela and said, "You can't tell from his face, but it was not a good way to die."

"What happened?"

"You see that syringe, right? I found a corresponding puncture wound on the back of his neck. In addition to that, he has scars on the front which indicate he was Tasered. You will see those if you move his collar."

"So he was first zapped with the Taser and then injected with something?"

"Can't tell yet which came first. But the injection alone didn't kill him. He must have thrown up in reaction to whatever was administered. Then came the pulmonary aspiration. Since he was incapacitated, he couldn't do much when he puked, and he choked on his vomit. You will see it if you open his mouth."

"Is that why his shirt has some stains? It's from the vomit?"

"Yes. Someone went to a lot of trouble to wipe it off his face and neck. All that remains are the stains. We will know more after the autopsy. Plus, we will be analyzing the contents of the syringe. There's not much in there, but I expect it should be enough to tell us what it is."

"Any prints on the syringe?"

"There are a few. We will check on those. And the wallet and license too."

"No signs of a struggle?"

"No. I didn't find any defense wounds, and his fingernails are clean. But as always, I can only confirm it after the autopsy."

"Sure. Any idea why his feet are bare?"

"Quite likely someone stole his footwear."

"Odd."

"It's been known to happen. Especially if he was wearing something expensive."

"But the socks too?"

"Maybe he didn't wear any."

"Maybe," said Angela, not quite convinced.

Angela and Paul put on gloves and booties. Since it was dark, they knew they would have to come back the next morning for a more thorough inspection. But they wanted to get a head start with a preliminary scan. Angela started inspecting the body, while Paul left to conduct a meticulous search of the area. She began with the feet, which, not surprisingly, were cold. They were also clean, indicating that he had not walked around barefoot. It seemed like someone took his footwear after he was dead. Next, she moved his shirt collar and found the Taser scars Shawna had mentioned. She continued with the front and then the rear of the body. A short while later she was done with the inspection. Her findings aligned with what Shawna had reported.

Meanwhile, Paul had combed the area. It was difficult to tell what was relevant to the crime since it was a well-traveled section, and anyone could have dropped something at any time. But he played it safe. He found a gold lapel pin that said "Purdue." He bagged it. That was all he had to show for his effort.

Once the search was complete, Angela joined him.

"Find anything?" she asked.

"Just this."

He showed her a clear evidence bag with his shiny find inside it. She took a closer look.

"It's a lapel pin from Purdue University. Gold. Found it two feet away from him," he said, indicating the corpse with his head.

"You think our killer might have dropped it?"

"Possible. Or it could be his," replied Paul, jerking his head towards Jay again.

"You know, I didn't find any keys on him. No car keys, no house keys. No cell phone either."

"The killer took those too?"

"Sure looks like it."

"Should we talk to the three musketeers now? All the businesses around are closed. Canvassing will have to wait until tomorrow."

"Yes. Let's do that. We should fingerprint them, too."

"You think they had something to do with it?"

"Probably not. But we should cover all possibilities."

Angela walked over with Paul to the guys who had found the body. Ashton was still watching over them dutifully. The witnesses nodded in agreement as she explained that they would be questioned and fingerprinted at the station. She hadn't expected it to be so easy. In the meantime, Paul instructed Ashton to maintain the crime scene until further notice. While Angela would have preferred to keep the witnesses separate, she didn't have enough resources to do so. Besides, she figured they wouldn't be able to say anything in the back seat of the car without the detectives hearing it. Angela and Paul drove off, with the guys huddled together in the rear.

TEN MINUTES LATER, they were back at the station. Angela recruited Officer Patrick to watch the witnesses and get them through fingerprinting.

"Which one of you made the call?" she asked.

Andy raised his hand. She and Paul walked him over to an interrogation room. Once settled in, she asked him to explain the events. He began by telling them how they had stumbled upon the body. Angela's ears perked up at the mention of the woman.

"This woman, what did she look like?"

"It all happened so fast. I didn't get much of a look. All I remember is, she was wearing a short skirt. Pink. Nice legs ... and ass," replied Andy, a smile reaching his lips as he savored the memory.

She had an urge to knock some sense into the guy. Here she was interviewing him for a murder investigation, and all he could do was talk dirty. Typical male.

"What about her face? Hair? Did you get a look? Something we can use to identify her?" she continued, keeping her annoyance in check.

"Umm ... not really. Like I said, it all happened so fast. One moment she was there and then she was gone."

"So you had time to admire her legs and her ass but you didn't see her face?"

"Hey, hey, it's not like I'm some pervert, okay? She had her back to us, so that's all I could see. She only turned for an instant before she ran away."

"Think harder. Try to remember. Any little information could be useful," Angela urged him.

Andy thought for a few seconds, then replied, "Well, I think she was blonde, shoulder-length hair. And she was white. Quite tall, guessing around six feet."

"That's good. Anything else?"

"Umm ... yeah, she was wearing a jacket. I think it was red. And she looked scared. That's all I remember."

"Not surprising she was frightened. Caught in the act. Which way did she run?"

"Through the alley. Away from the parking lot."

"I see. Do you have any connection with Purdue University?"

"No. Why do you ask?"

"Never mind. Thanks, Andy. Those are all the questions we have for you at this time. We have your contact information and may talk to you again if needed. Please don't discuss this with anyone else or it could hinder our investigation. Here's my card. Call me if you remember anything else."

Paul walked him back to Officer Patrick and returned with Stephen. Angela interviewed him, and then George after that. Unlike Andy, who seemed quite confident, they were nervous. It was something she often saw with people who hadn't directly encountered law enforcement before.

Stephen and George hadn't seen much. By the time they had looked, the woman was gone. They described their experience with the body, but it was nothing more than what Andy had told them. They had never been associated with Purdue either. The detectives walked out to the lobby with George. After confirming that all three had been fingerprinted, Angela allowed them to leave.

"That was promising. We have to find this mystery woman. We find her, and we might have our killer," she commented once they were gone.

"Quite a generic description, though. I hope we can find her on some security camera around there, assuming she actually exists. If these guys had anything to do with the murder, they could have made it all up."

"Right. If she does exist, we should find her prints on the evidence we found."

"So, what next?"

"Next-of-kin notification. It's sad he's gone. He was quite an icon."

"You knew him?"

"Not personally. He was the CEO of Intelligent Systems. One of the heavyweights in the AI space."

"And by AI you mean artificial intelligence?"

"Yes."

"How do you know so much about the tech industry?"

Angela smiled. "Kinda difficult to escape it, living in Silicon Valley. Plus, I was once a budding techie myself, so I try to keep up with what's going on."

"How did you end up as a cop?"

"I had taken some computer classes. Realized I didn't enjoy coding all that much, even though I love technology. My dad was a cop. I just drifted in that direction."

"Good for Sunnyvale DPS. Speaking of which, why the heck are we so perpetually understaffed?"

"Believe it or not, it's gotten a lot better since you joined. Not as good as, say, ten years ago, but still an improvement. Most cities in the area went through a rough time financially during the downturn. Law enforcement budgets were easy targets for balancing the numbers, what with all the outrage over huge overtime and pension payouts to cops. They didn't realize that after such big cuts to compensation, there wasn't as much incentive to risk life and limb. So cops left in droves, either to departments that still offered good money, or to better-paying professions. It even affected the number of recruits coming in each year. It's only after we hit rock bottom with crime that they decided to do something about it and restore some benefits. Then the recruiting drive began."

"Ah, and that's how I got in."

"Yes. We got lucky there. Even more so since you got a lateral transfer in as a detective. Under normal circumstances you would have had to start over in patrol."

"Boy, that's a relief. Thanks for the history lesson. Now, does Jay have any family?"

"Yes. A wife. No kids. We'll have to notify her."

"This wife, what does she look like?"

"No idea. You think she's the woman these guys saw?"

"It's possible. Spouses are usually *numero uno* on the suspect list."

"Yeah. Let's see if this one has anything to hide."

"Let's go, then. You have the address?"

"I admired the guy. Wasn't stalking him," replied Angela with an amused smile. "We'll have to look it up."

Paul chuckled. "Sure, let's do that."

THE WIFE

JANUARY 18

It was exactly 2:00 a.m. when Angela and Paul walked up the path to Jay Sharma's front door in San Jose. It took a few attempts at the doorbell before they heard movement inside. The door was soon opened by a beautiful Indian woman with sleep-laden eyes and an inquisitive look.

"Mrs. Sharma? I am Detective Angela White, and this is my partner, Paul Conley, from Sunnyvale DPS."

"DPS?"

"Department of Public Safety," clarified Angela, as she held out her badge.

"Oh. I see. Is that your police department?" asked Maya, a hint of anxiety in her voice.

"Yes, it is."

"What is this about?"

"May we come in? It will be better if we talk inside."

"Yes, please." Maya stepped aside to let them in.

Once they were all seated, Angela began.

"Well ... I'm afraid I have some bad news. We found a body, a man, and we have identified him as Jay Sharma."

Maya gasped in shock, her hand moving to her mouth.

"Jay ... Jay is dead?"

As she said this she leaned forward, her hands shaking. Her eyes welled up.

Angela rushed to comfort Maya. Paul brought her a glass of water from the kitchen. By now she was sobbing inconsolably. Her reaction was quite typical and not surprising. The unexpected demise of a spouse would be shocking for most people. But the suspicious detective in Angela wondered whether it was all an act.

"We are so sorry for your loss."

"How ... how did he ...?" Maya tried to ask in-between sobs.

"It's still early to be sure, but it appears he was poisoned."

"Poisoned?! Who would do such a thing?"

"We don't know yet. But we are trying our best to find out."

"Where ... where did you find him?"

"Behind one of the businesses in Sunnyvale downtown."

"Sunnyvale?"

"So you didn't know he would be going there today?" asked Angela, noting the confusion on Maya's face.

"No. He works in Milpitas. Didn't tell me about any plans after work."

"Perhaps he went there for a business meeting?"

"It's possible. But he didn't mention anything."

"Mrs. Sharma, did your husband have any enemies, anyone who would want to hurt him in this way?"

"Enemies ... no, no one I can think of. Are you sure this ... this was not ... not a random attack?" asked Maya, wiping her tears as she did so.

"We can't say yet. I assume he carried cash and credit cards?"

"Yes. In fact, he liked to carry a lot of cash. And he had some premium credit cards. Were those missing?"

"Yes. You should cancel the cards as soon as possible."

Maya nodded and took a sip of water. Angela hesitated before probing further. This was supposed to be a next-of-kin notification.

Would it be appropriate to interview her now? She decided to continue, since Maya was a lot more composed and didn't seem to mind the questions.

"Anything else of value we should know about?"

"A Rolex. And our wedding ring. That was expensive."

"We didn't find either. Another odd thing. His feet were bare."

"Bare? He always wore white socks and New Balance sneakers," Maya replied with a baffled expression.

"I see. Mrs. Sharma ..."

"You can call me Maya."

"Maya, did you notice anything unusual today?"

Maya considered the question for a moment, then responded, "No. It was like any other workday. We both dashed off early, and I expected him to be back by the time I got home. Usually I get home before him, but it was a busy day."

"Did you try to locate him once you got home?"

"Yes. I tried to call and text him but got no response. My neighbors didn't know anything either. Robert, his coworker, said Jay left work at seven p.m."

"Seven p.m.? And he is sure about this?"

"That's what he told me. I didn't probe further."

By now the strain was beginning to show on Maya's face. Angela glanced at Paul. He nodded to acknowledge that they should end the interview and let Maya recover.

"Maya, thank you for your cooperation. We understand this is a very difficult time. Is there someone we can call for you?"

"No, thank you. I will be fine."

"Are you sure?"

"Yes. Don't worry."

"Well, don't hesitate to contact us if you have any questions," said Angela as she handed her card to Maya. "Oh, one last thing. What car did Jay drive?"

"Tesla Model S. White."

"License plate?"

"He had a custom plate." Maya spelled it out.

"We'll look for it. Do you have a key?"

"There is a spare key here, but didn't you find one in his pocket?"

"No. No keys."

"He should have had the car key and the house keys. Never left home without them."

"Hmm ... Those were likely stolen as well. We would advise you to change your locks right away. If the killer knows where you live, he could easily get inside."

"Thank you. I will do that. You referred to the killer as a 'he.' You are certain a man did it?"

"Oh, no, no. It's just that most killers are men, so that came out of habit. We are open to all possibilities at this point. By the way, we didn't find a cell phone either. I assume he carried one?"

"Yes, he had an iPhone. So that was stolen too?"

"Quite likely."

"Oh. When can I see Jay?" asked Maya in a feeble tone.

"He is still at the crime scene. The coroner will move him once we are done there. We will contact you once he is ready. It could take a few days since we have to conduct an autopsy. That's when you can formally identify the body."

"And then I take him?"

"Yes."

"I see." Maya's voice grew feebler.

Angela wanted to ask for the car key but figured they had pushed Maya enough. She would try to locate the car first and get the key later.

AS SOON AS the detectives left, Maya crashed into bed, her body aching. She wanted to sleep, but the empty space in the bed next to her reminded her of her loss. She tried to get it out of her mind and finally, around 6:00 a.m., she fell asleep.

But it didn't last long. At 8:00 a.m. her doorbell rang. It was Anjali, looking concerned, even more so once she saw Maya's teary-eyed face.

"Maya, is everything okay? Did Jay get home last night?"

"They found him, Anjali. He ... he is dead," Maya struggled to say as she broke down in tears. Anjali gasped, but she composed herself and stepped in to comfort her. Maya related what had happened. Anjali stayed a while until she was sure her friend was doing okay.

"Maya, I have to get back to the kids. Mukesh has to leave for work. But do let me know if you need anything. I will check back on you later."

"Thanks, Anjali."

The door shut and Maya was all alone again. She called her boss and told him what had happened. She wouldn't be going in to work for a few days. Then she crawled back into bed to get some sleep, tears still flowing.

BREAKING NEWS
JANUARY 18

Angela arrived at the station, tired and bleary-eyed. She hadn't slept much, but she had a job to do. Besides, a new case always excited her. It was a challenge which she gladly accepted. But she wasn't prepared for what she saw once she stepped out of her car. A mob of reporters rushed her way as she started walking towards the station.

Angela sighed. This was the reason she hated cases involving famous people. Everyone was interested, with the media at the top of the pile. It had only been a few hours since the body was found, and it seemed like the entire world knew about it. Social media was buzzing with the news. Even some local newspapers had managed to squeeze in a small piece about it, though it had been late for their print window. All this, without any formal release of information from DPS. She was soon surrounded by the mob, but she tried to keep moving.

"Detective White, do you have anything to say about Jay's murder?" asked one reporter.

"Do you know who did it?" another one called.

"Is it true that his throat was slit?" Angela rolled her eyes as she continued walking. Where did that come from?

There were a few more inane questions before she stopped and replied. "There's a press conference at eleven a.m. You will get your answers there." Then she rushed into the welcoming arms of the building.

She walked to the chief's office and waited outside while Cynthia Crowley wrapped up the call she was on. Paul soon joined Angela, looking quite puffy-eyed himself. On the bright side, they would not have to be at the press conference. Cynthia was going to handle it herself, allowing her team to focus on the case. Hence the meeting, to brief her on the status. Ordinarily, they would be having this discussion with their lieutenant, but they didn't have one at present. He had retired around Christmas, and the vacancy had not yet been filled.

Cynthia had been promoted to chief the previous year, capping an impressive thirty-year career at Sunnyvale DPS. Angela would be the first to admit that Cynthia was not perfect, but she admired and respected the woman for her accomplishments and the way she ran the organization.

The door opened, and the Chief let them in. Standing at only five foot two, she was physically dwarfed by Angela and Paul, but she had a personality that commanded authority. She got right to the point as soon as everyone was seated.

"So, what do we have so far?"

Angela briefed her on what had happened and the evidence they had found.

"Any leads on the pin?"

"I checked Jay and Maya's online profiles, but I didn't find any connection to Purdue."

"So it could have been dropped by the killer?"

"It's possible. We will be considering it as we weigh suspects."

"And the woman in the pink skirt?"

"Nothing yet. We will check for security cameras in the area to see if we can identify her."

"What about the wife?"

"Can't rule her out just yet."

"Okay. Keep up the good work. This one is going to be in the spotlight, so we need quick progress."

"You got it, Cynthia."

"Fine. Now I have a press conference to attend. Keep me posted."

SOON THE DETECTIVES were back at the crime scene. It was important to inspect it in daylight to ensure nothing had been missed the previous night. The body, however, had been moved for the autopsy. Angela was surprised to see Officer Patrick managing the scene, given that he had been working the night before as well.

"Yeah, I know. Ended up with some shitty shifts this week." He smiled as they walked up. "You didn't get much sleep either, did you?"

"Story of my life," replied Paul with a chuckle.

Once again, they put on gloves and booties before stepping into the scene. Angela took the left half and Paul the right. The search was thorough but did not turn up anything new. Next, they moved on to the canvass. They each picked one side of the street and went to every business to find out if anyone had seen anything the night before. This took a little longer, with the eateries getting busier as it got closer to lunchtime. Paul did his best to block out the sight and aroma of the food and focus on the questioning. Unfortunately, no one had anything to report. A lot of the businesses didn't even have surveillance cameras. Of the few that did, some weren't turned on. Just having one in sight was considered enough of a deterrent. By the end, they were able to get copies of video from three establishments. They would be reviewing these once they returned to the station.

MAYA

JANUARY 19

Angela and Paul parked the car in front of Maya's house. It had been dark when they were there last, and Paul had not noticed the charming neighborhood. Every house on the street had its own unique identity. The distinctive architecture made quite an impression, giving each house a grand appearance. The streets were lined with lush green trees and well-maintained bushes. In the distance he could see the beautiful hills kissing the clouds. He would have loved to live in a place like this. But a home here would cost upwards of a million dollars. He knew it wouldn't happen in this lifetime.

The door was open before they got to it. Maya stood there looking drained, and her bloodshot eyes indicated she had been crying. Angela winced, knowing she was imposing on her too soon. But there was work to be done. A one-day break would be all Maya would get.

"Good morning, Maya. How are you holding up?" asked Angela.

"It has been difficult."

"That's understandable, but you do see this is important to make progress?"

"Yes, yes, I do. Would you like some tea? I was making some for myself."

"No, thank you," replied Angela before Paul could answer. She knew he wouldn't say no, but she wanted to keep it professional.

Disappointed, he scanned the kitchen. It looked like any regular kitchen, with the usual appliances. The sink was beginning to fill up with dishes. Not surprising, considering what Maya was going through. There was a large fruit bowl in the center of the island. Next to it stood a box of oatmeal. The plastic lid had a huge cut, as if someone had slashed it with a knife. He found it odd and was about to ask her about it, when he saw that she had caught him looking at it. She bit her lip and turned away as soon as their eyes met. He made a mental note of it and moved on. Something to think about after the interview. In the meantime, she quietly picked up the box and put it in the pantry.

Angela and Paul seated themselves on the couch while they waited for her. The house was tastefully decorated, and they surveyed it in admiration. There was a fireplace across from them. On the mantel stood a few photo frames with pictures of Maya and Jay. One from their wedding day. Another of them bundled up on what looked like a ski trip. They seemed happy.

A few minutes later, Maya was back with a piping hot cup of tea. Paul enviously observed her sipping it.

"Maya, how long were you married?" started Angela.

"A little over eight years."

"No kids?"

"No. We never got around to it."

"I know we asked you this earlier as well, but during the time you were together, do you know of anyone who might have wanted to harm your husband?"

Maya thought about it for a few seconds. "Well, the truth is, he wasn't easy to get along with, and he did annoy a lot of people. But I don't think it was reason enough for anyone to murder him. Except, now that I think of it ..."

"Yes, what is it, Maya?"

"There's Mark Harrison. You know, the SmartCloud CEO. He

had a falling out with Jay a few years ago, even threatened to kill him one time. But he's a nice man, and I don't think he would follow through. It was probably said in the heat of the moment."

"Ah, yes. I remember reading something about a lawsuit. Can you refresh my memory?" asked Angela, more for the benefit of Paul.

"Jay used to work with him at SmartCloud. Then Jay left to start his own venture in the same space. Mark felt blindsided and accused him of stealing IP, but Jay denied the claim. It infuriated Mark, and he filed a lawsuit, which was settled in Jay's favor last year. They had had huge fights on the subject before, but after this result it was crazy. That's when Mark made his threat."

"What did he say, exactly?" Angela tried to keep her excitement in check. This could be another promising lead.

"Oh, I don't know the exact words he used. Jay told me about it. He was actually happy. Happy to see Mark squirm."

"I see. This could be important. We will follow up on this. Anything between them after that?"

"No, that was the last I heard about Mark. Of course, Jay would gloat about his victory all the time, but I don't think he ever communicated with Mark directly after that."

Maya hesitated a bit, then added, "There is one other thing I think you should know about. It may mean nothing, but I might as well tell you."

"Go on. Every detail is important," urged Angela, intrigued.

"Around six months ago, Jay started receiving threatening letters in the mail, roughly one every two weeks. They were all about how someone would murder him because of something he had done in the past. At first, it looked like a practical joke, and we laughed it off. But they continued. He was unconcerned. I was worried. I asked him to report it to the police, but he destroyed them."

"So you don't have any of the letters?"

"No, but I did manage to take a picture of one before he burned it. And I was able to save one of the envelopes."

Maya unlocked her phone and started looking for the picture. While she searched, Angela asked, "Are the letters still coming?"

"No, they stopped last month. But I wasn't concerned anymore. I mean, why would someone go to the trouble of sending so many over the course of months? Doesn't make any sense. If this person was serious, he would have just done the deed without the drama." Maya stopped swiping. "Ah, found it."

She showed them the picture. It was a letter size sheet of white paper, which had been folded in half and unfolded. Nothing was written on it. Instead, everything was spelled out using letters cut out of a newspaper. Angela's first impression was that it was a prank. The letter said:

"Your time has come. Repent before it is too late. You will die for your sins you scumbag."

"How about the envelope? Can we see it?"

"Yes, I have it right here. I kept it ready since I knew you would return."

Maya walked over to the kitchen and took the envelope out of the top drawer. Once she was back, Angela noticed it had been crumpled and straightened out. There was no return address. Jay's name and address was on a printed label. The letter had been mailed from Oakland on November 13 the previous year. Any chance of viable fingerprints was slim, thought Angela. Still, she had Maya place it directly into an evidence bag.

"We will get this checked for prints and any other useful clues we can find. Do you mind sending us the pic of the letter?"

"Sure, I will send it now. Sorry about the condition of the envelope. I picked it up after Jay had crumpled it and thrown it in the bin."

"Don't worry about it. Were the other letters also mailed from Oakland?"

"Oh, I didn't check. I was so focused on the content."

"It's okay. Don't you find it interesting that they stopped a month before the murder?"

"Yes, I suppose so. In hindsight, I feel they might be related. But I still don't understand why someone would go to all that trouble."

"Maybe they were warning him, or rather, threatening him to do something or make amends for something. When nothing happened, the writer punished him. In any case, we will follow up on this as well. Were there any other threats of any kind? Any phone calls, emails?"

"None that I know of."

"Maya, now this might be a delicate question, but I have to ask. How was your relationship with Jay?"

"You think I had something to do with his death?" asked Maya, her eyes widening as her hand went up to her mouth.

"Please don't take it the wrong way. It's a standard question we have to ask. We have to cover all bases."

"Well, to be honest, he wasn't easy to live with. I can't say I was in love with him anymore. I guess he would say the same. But we managed somehow."

This was an interesting development, thought Angela.

"Did you hate him?"

"Hate him? At times, yes. But not enough to kill him, if that's what you mean."

"How did the two of you meet?" Angela tried a different approach.

"The traditional Indian way. It was an arranged marriage. My parents found his ad on a matrimonial website and invited his family over. I wasn't interested in getting married at the time, but once I met him, I liked him. He was handsome and dressed smartly. I felt an instant attraction. We saw each other often after that, and as I got to know him better, I started falling in love. He was an intelligent man and could hold a conversation on a variety of subjects. I accepted his proposal, and we got married a few months later."

"So you did love him at one point?"

"Yes. It's hard to believe, but I did. Things were different once we were together, and I got to see the real Jay. He was quite self-centered and uncaring. Didn't help with the chores at all. I was always so exhausted, managing work and home. It was crushing. He changed for the worse as time went by, and he became more successful in his career. There was an arrogance, an irritability. A total disregard for other people's feelings. So, yes, I found I couldn't love him anymore."

"That sounds awful. You must have fought a lot."

"Yes, we did. But nothing out of the ordinary. Most couples fight."

"But you still miss him?"

"What kind of a question is that? Of course, I miss him. He was still my husband and we had a life together!" replied Maya, raising her voice. Angela thought she saw her eyes well up a little.

"Is that why you never had children?"

"Why is that relevant?" asked Maya, showing no signs of backing down.

"It's okay. You don't have to answer that. Maya, where were you that evening?"

"So we are back to this? I didn't kill him. And if you really want to know, yes, I didn't want to have kids with him. It wouldn't be fair to them being raised in this environment."

"I understand. But please answer the question. Where were you?"

"I was working late and didn't get home until around ten p.m.," replied Maya, the calm returning to her voice.

"Anyone who can confirm that?"

"Yes, several members of my team were with me. You can talk to them."

"We certainly will. By the way, did either of you have any association with Purdue University?" Angela knew the answer from her own research but wanted to confirm it.

"Purdue? No, we both studied at universities in California."

"Thank you, Maya. We don't have any more questions. Sorry to bother you so soon after this tragedy, but we didn't have a choice."

"I understand. I am available in case you think of something else. Oh, and here is his car key. Did you find the car?"

"Not yet," replied Angela as the detectives made their way out the door.

ANGELA'S PHONE buzzed as soon as they stepped out of the house. She took the call, then turned to Paul after hanging up. "Quite a coincidence. We just got the car key, and they found Jay's car. It was still in the parking lot at Intelligent Systems."

"Hmm ... interesting. Did he Uber it to Sunnyvale? Or did someone drive him over?"

"Another possibility is that he drove there in his own car. We didn't find any keys on him. The killer could have driven his car back to Milpitas to throw us off track."

"That's one theory. Quite possible he was meeting someone there. We need his cell phone records, may get some leads. How is that coming along?"

"Phone company's dragging their heels as always. But I have my contact working on it."

"Skirting the laws?"

"Well, the way I look at it, we have the subpoena and are legally entitled to that data. We play by the rules, and we get them in a few weeks. Or I use my method, and we get them in a few days. We don't have the luxury of weeks. This will help us make progress on the case. The key is to only document any of this formally after we have obtained the records legally. That way we don't get into any trouble."

"I like your approach. By the way, did you see the oatmeal box?"

"Uh-huh."

"What was the deal with that? She was worried we saw it."

"I don't know. Perhaps she did it out of frustration and was embarrassed. It's been a huge loss for her. People cope in different ways. I wouldn't worry about it."

"Just odd, that's all."

ONCE THE DETECTIVES LEFT, Maya closed the door and walked back inside. It was the second time this week she had been careless. It was quite unlike her. What was she thinking, leaving the oatmeal out? She resolved to be more careful from here on.

Talking about those early days with Jay brought back a flood of memories. The first time their lips had met, that electric feeling that ran through her. She had kissed before, but what she had experienced with him had been special. She remembered the time he had tried to take it to the next level, but she had refused, preferring to wait until they were married. And how could she forget her disappointment when she made love for the first time, on their honeymoon, only to discover what a lousy and selfish lover he was. To think she had saved her virginity for that. She couldn't help but think about Mohit, her neighbor and study partner back in India in her teenage years. Their platonic relationship had developed into something more when they had shared their first kiss during a homework session in her bedroom. Her mother walked in on them before they could take it any further. A severe tongue-lashing, and a month of stern treatment from her mother made her resolve to be a decent Indian girl and not give in to boys until marriage. What a terrible decision, in hindsight.

Wearily, she plopped herself on the couch. She had spent most of the previous day talking to her and Jay's parents. Breaking the news to them had been hard. They were understandably devastated. What made it worse was the fact that, due to their health problems, neither set would be able to visit. Maya had slept after those long, draining conversations. She had awoken later in the evening when Anjali had come over with a home-cooked meal. A steaming bowl of rice and lentils prepared with Indian spices. Simple food. Comfort food. Just like her mother would have made it. Maya had wolfed it down, so thankful she had such a caring friend and neighbor. Her phone showed a lot of missed calls from her friends and coworkers. The news was spreading. But she hadn't the energy to call back. It could wait a few days.

MARK HARRISON
JANUARY 20

It was a rainy, windy Saturday morning. Paul's mood matched the gloomy weather.

"I thought California had a great climate. Why did I bother moving?"

"Oh, don't complain. It's not like it rains a lot around here. We need it. Besides, everything looks so pretty."

"It's beautiful, yes. But I prefer enjoying it from my couch, not driving all over the place."

"You sound like my old man, Mr. Grumpy."

Paul laughed as he eased the car into one of the visitor parking spots in the swanky Los Gatos apartment complex. They were there to question Mark Harrison. He had said he would be home, since with the downpour he couldn't go golfing anyway. They ran over to the apartment to get out of the rain. It was a full minute before the door opened. Mark was in workout clothes, all sweaty. He was an imposing six foot two and in great shape for his forty-eight years. However, his face made him look older. Angela got the feeling something was troubling him, and the broad smile could not hide it. She made the introductions.

"Please come in. Sorry for the delay in getting to the door. I was burning off some calories on the treadmill. Helps work the stress off. A CEO's job is never easy."

The place was clean and tidy but minimally furnished. Some moving boxes were sitting in the corner, still unopened.

"You moving?" asked Paul.

"Oh, no. Those are from when I moved in last year. After the divorce. My ex is lording it over the mansion now while I survive here temporarily. Someday I will get done unpacking."

As soon as they sat down, Mark asked, "So, what do you want to know?"

"You knew Jay well?"

"Yes, quite well. We worked together for a long time. Unfortunate business. Huge loss," he replied. On getting no reaction, he added, "I really mean that."

"We hear you and he were close at one point, but then there was a falling out," said Angela.

"Yes, it was awful, what he did to me. He was one of the early employees at SmartCloud. I saw his potential and mentored him. He was crucial to our success. I liked him. Our families enjoyed hanging out together. But then he cheated me. Stole our IP and trotted off to start his own venture."

"But didn't the courts rule in his favor? That he didn't steal any IP. Intelligent Systems developed their solution independently, and your accusations were just a way to distract and financially bleed his startup?"

"Utter nonsense. Most of the time I don't think these legal folks know what they're talking about. Besides, Jay was a super smart guy, maybe a little too smart. He figured out a way to work it in his favor. I hated his guts after that."

"Enough to murder him?"

"What? No! Are you crazy? Why would I do that? Not worth it for me. I would rather kill in the marketplace."

"Where were you that evening?"

"Ha! So you seriously think I did it?" asked Mark, the color rising in his cheeks.

"Just answer the question. We know you threatened him."

"In the heat of battle, yes. That doesn't mean I would actually do it! I mean, the guy was gloating all around about how I was a liar and he had beaten me. That cheating scumbag."

Angela stole a quick glance at Paul. She was sure he had noticed it too. Was it a coincidence that Mark had used the term "scumbag" to describe Jay? Had he written the threatening note?

"Coming back to my question, where were you that evening?"

"I was at work till around six thirty, and then I went over to Sha Sha Shawarma for dinner. I was there till around eight. Then I came home."

"So you were in Sunnyvale downtown?"

"I know, so close to where he died."

"Were you with anyone?"

"Nope, not a soul. I drove there alone, dined alone, and drove back alone. Alas, no alibi. My sad little single life."

How convenient, thought Angela.

"We checked your bio. It says you graduated from Purdue."

"That is correct. Seems like a lifetime ago."

"Do you own a Purdue lapel pin?"

"Yes, I do. It's a beautiful gold one I bought a while back."

"Can I see it?"

"You a Boilermaker too?" replied Mark, referring to the school mascot.

"No, but this is relevant to the investigation."

"Oh. Sure, give me a minute."

Five minutes later he was back, minus the pin.

"It's the damnedest thing, I can't find it. I swear I wore it a few days ago."

"You lost it?"

"I don't know. Maybe."

"Is it this one?" Angela showed him the one they had found. It was in the evidence bag, so he took some time inspecting it.

"I'll be damned. Yes, that looks like mine. Where did you find it?"

"Right next to Jay's body."

"Oh," said Mark, his face reddening again. "I see where you are going with this. But anyone could own one. And even if it is mine, I could have dropped it at any time. I am in the area quite often, given that I work close by."

"You hated Jay. You threatened to kill him. You don't have an alibi, and we found your pin right next to his body. Looks fishy."

"I didn't do anything. Why don't you believe me? I repeat, I did not have anything to do with his death."

"Let's hope for your sake that you are telling the truth. But we will have to search your apartment."

"You kidding me? Do you have a warrant?"

"No. We don't. But it shouldn't be difficult to get one."

"Then go get it."

"This will go a lot easier if you give us verbal assent. Saves everyone time and effort. Surely as a CEO you appreciate doing things efficiently."

Angela could tell that her appeal had hit the spot. Mark soon confirmed it by agreeing to the search. To be on the safe side, Paul got the acknowledgement on video. The detectives didn't waste any more time and got to work. In the bathroom cabinet Angela found a bottle of Prozac prescribed to Mark. So, he was depressed. Was that the trouble she had read in his face? She continued the search. But an hour later they were done, with nothing to show for their efforts. They left the apartment, Mark's last words echoing in Angela's head.

"I told you I have nothing to hide."

MARK ENTERED the kitchen once the detectives departed. He filled a glass to the brim with water and downed it with big gulps. It didn't help. He decided resistance was futile and reached for the bottle of Macallan. It had been a while since he had completed his workout, but he was sweating again. They suspected him. If they kept digging, what else would they discover? The thought worried him as he chugged on the bottle, trying to find some peace.

THE NEIGHBORS
JANUARY 20

After talking to Mark, Angela and Paul headed to San Jose to question Maya's neighbors. It had stopped raining. But Paul still looked a little morose.

"What's eating you, Grumps?" asked Angela in an attempt to cheer him up.

"Thinking about Mark."

"What about him?"

"His divorce. He must have gone through hell. I know I did."

"I remember. You told me you were miserable. So miserable that you had to leave Kansas to make a fresh start here."

"Yep."

"I'm sorry. You never told me much more than that. Were you married long?"

"Fifteen years. To my high school sweetheart, Brigette," Paul replied with a far-off gaze, faint smile on his face. "Well, here we are," he continued as Angela parked the car in front of Anjali's house.

The detectives stepped out and walked up to the door. Angela went for the doorbell. She could hear music and some kids inside, and soon enough the door was opened by Anjali, looking harried. Two toddlers followed, screaming at the top of their lungs. The two girls appeared identical, and their smiles indicated they had been up to some serious mischief.

"Twins?" asked Angela. "They are so cute."

"Yes. But right now, they are little devils."

Angela introduced herself and explained why they were there. She noticed Anjali's face harden a bit as she let them in. The girls followed quietly behind, trying to be on their best behavior. A variety of toys was strewn all over the living room. The TV was on and playing some Bollywood song. Everyone on screen was decked up and dancing. It was a catchy tune, and Angela knew that under different circumstances Paul would have busted some moves by now. Anjali turned off the TV but was met with howls of protest from the twins. She caved and turned it back on, this time with lowered volume. Without the music the actors looked funny, as if they were uncomfortable and were trying to twist their way out of the discomfort.

"Sorry about the mess," said Anjali.

"Don't apologize, I assume one can be a handful. I don't know how you manage two."

"We survive," replied Anjali's husband Mukesh as he came down the stairs. They all seated themselves for the questioning.

"Do you know the Sharmas well?" began Angela.

"Very well. We are good friends," Anjali replied.

"And how long have you known them?"

"Around two years now. That's when we moved in. Maya was so welcoming."

"And Jay?"

"What about Jay?"

"What did you think of him?"

"Like I said, we were good friends. It's just that I am really close to Maya. We spend a lot of time together."

"When was the last time you saw him?"

"On the weekend. They were here for dinner Saturday night."

"And did everything seem okay?"

"Yes. As normal as ever."

"How would you describe their relationship? Did they get along well?"

"You don't think she had something to do with it?" asked Anjali, looking quite horrified.

"Mrs. Bhatia, it's a routine question. As you might already know, spouses are often high up on the suspect list."

"Well, in my opinion they got along well."

"And Mr. Bhatia, how about you? What did you think about the Sharmas' relationship?"

"Er ... I think they made a good couple," Mukesh backed up his wife.

"So neither of you thought they had issues? Any fights?"

"Not that I know of," replied Anjali. Mukesh nodded his assent.

"And she never told you about any problems? You said you are close. She must have discussed something with you?"

"No, nothing at all."

Angela could sense that Anjali was lying. But why? Was she trying to protect her friend? It didn't add up, considering that Maya herself had confessed about her marital problems. She decided to move on with the questioning.

"Did you notice anything unusual on the day of the murder?"

"No, it was like any other day. Only when Maya called me that night did I feel something was wrong. She was so anxious that Jay was not home and was not answering her calls."

"Around what time was this?"

"Um ... I would say sometime around ten, ten thirty."

"Do you know what time she got home that night?"

"No idea."

"And anything from her after this call?"

"No. We assumed everything was okay. But I did go over to check on her the next morning. That's when I found out."

"How did she seem that morning?"

"Distraught. As one would expect."

"Thank you, Mr. and Mrs. Bhatia. We don't have any further questions for now. If we do need anything later, we will reach out to you. Again, thanks so much for your time."

As Angela was about to turn away, she noticed the twins standing and smiling at her. She returned the smile.

"What are your names?" she asked.

"Zara."

"Sara."

"Those are beautiful names. See you now. Be good."

"Bye," said the girls in unison as Angela stepped out of the house.

———————

"SHE WAS LYING, WASN'T SHE?" said Paul as soon as they were far enough from Anjali's house.

"They both were. Amateurs. It was so obvious."

"Yeah. I don't think they had anything to do with it, though."

"I agree. Now let's see what this other neighbor has for us. It better be worth this drive to San Jose."

They walked past Maya's house over to the house of Weilin and Joshua Zhang. Strains of a beautiful piano piece emanated from the house. Neither of them could identify it, but they enjoyed the performance as they waited. It was a pleasant break from the somber task at hand.

The music stopped. The door opened to reveal a young girl of about ten. Behind her, an older woman approached. Angela introduced herself and explained why they were there.

"Please come in. I am Weilin. This is my daughter Lily."

Lily skipped back to the piano and resumed the piece as they followed Weilin into the pleasantly furnished living room. Joshua was seated on a couch, tapping away at his laptop. They exchanged pleasantries and got down to business.

"Have you lived here long?" asked Angela.

"Yes, almost fifteen years."

"And the Sharmas moved in around three years ago?"

"Oh, is it three years already? Yes, they have been here a while now."

"So you know them well?"

"Nah. We don't talk much."

"Why is that? Any trouble?"

"No, no. No trouble, but that's how life is in this country, right? People keep to themselves. Not like back home."

"So you wouldn't know about their relationship? Whether they got along well?"

"Oh, they were always fighting."

"How do you know that?" asked Angela as she leaned in. At least one neighbor was telling the truth about the fights.

"We can hear them sometimes. He is ... umm ... was loud when he got angry. And she can yell too."

"We noticed there is quite a distance between your houses. Do the voices carry that far?"

"You think I am lying?" asked Weilin in a stern tone. Her right eyebrow had moved up a notch.

"Sorry, that's not what I was implying. Just trying to clarify the details."

"You see, sometimes they have their windows open. If our windows are open too, we can hear them."

"Any idea what they fought about?"

"Oh, we didn't care. But the little bit we heard would be the usual arguments between husband and wife, nothing special."

"Did they have any fights recently? Around the seventeenth in particular."

"Oh, yes. That morning I was out in the backyard getting some lemons from our tree. That's when I heard them."

"It's winter. Were their windows open?" Angela was not entirely convinced. But she used a cautious tone, not wanting to rile up

Weilin again. She needed the Zhangs to cooperate and give her whatever useful information they had.

"It had been quite warm that week. In fact, I do remember closing the windows later that evening since it got cold again."

Angela nodded in agreement. Yes, she did remember the weather had changed that day.

"What did you hear?"

"That fight was different. It sounded like she accused him of an affair. And she said she would kill him."

"You sure that's what you heard?"

"Yes. But I don't think it means anything. I mean that's the kind of thing you say when you are angry, right? In fact, I told Joshua earlier this morning that I was going to kill him," laughed Weilin.

Joshua's face broke into a meek smile. "That's what happens when I leave my clothes on the floor."

Angela couldn't resist a smile herself before getting back to the interview. A threat was still a threat and couldn't be discounted under the circumstances.

"What happened after that?"

"Not much that I could hear. It sounded like he sped off in his car soon after that."

"Thank you for that information, Mrs. Zhang. We will check on it. Anything else different that day?"

"Well, just that she called me that night to ask whether I had seen or heard from Jay. I could tell she was worried about him. He wasn't home, and she couldn't reach him either."

"Around what time was that?"

"It was sometime after ten p.m. Not sure what time exactly. Soon after she got home, I think."

"Did she usually get home that late?"

"Sometimes."

"Thank you for your time. We have no further questions."

By this time Lily had moved onto a different piece. Angela knew this one. It was "Für Elise" by Beethoven. The notes flowed effortlessly, making their entrance at just the right moment and enveloping the listeners in their magical world. She was tempted to stay back and enjoy the performance. She could see Paul was enthralled too. But they had work to do.

"NOW, THAT WAS INTERESTING," remarked Paul once they were in the car.

"She confirmed about the fights. Something that Anjali lied about. I guess she wasn't worried about protecting her neighbor. Maya didn't tell us they had such a heated argument that morning. If she suspected him of cheating on her, I can see how she would be angry enough to threaten him. But was it enough for her to act on that threat?"

"Well, we just have to grill Maya about it, don't we?"

"Yes, we do."

MAYA AGAIN
JANUARY 21

Angela spent the morning attending Jay's autopsy at the Santa Clara County Medical Examiner-Coroner's office in San Jose. A fifteen-minute drive later, she was back at the station and walked over to Paul.

"We have the autopsy results. He died of asphyxiation. Choked on his own vomit like we suspected. The syringe contained a lethal dose of concentrated cocaine in a solution of liquid nicotine. His body reacted to the poison by throwing up. Even without the vomit, the poison would have killed him eventually."

"Interesting. I remember reading about this guy who poisoned his wife with liquid nicotine a few years ago. The cocaine adds a creative touch. Do we have a time of death?"

"Sometime between six p.m. and eight p.m. I guess that clears Maya."

"Not so quick. We haven't confirmed her alibi yet."

"Right. Let's not mention any of this when we question her today. I want to hear her side of the story after what Weilin told us."

Soon Angela was driving back to San Jose to meet Maya, Paul by her side. It was a bright, sunny day, and he had left his grump at home. She was delighted to hear no whining. It was one of the rare times of day when there was no traffic clogging 101-S, and they made it in under twenty minutes.

"You are looking a lot better today," she commented to Maya once they were inside.

"It was tough the last few days, but this morning is better indeed. We have a wonderful view of the hills from the bedroom window. I just sat there, gazing at the snow-dusted hilltops. That soothed me and helped take my mind off things. I love the snow. Have always loved it. My best memories of childhood are from a family trip to Pahalgam. It's a small town in northern India. It was the first time I saw snow. Oh, how excited I was. Such a beautiful place."

Angela began to get a little irritated as Maya rambled on. She wanted to get to business. But she figured, under the circumstances, Maya deserved some slack. The wistful look in Maya's eyes was difficult to ignore.

"You are living in the wrong state if you love snow," commented Paul.

"Oh, I don't think I could handle too much of it. But I like that I can make a quick trip to Tahoe or Yosemite if I crave it. We made these trips when we first got married, Jay and I. He was such a different person when we were on vacation. More relaxed, more patient. If it were up to me, we would always be on holiday. It's a pity we didn't do that anymore after that first year."

"We're on the same page there. I don't mind being on perpetual break," chuckled Paul.

Maya smiled. Then noticing Angela's serious face, she said, "I'm so sorry. Silly me, going on and on. You are here to talk about the case. Any progress?"

"We are still waiting on the autopsy results. But we did find his car," replied Angela, glad to be back on track.

"Oh. Where was it?"

"At Intelligent Systems."

Maya gave a confused look.

"I guess you're wondering how he got to Sunnyvale without his car?"

"Yes."

"We don't know yet. We will be keeping the car until the investigation is complete."

"That should be fine. I have my own car."

"In the meantime, we do have some more questions for you."

"Sure, go ahead."

"Last time, you said you and Jay didn't get along well and you fought a lot."

"Right. But nothing more than the usual arguments couples have. We had learned to stay out of each other's way as much as possible."

"So no major fights? No violence or threats?"

"No, nothing like that."

"We were talking to your neighbors, and we heard you had a nasty fight that morning. Something about an affair? And you threatened to kill him."

Maya bit her lip as her eyebrows furrowed. "Oh," she said. "Weilin is lying again. I don't know why she enjoys it so much. Nothing of the sort happened. It was a simple quarrel about the usual stuff. Nothing fantastic like she says."

"Maya, we hope you are telling the truth. Because we have other ways of finding out. And if we find out you are lying, it will look very bad for you."

"It *is* the truth. Surely you don't believe Weilin over me? How could she have heard anything? She wasn't here."

"We are just doing our job, Maya. Now, what did you mean when you said she was lying *again*?"

"Of course, she didn't tell you about the incident. Why would she? It would be so embarrassing for her."

"What incident?"

"She called the cops on Jay and me last year. She claimed she heard us fighting and was worried for my safety."

"And were you in any danger?"

"Not even close. When the cops arrived, we were enjoying a *Game of Thrones* binge. It was so awkward, having to tell them it was a false alarm. I see Weilin hasn't learned her lesson. She sure has a wild imagination."

"Do you remember the date?"

"No. It was a minor nuisance. Can't remember dates for that. Why don't you ask her?"

Angela made a mental note to follow up with SJPD about this domestic call. She hadn't found anything when she had done her research on the Sharmas. But she had only searched the Sunnyvale DPS database. She didn't have access to records from other jurisdictions.

"Coming back to the fight that morning. You didn't suspect Jay of cheating on you?"

"Does it really matter whether I had any suspicions? The point is, it had nothing to do with that."

"Well, it's a simple question. Did you think he was cheating?"

"No. I did not. Happy?"

Angela realized she was not getting anywhere with this. She wondered why Maya was so cagey. Perhaps she was playing it safe, waiting for her alibi to be confirmed first? Or was it the emotions building up from such a tragic event in her life? She decided to pick this up again after a few days, once she had more information from her investigation. She expected Maya would be much calmer then.

"Maya, one last thing. We need your fingerprints."

"Oh," said Maya, a mixture of fear and confusion on her face. "You still think I did it. You ... you need them now?"

"No. But we will be sending over a tech later today. Unless you prefer coming over to the station."

"Home is fine."

Interview complete, the detectives bid adieu.

"I AM SURE SHE WAS LYING," said Angela as soon as they were in the car.

"Why would she lie? She has a strong alibi."

"An alibi which we still have to confirm. And she doesn't know about the autopsy results yet. It would depend on our time of death estimate. She's trying to be careful."

"Maybe."

"First, I want to find out more about that night Weilin called the cops," said Angela as she placed a call to Officer Fielding at SJPD. Chris Fielding was a close friend, and they often interacted to cut the red tape and obtain information quickly. He picked up, and she explained what she needed.

"You got a date for me?"

"No, just the name and address. But it was sometime last year."

"That should work."

Angela could hear him typing furiously as he searched the database for the incident.

"Found it. It was August 7. Roberts and Jones were called out for a domestic disturbance reported by a neighbor."

"Awesome. What happened?"

"It says here it was a false alarm. They spoke to the couple, and everything looked normal. The Sharmas were watching TV turned up loud and figured that's what spooked the neighbor."

"And was it turned up loud?"

"Huh?"

"The TV. The officers would have heard it when they arrived. Was it that loud? Loud enough to startle a neighbor?"

"Good question. But the report doesn't say much else."

"Thanks, Chris. You have been helpful, as always."

"So, you treating me to lunch, or what?" asked Chris with a chuckle.

"Sure thing. Sure thing," laughed Angela as she hung up.

MAYA LAY IN BED, wide awake. The conversation with the detectives had left her feeling uneasy. She had lied to them about Jay's fidelity, but did she have to tell them everything? She was convinced it would be wrong to tell them about Gauri. That smart, caring woman who once worked with Jay at Intelligent Systems. It was roughly two years ago when Gauri had revealed the ugly truth about him. Even though Maya had suspected he was up to no good, she had been shocked by the revelation. Suspecting your husband was one thing, getting confirmation about it was something else. Gauri had detailed how Jay, once a trusted friend and coworker, had started harassing her, trying to kiss and grope her, friendly hugs turning into much more. Not knowing what to do, she had tried to ignore it. Then one day he had propositioned her outright, and she had decided that enough was enough. That was the day she quit her job and, embarrassed, stayed away from Maya as well. Until the day Maya had bumped into her at a bookstore and demanded the truth. Maya had felt outraged at first, spewing venom on Gauri, but once she had time to think about it, she had realized it was not Gauri's fault at all. The hapless woman was a victim, who, well aware of the toxic culture pervading the tech industry, knew that complaining to HR or going public with the news would only hurt her. A powerful man like Jay would emerge unscathed. Did Maya want to tell the detectives about her and expose her to unwanted scrutiny? No, it was a sensible decision to keep Gauri's secret a secret. Thinking through it all calmed Maya, and she was able to fall asleep after a while.

An hour later, she was awakened by a sound coming from the walk-in closet. She turned to her side and noticed Jay was not in bed. What was he doing shuffling around in the middle of the night? Perhaps he couldn't sleep. A disgusting odor hit her, as if she had just dived into a garbage truck. But she closed her eyes, trying to get back to sleep. Suddenly, she remembered – Jay was dead! What was making that sound then? Scared, she opened her eyes and saw a figure tiptoe across the room towards the door. She dared not move until the figure walked out of the bedroom, through the loft and started down the stairs. Then she got out of bed and silently closed the door, locking it. Maya dialed 911 and was relieved to get an immediate response.

"911 operator. What is your emergency?"

"I have an intruder in the house," she whispered, worried the man might hear her.

"I am sorry, ma'am, can you repeat?"

"There's an intruder in my house," louder this time.

"Is the intruder still in the house?"

"I don't know. He went downstairs. I am still in my room upstairs."

"And are you safe, ma'am?"

"Yes, I am fine."

"Do you know if he is armed?"

"I don't know."

"What's your address?"

She was about to respond when she heard something outside the room. Was it a creak? Was the intruder returning?

"Ma'am, what's your address?"

Maya moved through the bathroom to the walk-in closet before responding. She wanted to be in a safe position in case the intruder was outside. More importantly, she didn't want him to hear her. She responded with the information and was assured that help would be there in a few minutes. Then she waited, stomach fluttering and ears sensitive to the slightest sound.

While she waited, her thoughts drifted to the first time cops had shown up at her door. It was that summer night the previous year when she and Jay had had their massive row. They had been loud and vocal, with Jay taking it a step further by throwing things around. Sometime during the fight, they heard the doorbell. They stopped and cleaned up quickly, wondering who it was. Whatever problems they may have had, they agreed that they did not want any outsider to learn about them. She had composed herself and answered, shocked to find two SJPD officers outside. They had asked her if she was okay, stating that they had received a domestic disturbance report from a neighbor. She had replied that they were mistaken. Once they had left, she wondered who had placed the call and had concluded it must be Weilin. Though she had never admitted it, she was thankful Weilin had taken action. It had helped end a most distressing argument.

Maya was brought back to the present when she saw lights outside. The cops were here. She picked up a pair of scissors, in case the intruder was still in the house. She put her ear to the bedroom door and listened for a few seconds. Once she was sure no one was on the other side, she crept down the stairs, careful not to make a sound. She stopped at the last step and tried to listen, while scanning the darkness for any signs of life. Convinced that no one was present, she sneaked towards the front door, weapon ready for attack if the need arose. Two cops stood outside. They introduced themselves as Officers Garcia and Mendez from San Jose PD. Behind them, she could see two squad cars and two more men in uniform. She switched on the light and let them in. Then she recounted what had happened.

Officer Mendez stayed with her while the other officers searched the place. They returned a few minutes later confirming that there was no one else in the house.

"Maya, do you know if anything is missing?" asked Officer Garcia.

"I don't know. Nothing out of place here. Should I check the bedroom? I think he spent most of his time there."

"Yes, please do while we inspect the entry points."

Maya went up to the bedroom, still gripping the scissors tightly. Even with the assurance of having cops in the house and knowing that the intruder had left, she was scared. The odor hit her again as she entered the closet. It was quite evident someone had gone through her things. A quick scan confirmed that all her jewelry was gone. Expensive stuff. If only she had been conscientious enough to store it in the safe deposit box at the bank. If Jay were still around, she would have received a thorough scolding for being so careless. Disappointed, she returned downstairs and reported her findings. Officer Garcia offered his sympathy.

"Anything else missing?"

"Nothing obvious. It will take me a little longer to confirm."

"That's alright. You don't have to do it right away. At least this gives us an idea about his motives. Quite likely a regular burglar."

"Maya, did you lock the doors and windows before you went to bed?" asked Officer Mendez.

"Yes, I did. I always check before turning in for the night."

"Interesting. We didn't find any signs of forced entry. We noticed you have an alarm system. Did you arm it?"

"No. I only do that when I leave the house."

"Anyone else who has the keys?"

"Only Jay, my husband, and I. But his were lost a few days ago."

"How did that happen?"

"He ... he was murdered. The keys were not found."

"Oh, sorry to hear that. You should change your locks first thing tomorrow morning. And please use your alarm system. Always."

"Yes, I will be more careful next time," replied Maya, realizing that Angela and Paul had instructed her to replace the locks as well. If only she had acted on that advice. But with so much going on, where was the time to do that? She resolved to follow through this time and get it done the next morning.

"Is there some place you can go tonight? It's dangerous for you to stay here until the locks are changed."

"I can go over next door."

By this time some of the neighbors were at their doors, awakened by the sound and lights. She noticed Mukesh outside his house and told him what had happened. She asked him if she could sleep at their place and he agreed. The officers left once they had ensured that she was in safe hands. They would investigate the robbery and keep her updated on the progress.

Soon Maya was in the Bhatias' comfortable guest bed. She knew she should feel secure here, but she was still shaken up. How had the thief entered the house? Did he have the keys? If so, was this the same person who had taken the keys from Jay? She tried to get the thoughts out of her head but failed. Sleep was impossible after what had happened. Too bad she had left her sleeping pills at home.

MARGARET LANE
JANUARY 22

Margaret woke up in a cold sweat, her head pounding. She didn't need the clock to know it was 2:00 a.m. It had happened again. Funny how it always occurred at the same time. At sixty-five, she was getting too old for this, and she wished it would stop. In fact, she had wanted it to end for as long as she could remember. But it never did. One more vision to add to the collection. She reflected on this latest one. A knee-length formal black skirt, leading into slender, fair-skinned legs and ending in yellow pumps. Lying by the rail tracks. From the intensity of the episode, she estimated a day or two. If only she had some more clues as to the identity of the victim. That was one of the frustrating parts about her visions. Most of the time she did not have enough information. She felt so powerless that it intensified her suffering, that feeling of knowing someone was about to die, yet she couldn't do anything about it. The few times that she did have sufficient details, people did not believe her. They wrote her off as a crazy woman. What use was this gift if she couldn't help anyone? Or was it even a gift at all? Sometimes she felt it was a curse.

Margaret had these visions even as a child. At the time she didn't understand what it was. Neither did her parents. Initially they thought they were just regular nightmares. They thought, perhaps, this was the result of some violent horror movie she had seen. As things got worse, they started visiting various doctors, but with no result. The doctors were clueless. Her parents slowly began to understand the gravity of the problem. They realized this was probably why she had been such a fussy baby, waking up crying in the middle of the night and not stopping until hours later.

Her school years were quite miserable too. The visions haunted her. She dared not share them with anyone. It resulted in her becoming withdrawn. She did have a few friends, but she was unable to enjoy her childhood in that carefree manner that most children do. Some of the kids mocked her and called her weird. Of course, somewhere along the way she also figured out a way to use the visions to her advantage. Sometimes she would fake them and act distressed to garner some sympathy from her parents. At times like these, they would cave in to whatever demands she had.

It was not until she turned fifteen that she truly understood what the visions were all about. One morning, she awoke to a shocking headline on the front page of the newspaper. A famous senator had been assassinated. Below the bold letters was a photograph showing him sprawled in someone's lap, splotches of blood in a couple of places on his white shirt. These were the spots where he had been shot. Around him stood a lot of people, looking concerned. This was the first time most people around the nation, and the world, were seeing this scene. The people who had been present at the scene had witnessed this the previous day. But Margaret had seen this, or at least part of this, a week earlier. As with all her visions, at the time she had dismissed it as another weird dream. However, after seeing this photograph the true significance of the dreams dawned on her. From there on she was obsessed with understanding it better. She started documenting the episodes extensively and perused the news for any deaths that matched what she had seen. With time, she had enough data to notice patterns. She deduced that the intensity of the vision was correlated with how soon the death would occur. There were times when she was aware enough during the occurrence that she tried to see more. She was successful sometimes, and it helped her figure out more about the victims so that they could be warned in advance.

IT WAS 8:00 a.m. Margaret had struggled to fall asleep, the episode weighing on her mind. But she had eventually succeeded. Now she was awakened by the sound of the garbage truck. It occurred to her that she had not put out the trash cans. She hurried to drag them out to the curb. On her way back to the house, she noticed her next-door neighbor, Brenda Donovan, stepping out of her home. Margaret waved to her and wished her good morning. Brenda smiled back faintly. She and her husband, Jason, had once been friendly and Margaret had loved spending time with their kids, six-year-old Sarah and nine-year-old Jacob. However, that had changed once they had learned about the visions. They had started becoming distant, something Margaret was quite used to with other people.

Margaret felt Brenda was a beautiful woman and always dressed immaculately. As Brenda walked over to her car, Margaret looked her over admiringly and froze. The black skirt on Brenda's slender figure stopped at her knees. On her feet were a pair of bright yellow pumps. She commuted to San Francisco and often took Caltrain. Margaret's head was spinning. She couldn't stand the thought of the kids losing their mother. She rushed over to her in a panic and blurted, "Brenda, are you taking the train today?"

"Yes. Margaret, are you okay? You don't look too good."

"Don't go."

"What do you mean?"

"Don't go in to work."

"Why not?" asked Brenda, sounding exasperated. "I have important meetings. I must go."

"Drive then. But don't take the train. Something terrible is going to happen on the tracks."

"I can't drive. The traffic is insane. What's going to happen anyway?"

"You ... you will die if you take the train."

"Is this some sort of joke? Another one of your 'visions'? I have to leave now, or I'll miss the eight thirty."

"No, no Brenda. I saw it. You will die. Please, don't go," implored Margaret.

By this time she was gripping Brenda's arm tightly.

"Let go, crazy woman!"

Brenda shook off Margaret's hands and got into the car. Then she drove off as Margaret looked on, falling completely to pieces. She was shaking and in tears, not knowing what to do. She ran to Brenda's and rang the doorbell. Jason soon appeared, concerned once he saw the state she was in.

"Margaret, what's going on?"

"Brenda ... Brenda ..." was all she was able to say.

"What happened to Brenda?" He stepped out of the house to check, and seeing the car gone, he turned to her.

"Margaret! What about Brenda?"

"She ... she is taking the train. I ... I told her not to ... not to take the train. Stop ... stop her."

"Why? She always takes it."

"She's going to die."

"What nonsense is this?"

"I had a vision."

"Oh, not that again! Leave!"

"Please believe me. You have to warn her!"

"Leave, Margaret! Now!"

He pushed her away and shut the door. She walked back to her house, dismayed. The day was spent worrying and watching for her neighbor to return. But Brenda didn't come.

At around 8:00 p.m. Margaret noticed lights outside. There was a cop car parked in front of Brenda's house. A few minutes later the doorbell sounded. It was Jason along with two officers from SJPD. He looked pale and teary-eyed. It was enough to tell her that the worst had come true. She knew the officers, and they remembered her as well. How could they not? She had gone to them often with warnings about her visions, only to be laughed off. But this time they listened. Jason had told them about the incident earlier that morning. She explained the vision. It matched what they had seen. Brenda was indeed found dead on the tracks. They weren't sure yet whether she had fallen, been pushed by someone or, worse, jumped of her own volition. Margaret was devastated. If only people took her seriously.

YUMMY TUMMY
JANUARY 22

Maya worked at one of the up-and-coming food delivery startups, Yummy Tummy, which was headquartered in Sunnyvale. It was a single-story building in a cluster of office buildings close to downtown. This morning Angela and Paul planned to interview Maya's colleagues to verify her alibi. Yummy Tummy had twenty employees, of which five had been in the meeting with Maya that night. They would be talking to all five.

Angela got there a few minutes after 10:00 a.m., having called Paul to tell him she would be late. She parked her car next to his and got out, trying to ignore the pounding headache.

"Looks like someone had a hot date last night. Not much sleep?" he remarked with a mischievous smile. He had got there shortly before ten.

Angela gave him an unamused look.

"More like a date from hell."

"What happened? You were raving about him before the date."

"Yeah, he seemed great online. In fact, in person as well. It began well, until he got to his third drink. Then the alcohol took over. Started talking dirty to me right there in the restaurant. So I left. Silly me tried to keep pace with his drinking, hence the terrible hangover. Sorry, I'm late."

"My sympathies. No need to apologize. Happens to the best of us."

"Men are such jerks!"

"Hey, not all of us!"

"Okay, *almost* all men are jerks. Now, can we get to work?"

Jessica Blosco, the head of HR, was there to receive them. She would be helping them get through the interviews. She walked them over to a vacant conference room right next to an open office area which was mostly empty.

"It will fill up soon. Ten a.m. is kinda early for our engineers," she clarified with a smile. "But everyone you will be talking to is already here as per your request."

Paul had heard a bit about Silicon Valley startups and the cool workplaces and perks. He had hoped to check it out. But this one was quite no-frills. His face fell. Jessica seemed to note his disappointment.

"We run a tight ship around here. Only necessary expenditures until we hit profitability. Someday we will move into a grand office building with all the perks. I'll get John for you."

John Connolly appeared a couple of minutes later. He was a lumbering six foot three inches and moved at a languid pace. He greeted them and eased himself into the chair across from the detectives, spending a considerable amount of time ensuring he had enough leg room. Once he was comfortable, he looked up, first at Angela and then at Paul.

"John, thank you for taking the time for this today," said Angela.

"No problem. Anything I can do to help."

"Have you been here long?"

"Two years. I was employee number five."

"So I assume you know Maya well?"

"Yes. We started on the same day and have worked together

closely. It's a small outfit. Everyone knows everyone. Quite sad about her husband."

Angela nodded. Time to get to business.

"Where were you on the evening of January seventeenth?"

"I was right here in this conference room with Maya and the rest of the team. From around four p.m. to around nine p.m."

"You often work that late?"

"Hey, it's a startup, man. Working late nights and weekends is the norm. But that week was more focused since we were close to a major release."

"And Maya was there the entire time?"

"I wasn't keeping tabs on people, but as I recall, she joined a few minutes after we all came in. Then she was gone later briefly, can't say what time. Of course, this is apart from the bio breaks everyone takes. No one tracks that," he replied with a smile.

"Can you be more specific? How long was she gone for?"

"I'd reckon not more than fifteen to twenty minutes. Actually, now I remember. It was a short while before we all dispersed for the day."

"And how did she seem the whole time? Anything out of the ordinary?"

"No. She was running things as usual. Like I said, I didn't really notice much. I have more of a heads-down approach to work."

But you remember when she came and went, thought Angela.

"Thanks again, John. We don't have any more questions for you."

Next up was Scott Morrison. Paul's mouth fell open when he saw him walk in. He knew the dress code in the tech industry was lax, but this was something he had not expected at all. Scott was dressed in a graphic t-shirt and shorts, topped with a baseball cap worn backwards. He looked more suited for a trip to the ball game than someone doing important work. To make things worse, he was chewing gum in the most annoying way. If there was one thing that irritated Paul, it was people ruminating in that dramatic fashion. He had the urge to whack Scott hard across the face and watch the gum fly out in one direction while the cap flew off in another. But he kept his cool and behaved like the true professional that he was. Scott didn't make it easy, though. He was another one of those kids fresh out of college who couldn't keep his eyes off his phone. He didn't acknowledge them as he sat down, busy typing away on his precious toy. The detectives waited a few moments, until he finally deigned to look up, only for a couple of seconds, and said, "Oh, ready when you are," and went back to his first love. Paul looked at Angela, Angela looked back at Paul. They shrugged and decided to get on with it.

"Scott, you were with the rest of the team on the evening of January seventeenth?" she asked.

"Last Wednesday? Yeah," he answered, still glued to his phone.

"And was Maya in the room throughout?"

"I guess so."

"She didn't go anywhere?"

"I don't know. I was busy working."

More likely busy kissing your phone, thought Angela.

"So you don't know if she was around?"

"Nope."

By now she was convinced that a visit to the dentist was more agreeable than talking to him.

"Okay, Scott. We are done here."

He got up and walked out, still admiring the glowing device in his hand.

"Now that was super fruitful," said Paul wryly.

"I wonder whether he does any work or just gets paid to fondle that thing."

The next two interviews were less dramatic. Everyone confirmed that Maya had indeed been in the room all evening, except for a short interval where she had stepped out.

Last one in was Mary Abrams, looking a lot younger than her sixty-three years. She had bright, intelligent eyes and exuded a calm that usually only came with age. She started talking before either of the detectives could get a word in.

"What do you want to know? I am a very perceptive woman and have known Maya a long time. I can assure you, she is incapable of murder."

If you're so smart, why don't you do my job, thought Angela, resisting the urge to roll her eyes.

"That's for us to decide, Mary. Please answer our questions truthfully."

"Sure, go ahead."

"Was Maya with you the evening of January seventeenth?"

"Yes, from four p.m. until we wrapped up around nine p.m. Except, she left around eight fifteen and didn't get back for another thirty minutes."

"You sure about the time?"

"Absolutely. I don't miss a thing."

Of course, you don't, Ms. Perfect. Angela hoped it wasn't misplaced confidence.

"Anything unusual about her that evening?"

"She is usually very calm and focused. But that day she seemed a little distracted. Like she would rather be somewhere else. One more thing. She received a text a short while before she took that break. She was nervous after that. And she looked a bit rattled after she returned."

"That's an interesting observation. No one else mentioned it."

"Like I said, I am very perceptive."

"Anything else you would like to add?"

"No, that's all I've got."

"Thank you, Mary. We are done with the interview."

They would have to ask Maya about Mary's observation. Maybe there was something there. But the interviews confirmed Maya's alibi. All that remained was to check the security cameras for a final confirmation.

On their way out, they stopped by the security room and requested the surveillance footage for January 17. Over the next couple of hours, they reviewed it from 6:00 p.m. to past 8:00 p.m. They didn't see Maya leave the building until after 8:15 p.m.

The next morning they performed the same exercise at Intelligent Systems. They noted in the recording that Jay had left the building at 7:00 p.m., never to return. That further narrowed down the time of death to between 7:00 p.m. and 8:00 p.m.

SYNC UP

JANUARY 23

Angela and Paul were in Cynthia's office for a sync-up on case status. It had been six days since the incident, and she was being hounded for an update. That was the problem with such high-profile cases, thought Angela. The pressure was enormous when everyone was watching.

"What's our progress so far?"

"We have a total of three potential suspects. Maya, Mark Harrison, and the woman in the pink skirt. We know both Maya and Mark had motive, but neither of their prints match what we collected at the crime scene. Maya has a strong alibi, so we are almost ready to rule her out. Mark has no alibi, was near the crime scene, and we found his pin there. The witnesses are clean. Their prints didn't match. Oh, and we also have to follow up on those letters."

"You really serious about the letters?"

"Well, it may lead to nothing, but I think we would be negligent not to pursue it."

"What about the prints on the wallet?"

"That's a different set from those on the syringe. Doesn't match any of the suspects' or Jay's prints."

"The woman. Anything on her?"

"Oddly enough, not many businesses in the area have security cameras. The few we reviewed didn't have her. There was one where we saw a woman that matched the description, but it was not clear enough for identification. That's a dead end for now. Besides, she was seen with the body at nine p.m. Time of death is sometime between seven p.m. and eight p.m. It is quite possible she had nothing to do with it, and she just stumbled upon it."

"Hmm ... but she may have some information about it. She could have seen the killer."

"Right. That's another reason we haven't given up on her. We will keep looking."

"So at this point Mark is the only viable lead? Let's get some strong evidence. Someone must have seen something. It's a busy enough area. I can't believe a man was murdered there, and no one saw anything."

"You're assuming he was murdered where we found him. It's entirely possible it was done elsewhere, and the body was dropped at Sha Sha."

"Why would someone do that? It doesn't make sense. If I wanted to dispose of a body, I would dump it somewhere no one would find it."

"Maybe the killer wanted it to be found. Remember, Jay died between seven p.m. and eight p.m., but the body was only spotted at nine p.m. It's highly unlikely it was there for over an hour, and no one saw it. That's why we suspect he was killed elsewhere."

"I see your point. But then why was the syringe still on him? It would have fallen off during the move."

"Maybe it was meant to be found too."

"But why?"

"Beats me."

"So far we have been focused on motive. What about the robbery angle?"

"We are not ruling it out. It could have been a simple robbery gone wrong. But we feel that was not the motive. This looked planned. I mean, why the poison? It would be more likely to see a gun or knife used, or even a plain old whack on the head with any random object. The theft may have been staged after the murder to put us on the wrong track."

"Possible. Well, you know what you have to do. Just do it fast and get these people off my back."

"Do you think we should bring Mark in? That might put pressure on him and prompt him to confess."

"No, nothing rash until we have strong evidence. I don't want any scandals. He is a man in a powerful position and the world is watching. Don't forget Lamar."

"Lamar?" asked Paul with a blank expression.

"Right, you don't know. That was before your time," replied Cynthia.

"Lamar James. A successful businessman suspected of killing his neighbor. He was arrested, even though the evidence was thin. The DA refused to prosecute. Frankly, I was surprised we got the arrest warrant," Angela chimed in.

"So he went free?"

"Yes. He did. But not before there were widespread protests. Lamar was African American, and this was seen as yet another racially motivated case of police heavy-handedness. Our chief at the time, Ryan Hartford, was forced to resign. The judge who issued the warrant narrowly survived a recall."

"Is that when you became chief?" asked Paul, turning to Cynthia.

"Yes. I got lucky with that promotion, and I want to ensure we don't make such mistakes again."

"Seems harsh though, what happened to Hartford."

"Well, truth be told, this wasn't the only reason he faced the heat. He was heard making a snide comment to the effect that Lamar should have been happy he was only arrested and not shot down like so many other African American men across the country."

"What an ass! I'm glad we have you, Cynthia," Paul smiled. "Did we ever nab the real killer?"

"Nope. The case was dead by the time you joined. Oh, one more thing before I forget. This could be important."

Angela leaned forward, eager to hear what juicy tidbit Cynthia was going to share with them.

"A Sunnyvale woman has been reported missing. The name is Betty Liu, twenty-four years old. Here's the kicker. She worked at Intelligent Systems and she was last seen on the seventeenth."

"She worked for Jay? Disappeared on the same night he was killed? Can't be a coincidence," said Angela, her hazel eyes sparkling.

"Exactly. She was last seen at work around seven p.m. She lives with her mother and sister. They were worried when she didn't get home that night, but they waited a day before reporting her missing. They figured she was spending the night at a friend's place. It wasn't unusual for her to do that."

"It's only been six days. She might turn up."

"Possibly. But I have Wilson and Shibata doing some preliminary investigation."

Angela cringed at the mention of Shibata. Cynthia noticed it but continued on.

"They didn't get much from the family. A friend told them Betty had a boyfriend, but she didn't know who it was. Apparently, Betty was very secretive about it. They are still talking to her other friends and coworkers. I'll keep you posted."

"I hope she's alive and well. Or it would seem someone is going around killing Intelligent Systems employees."

INTELLIGENT SYSTEMS

JANUARY 25

The Intelligent Systems headquarters was located in Milpitas. It was a single, three-storied building, and the contrast from Yummy Tummy was clear. The interiors were glitzy, with cool features. A fountain here, a waterfall there. A wide array of snacks were available for the employees. This was more like the tech world he had read about, thought Paul. He was there with Angela to question Jay's coworkers. Robert Cruz, who was the Chief Technology Officer, had volunteered to help them out with the interviews. Angela decided to begin with Robert himself.

"Robert, can you tell us about that evening. What time did Jay leave?"

"He left around seven p.m. I remember because it was early by his standards, and he stopped by to say goodbye."

"Did you notice anything unusual?"

"No. He looked pretty upbeat, as if he had something fun planned. I don't recall anything unusual."

"How well did you know him?"

"We were co-founders. We had worked together a long time ago, and he reached out to me when he had the idea to start his own thing. So, I did know him well professionally. Personally, not that much."

"Can we assume you got along well, then?"

"Well, I wouldn't say that. To be honest, he could be a real jerk at times, and I didn't like to hang out with him outside of work."

"You didn't like him, yet you decided to found a company with him?"

"Look, I am a practical guy. When I heard his pitch, I knew this was going to be a success. I was stuck in a dead-end job at the time, and this seemed like a great opportunity. I couldn't pass that up. It has worked out well so far."

"What about these problems with Mark Harrison and Smart-Cloud? Any truth to those accusations?"

"We didn't steal anything. Our product was completely designed and developed by our team here. Even the ideas are all ours. That was dirty tactics by Mark. Anything to squash a rising competitor."

"So, do you see Mark as a possible suspect? He would have loved to see Jay dead, right?"

"Oh, I can't comment on that. I don't know the guy. In any case, that's not how we settle scores in tech."

"How about you? You didn't like Jay. Did you ever wish he was gone?"

"What kind of questioning is this? I don't go around whacking people I don't like. Now, have I ever wished him dead? I have to admit, yes, a few times. But I would never kill anyone."

"You were co-founders, yet he ended up as CEO. You must have wanted the top job, too."

"Ha! You think I knocked him off so I could become CEO? Look, it's pretty simple. I'm a technical guy and don't have much business sense. Jay, on the other hand, was a smart cookie. He was cut out for it. I don't think I could ever fit in. Besides, it's up to the board who gets picked for the role."

"Anyone else here at Intelligent Systems who could have a motive to kill him?"

"No one I know of. People are happy working here. Like I said, he could be a jerk, and may have rubbed some the wrong way, but nothing so extreme. He was great at what he did, and he was respected as a leader."

"How about his wife, Maya? How well do you know her?"

"We have met a few times at company socials. They also attended my daughter's birthday party last year. You know, she called me that evening to inquire about Jay. She was worried he wasn't home."

"Around what time was that?"

"It was pretty late. Sometime after ten, I think."

"What did she say?"

"Oh, nothing much. She expressed her concern, and I told her what I knew – basically what I told you. And that was that."

"Since we are here, might as well ask you. Do you know Betty Liu?"

"Yes, of course. She was one of our best engineers. Came to us fresh out of MIT. Friendly girl."

"You said 'was'. Doesn't she still work here?"

"Did I? I guess I did. It's just that she hasn't been around much lately. The thing is, something went wrong in the last few months. Her results deteriorated. She started getting irritable. Some health problems, people thought. There were rumors that she was involved with Jay. It may have been boyfriend issues."

Angela brightened at that piece of information. Had Jay been having an affair with Betty? That connection might explain why both of them ran into trouble that day. And was that what Maya and Jay had fought about?

"And what do you think? Were they involved?"

"It's possible. They had always been quite close. But lately they were awkward around each other. Betty in particular seemed to fall apart in his presence."

"When did you see her last?"

"Can't remember. It's been a few days for sure. Why are you so interested in her?"

"Her family reported her missing. She disappeared that same evening."

"Oh, I had no idea. I assumed she was out sick again. This is terrible. Now that you mention it, I remember when I last saw her. It was when Jay left that evening. Betty's desk is close to my office. I saw her get up and follow him."

"So it's possible they went out together? On a date?"

"I guess. Perhaps that's why he looked so happy."

"Thanks, Robert. Can we talk to some others now?"

"Sure, I will bring in the next one."

The rest of the interviews were uneventful. They didn't learn much more that would help with the investigation. But they did get confirmation that Jay and Betty had been involved romantically, and the relationship had gone sour recently. Angela wondered whether Betty could have killed him.

Just as they were about to leave, Robert said, "Oh, I blanked out when you asked about employees with motive."

Angela perked up and looked at him, waiting for the potential lead.

"It's an ex-employee, Praveen Sood. Jay fired him around six months back. They had a big row when Jay told him. He had to be escorted out by security. He even threatened to kill Jay."

"But that was a long time ago. Why would he wait until now to do anything? Usually in such cases the reaction is very quick."

"I don't know about that. Just thought I should let you know."

"Thanks. It's good that you did. Do you have his contact info? We would like to talk to him."

"Sure, I think I still have his number."

Angela noted the details. No harm in talking to the guy.

PRAVEEN SOOD
JANUARY 27

Praveen Sood lived in a two-bedroom apartment in Santa Clara with his wife, Rashmi, and their seven-year-old daughter, Priya. Angela and Paul arrived a few minutes after 11:00 a.m. and climbed the stairs to the second floor. Rashmi opened the door and looked at them with an inquiring expression.

"Mrs. Sood?"

"Yes?"

The detectives flashed their identification and introduced themselves.

"We have some questions for your husband," said Angela.

Rashmi turned pale. "What is this about?"

"It's regarding the murder of Jay Sharma. We believe Praveen worked with him?"

"Yes, he did. Please come in."

Angela stepped into the living room and saw Praveen seated on the floor, next to his daughter. A few sheets of chart paper were on the floor, interspersed with craft materials. Newspapers were scattered to one side. Some of the chart papers had pictures on them, alongside text cut out from newspapers. It seemed they were working on a school project. But all Angela could think of was the threatening letters Jay had received.

Praveen and Priya looked up as they walked in, and the detectives reintroduced themselves. Rashmi took her daughter into the bedroom.

"Praveen, we are investigating the murder of Jay Sharma, and we have some questions for you. We understand you have worked with him in the past."

"Yes, I did, until six months ago."

"And what happened then?"

"He fired me."

"Why was that?"

"The guy had a huge ego. He didn't like that my ideas were different from his and that I had the guts to defend them. We had clashed one time too many. That day we had another disagreement on technical direction. He decided enough was enough."

"We hear there was quite a row."

"Yes, Jay was his usual arrogant self. And, of course, I was furious at being let go."

"Why did you care if he sacked you? It seems you weren't happy there anyway."

"Like most people, I would have preferred to leave on my own terms. Besides, he did it a week before a major stock vest. That would have been a lot of money once we went public. It was not fair after all the hard work I put in."

"You threatened to kill him?"

"In the heat of the moment, yes. But I didn't mean it, of course."

"Where were you on the evening of January seventeenth?"

"Hmm ... let me see." Praveen paused to consult his phone. "I was at home. Left work early for a parent-teacher meeting at Priya's school."

"Can anyone vouch for that?"

"You want an alibi? Am I a suspect?"

"It's a routine question. We have to consider every possibility."

"Rashmi and Priya were with me the whole time."

"So, no one other than your family."

"That is correct."

"Where do you work now?"

"At SmartCloud."

"Ah. With Mark Harrison. Interesting."

"Not sure what you mean by that. SmartCloud is in the same space. They were hiring and it was a good fit for me."

Angela gave him a silent stare.

"Well, okay, I will admit it was very satisfying going over to Jay's archrival, but that was secondary."

"Ever discuss the legal controversy with Mark?"

"It was unavoidable. The case was ongoing and then, with the verdict, everyone was talking about it at work. He vented to me a few times. He was obsessed with the whole thing. It was a relief when it was over. He was furious, but at least things went back to normal after that."

"Did he ever say he wanted to harm Jay?"

"You mean whether he wanted to murder him?"

"Yes, that's what I meant."

"No. I don't think he would do that. It's not easy taking a man's life. Why risk the consequences? He was more interested in the success of his business."

"How about you? Would you kill?"

"I don't see the point. Whatever happened, I have moved on. This is little stuff that happens in life. You can't go around killing people. Besides, it's not worth the risk. I have a family to take care of."

"One more thing. Have you ever been associated with Purdue University?"

"No. I went to Georgia Tech."

That matched the information Angela had found in her research.

"That's all the questions we have, Praveen. Thanks for your time. Do contact us if you think of anything else that might be relevant."

AS PRAVEEN WATCHED THEM LEAVE, Rashmi appeared from the bedroom.

"Why didn't you tell them?"

"They don't need to know everything. I don't want any trouble."

"But what if they find out? That would be serious trouble."

"Don't worry. They won't find out. They won't."

Rashmi went quiet. No use arguing with Praveen. But she was worried.

ONCE OUTSIDE, Paul turned to Angela, "You think he is telling the truth?"

"I believed him. He seemed sincere enough. In any case, I'll pull his phone records to confirm the alibi."

"I wonder whether our focus on alibis is misplaced. I mean, some of these people, like Mark and Maya, these are rich people. They could pay someone to do a hit."

"And how would they find a hitman? Besides, they're smart enough not to outsource such work. Loose lips sink ships. The more people know about it, the higher the chances they could get caught because someone squawked."

"Point taken. All I'm saying is, let's not rule out the possibility."

"Agreed."

MEGHNA RAO
FEBRUARY 2

Angela knew she was close. Close enough to hear him above the throbs of her racing heart. Her gun was cocked and ready, finger on the trigger. She detected movement in the distance and fired. He fired back, the bullet whizzing past, inches from her face. She took another shot. There was a cry, followed by the sound of a body slumping to the ground. Angela ran towards the thud and saw the motionless body. It was him! Angela White, the rookie FBI agent, had brought down Dirty Dan, the serial killer they had been chasing for months. She heard footsteps behind her and turned around. It was the rest of her team, every member beaming. A successful mission at last. After a round of high fives, she looked back towards her prize and found herself staring at two wide-open eyes. A flash of light appeared in front of those eyes, accompanied by a bang and a piercing ache in her chest as she collapsed. Dan's shot had hit its mark.

Angela woke up in a sweat and saw the light for what it was. Sunbeams streaming in through the blinds. She realized it was just a dream and let out a relieved sigh. It had seemed so real. She was doing well as a detective and had a bright future in the force, but she knew she was capable of so much more. One of these days she would get around to turning in her job application to the FBI.

Now that she was awake, Angela decided to make the most of it by hitting work early. She was rewarded for the early start. Her contact had sent her the phone records for Jay, Maya and Mark. She spent the next few hours scrutinizing the data. The first thing she noticed was that Jay had texted someone shortly after 7:00 p.m., around the time he was seen last. Could it be the killer? Or at least someone he was meeting that evening? Maybe someone who could shed some light on what happened next. It did not match Betty's number. His location data showed he was at work until around 7:15 p.m., at which point his phone was switched off and never turned on again. Why was it turned off at that time? Did Jay do it himself? Or was it the killer? Something to think about.

Next, she moved on to Maya's records. The data showed she was in the office all evening. The logs didn't have anything interesting either, except for a text she had received at 7:25 p.m. Angela deduced this was the one Mary had mentioned. The one that had got Maya nervous. Yes, Angela would have to ask her about it.

Mark's records didn't reveal anything new. No suspicious calls or texts that evening. Location data confirmed what he had told them. He was at work until 6:22 p.m., and then he drove over to Sha Sha. He was there until 8:00 p.m., after which he went home to Los Gatos.

She went back to that last text from Jay. A little more research revealed that the number belonged to Meghna Rao. Could this be the woman in the pink skirt?

Angela walked over to Paul to fill him in on her findings. He was polishing off a chocolate doughnut and licking his fingers when she appeared.

"Any good?"

"Delish! You should try one," he replied, offering the box full of sinful delights.

"Thanks. I'll pass. We have to talk to this woman, Meghna Rao."

"Who's that?"

"Come on. I'll bring you up to date."

He stood up and joined her, but not before grabbing one more doughnut for the road.

MEGHNA RAO WAS the CTO at Vroom, one of the prominent companies working on self-driving car technology. She was smart, articulate and a visionary. At thirty-two years old, she was already widely respected in the tech industry.

Meghna had gone through a busy few weeks at work, but it had been worth the effort. It was the last day of Vroom's two-day conference, the first ever organized by the company. She stood on stage to present the product demo and introduce the features to the captive audience. Vroom had a sprawling test facility in Stockton, where they put the cars through their paces. It spanned a few square blocks and was designed like a real city, complete with traffic lights, streets and the works. She streamed in the live demo where the car aced the drive across "town," through various conditions like rain and snow, day and night. As the applause from the audience died down, she showed off another stream from the streets of San Francisco. The car weaved through the horrendous traffic and scores of pedestrians like a pro. The ovation grew louder. There was no doubt Vroom was way ahead of the competition.

Meghna couldn't resist picking a page from her idol's playbook as she said, "One more thing," and pulled a phone out of her pocket. She demonstrated how she could remotely control the car from the phone, moving it around at her whim. Next up were some more controls, turning on the heat, starting the wipers and so on. The crowd went wild, and she soaked in all the adulation. This was awesome.

Exhaustion set in by the end, and when she got home around 3:00 p.m. she was looking forward to a weekend of R&R as a reward

for all the hard work. The doorbell chirped just as she was getting
into bed for a quick nap. She sighed and walked over to the door.
There was a man and a woman, both tall and dressed in suits. The
woman spoke first.

"Meghna Rao? Detective Angela White, and this is my partner
Paul Conley. We would like to speak with you regarding a case."

Meghna studied the badges they presented.

"Sure, come in."

"We are investigating the death of Jay Sharma. We believe you
knew him?"

"If you mean the CEO of Intelligent Systems, then yes, I did
know him professionally. Tragic."

"How long had you known him?"

"Hmm ... let me see. I recall we first met at a networking event a
few years ago. We were working on related technology and got talking. After that we were in touch every now and then to catch up on
the latest advances."

"When was the last time you saw him?"

"It was a couple of days before he died. Bumped into him at
Cinebar. We had a short discussion and that was it."

"And no communication after that?"

"No," replied Meghna. Then she added, "Wait, I remember. He
did text me that evening. The evening he died. But I was swamped at
work and did not get a chance to respond."

"What did he say?"

"Oh, he wanted to meet sometime to carry our discussions
further."

"Can we see it?"

"I'm sorry, I deleted it. I was cleaning up my phone over the
weekend to make some space."

"If you don't mind, we would like to take a look," continued
Angela.

"You want to check my phone? Am I a suspect?" Meghna replied
with a quizzical look.

"No, you are not a suspect yet. But we are pursuing all possibilities. We don't have a warrant, but if you agree now it will save everyone a lot of trouble. All we want to do is review your messages."

She considered the request for a few seconds, then unlocked the phone and handed it over. Angela took a couple of minutes to search, handing it back once she was done.

"Where were you between seven p.m. and eight p.m. that night?"

"I was at work. But I did step out for a bit between seven and seven thirty."

"Where did you go during that time?"

"To our garage to check on something."

"Can anyone confirm your alibi?"

"I was with my team the entire evening, except for those thirty minutes. Any one of them can vouch for me."

"How about the garage? Did anyone see you there?"

"No, I was alone. At least, I did not see anyone."

"And what time did you leave work?"

"Around nine p.m. Along with the rest of the team."

"Do you, by any chance, have any association with Purdue University?"

"No, none at all."

"Thanks for your time, Meghna. We'll get in touch if we have any more questions," said Angela as she stood up to leave.

Meghna heaved a sigh of relief once they were gone. She was exhausted, and talking to detectives about a murder case was the last thing she wanted to do. On the flip side, it was a novel experience. She had never talked to cops before, so perhaps that counted for something. She undressed and crashed into bed, hoping for no more disturbances. But she just lay there, unable to sleep.

All Meghna could think of was that evening three years ago, when she had first laid eyes on Jay. She was at an AI networking mixer, trapped in conversation with some guy who was more interested in discussing his awful marriage than technology. As her eyes had started to glaze over, she had spotted Jay across the room, staring at her intently. She felt an instant attraction and sensed that the feeling was mutual. After some concerted effort she had managed to excuse herself and walk over to the bar, where he joined her and tried to flirt his way into her heart. He looked even better up close, tall and poised. She had noticed the ring on his left hand, and he had assured her he wouldn't be married for long. By the end of the evening, he had convinced her to have dinner with him later that week.

And now he was dead. She had told them that the relationship was purely professional. Was that a mistake?

"SO, WHAT DID YOU THINK?" asked Paul once they were in the car.

"Well, she was out for a full thirty minutes. Her office is only five minutes from Jay's. Plenty of time to kill him and get back. Though not enough time to dump the body in Sunnyvale. Quite unlikely she did it. But I wouldn't rule her out until we've confirmed her alibi."

"I agree. Let's see what her coworkers have to say about it. But if she did do it, what would be her motive?"

"I don't know. I guess we have to find out if she has one."

WHEN THE DETECTIVES returned to Sunnyvale, they spotted Detective John Shibata. Angela wanted to get back to her desk, but Paul walked up to him to ask about progress on the Betty Liu case. She reluctantly followed. She didn't want to miss out on any crucial information.

"Well, well, well, if it isn't Beauty and the Beast," he remarked as he saw them approach.

Big Bad Wolf, thought Angela.

"Doll, you get prettier by the day," he continued with a smirk on his face, giving her the once-over.

"Shut the fuck up, John."

"Ouch! Bitchier too."

Shibata was by far the best detective on the force, and the most experienced as well. He was well respected by his peers, but he was trouble when it came to women, especially Angela. It was another year until he retired. She was counting the days. She had reported this behavior to Cynthia, but nothing had happened. Angela knew this was because it would not be easy to discipline him, what with his popularity as well as his ability. It would be a political game, and Cynthia didn't want to take on this challenging task so early in her tenure.

"Don't worry, Hansel and Gretel. I have good news for you," he continued, undeterred. "We got her phone records this morning. Nothing significant in terms of calls and texts, except plenty of outgoing to Jay Sharma with no response. That was not surprising, considering what we found out from her coworkers. But the location history for that evening was interesting. She was at work until around seven fifteen p.m., at which point she started moving. But then there's a long gap."

"Phone turned off? Jay's phone also went off the grid around the same time. Did hers come back on?" asked Paul.

"Yes. Around eight twenty p.m. we start seeing data again. Guess where she was?"

"Sha Sha Shawarma?" replied Angela.

"Bingo! She was there for a few minutes, and then she was in motion again. But the data is gone again after a while. Nothing after that."

"Seems like she was with Jay throughout. They moved from Intelligent Systems at the same time. They both ended up at Sha Sha a while later. That would explain why his car was still at work. She drove him to Sha Sha in her car. I'm beginning to think Betty killed him and then disappeared."

"Betty? No way! From what I hear she was a little thing, not that strong. She couldn't have attacked him and succeeded."

"That's where the Taser would come in," said Angela. "The killer didn't need strength to kill him. Shock him with the Taser first, and then inject the poison. And remember, she was mad at him. Sufficient motive for murder. Of course, we don't have any evidence. We have to find her first."

"We searched her house. Nothing suspicious there. Nothing to tie her to the murder. And if she planned on killing him and absconding, how come she didn't take any belongings with her?"

"Maybe it wasn't planned. It's possible they quarreled, and she killed him in a fit of rage. Then she panicked and fled."

"If it was unplanned, how come she showed up with a Taser and a syringe loaded with poison?" countered Shibata.

"You got me there. I know it's not adding up, but it does look like she had something to do with it. Did you find her car?"

"No, not yet. We are working day and night to find her. Hopefully, we will soon."

"I hope so too," replied Paul.

BETTY LIU
JANUARY 17

The alarm blared at 7:00 a.m. and jolted Betty out of her slumber. She couldn't remember the last time she had slept so soundly. The last couple of months, she had spent most nights tossing and turning, and was awake before the alarm rang. One thing was unchanged, though. She didn't want to get out of bed. There was a complete lack of will to rise and face the day ahead. She was convinced she was spiraling into depression, if she wasn't depressed already. Still, she put in the effort and got up. There was no choice anymore. Her month-long break from work was over, and she had to go in if she was to retain her job. She had received a few warnings about her performance prior to the time off. There was no point risking it. Too bad the hiatus hadn't helped her recover. In fact, it had made things worse. With nothing to do, her thoughts had taken over and the results were not good.

On her return to work, she had hoped it would keep her mind occupied and help her stay out of trouble. But in the two days that she had been back, she had been unable to focus. The unhappy thoughts refused to go away. It didn't help that she was on the same floor as Jay and saw him several times a day. It brought back some fond memories, which were quickly overshadowed by the unpleasant ones. She had loved him once, still loved him now. He had loved her, too. But that had changed once she had told him. Suddenly, he didn't want anything to do with her. He had reminded her he was married, and he couldn't leave his wife. Betty had been used and discarded. She had not expected it, but he had turned out to be just like every other no good, cheating husband she had heard about.

Betty took a quick shower and got dressed. Breakfast with her mother and sister cheered her up a little, but the hollowness inside her persisted. She hadn't told them her shameful secret yet. Time was running out, and she would have to soon. But she didn't know how to.

Once she got in to work, she tried to concentrate. She had been a brilliant student and had finished top of her class at MIT. In her career too, she had excelled. Until things went south with Jay. Now she had lost the respect of her colleagues. Not only because of her poor performance, but also because most of them knew about her involvement with him. She was the other woman, the tramp who was having an affair with a married man. Behind her back, and sometimes in her presence, they gossiped about her, and how she still had a job only because of her relationship with him. She had made a terrible mistake, yes. She should have stayed away from him. She saw that now. But only after it was too late. On the bright side, there were a couple of coworkers who continued to be friendly with her. They made it somewhat bearable.

Somehow, she got through the day. It was 7:00 p.m. She was glad another workday was coming to a close. It hadn't gone as well as she had hoped, but she had hung in there. She would have to do better tomorrow. Glancing up from her screen, she saw Jay talking to Robert. In a minute he walked away, leaving for the day. Betty decided to leave too. She would catch up with him and confront him one last time.

VROOM

FEBRUARY 5

Angela and Paul walked into the lobby of Vroom. The office was only a couple of blocks away from Intelligent Systems. It was to be a day of interviews with Meghna's coworkers. She had a tight alibi, and they had to confirm that it held up. They signed in at the reception and Tim Rather from HR ushered them in. As he walked them over to the conference room, Paul marveled at the plush interiors and the cool vibe of the place. It was an open layout with rows of spacious desks interspersed with some lounge areas. Software developers were either furiously typing away or staring down their massive screens. Some of them had multiple monitors, with an array of open windows. Others were slouched over their laptops in the lounge areas. There was a large game room with air-hockey, foosball, and ping-pong tables right next to the break room, which was stocked with a variety of healthy, gourmet foods and exotic coffees.

Wow, this was the life. Paul questioned what he was doing in his job. These kids had it all. Extravagant salaries, bonuses, stock options, cool work environment, and all kinds of perks, from the food and entertainment to onsite massages. Then he explained to himself, he was making a positive impact on the world. He was cleaning up the scum, not wasting his life building some silly app, or some unnecessary and overpriced tech gadget. But it would be nice if he was compensated better for his troubles, or at least got some of these luxuries. Instead, with his pay, he was stuck renting a tiny apartment in faraway Mountain House and enduring the long drive every day. He could not afford anything near work. The irony was that these techies earned enough to buy homes in the area, but they also had the option to work from home. He couldn't avoid his commute – try checking out a crime scene over Webex or interrogating a suspect over Zoom.

He seated himself in the conference room, aptly called Cape Fear. The rooms on that floor were all named after Robert de Niro movies. Paul had given Tim the list of people they wanted to interrogate in advance. Tim left to bring in the first one.

First up was Daniel, a blond guy, fresh out of college. He had been working there for six months. He looked nervous, which was not surprising since a police interview isn't a common experience for most people. It also didn't help that he seemed to be enchanted by Angela and couldn't resist staring at her. She tried to put him at ease by going over some basic questions. Like her, he was a local. During his time at Stanford, he had interned at Vroom one summer. After graduating, he had decided to come back for a full-time position. He loved it there and was excited to help advance the technology of the future. According to him, autonomous cars would be ubiquitous within a few years and would solve several problems.

"Daniel, I know it's been a while, but can you tell us about the evening of the seventeenth? Who was present here and what went on?"

"Um ... the entire team was here. We have a launch coming up later this month, so it's been crunch time for some time now. A lot of late nights and weekends at work. That week in particular, we got together in Godfather around five p.m. and were there until around nine p.m."

"I am guessing Godfather is another conference room around

here?" asked Paul, a bit amused. Technically, it should have been Godfather II, he thought.

"Yeah, it's the large one around the corner."

"Was Meghna present throughout?"

"I guess so. I can't say about that night in particular, but she had a habit of stepping out for a short while after dinner every night."

"Do you recall what time she left and how long she was gone?"

"Um ... it couldn't have been more than ten to fifteen minutes, I think. But then, I was busy working, and didn't pay much attention. As for the time, we would get done eating around seven p.m."

"I understand there was a routine all week, but I am particularly interested in the seventeenth. Was it the same? Any different? I could really use your help here."

"As far as I can remember, she stuck to the routine every day. Sorry, but it was a while ago, and there was nothing special about that night."

"Do you recall how she seemed that night? Anything unusual about her?"

"No. Nothing odd about her all week."

"Thanks, Daniel. That's all we have for now."

He departed, stealing a few more glances at Angela, who obliged with a polite smile.

"Well, I think you got yourself an admirer," joked Paul as she watched Daniel walk off.

"Yeah, I bet he's a really mature guy I would get along great with. That's what I need, a little kid to look after."

They were still enjoying the laugh as the next one on the list walked in. Joanna was a thirty-three-year-old developer who had been at Vroom ever since it was founded five years ago.

"Joanna, we have some questions about the evening of January seventeenth. We hear you were all working late in one of the conference rooms."

"Yes, that's correct. We were there from around five p.m. to nine p.m."

"Meghna too?"

"She was, except for a short period when she left. She said she had to make a phone call."

"Oh, she told you why she was leaving?"

"Yes, I don't know why she mentioned it. Maybe because I had told her earlier that I wanted to discuss something. She wanted me to know she would return."

"And what time did she leave?"

"This was around seven."

"You sure about that?"

"Yes, I remember looking at the time. She was back in thirty minutes."

"You sure about that too?"

"Yes. Bad habit I have. Can't resist looking at the time every few minutes."

"How did she seem that evening? Did she look stressed or nervous?"

"No, she looked relaxed like she always is. Calm and in control."

"Anything else you want to add? Anything that might help us?"

"No, can't think of anything."

"Thanks, Joanna. We wish everyone we talk to was as precise as you are."

"It's a good thing not everyone is mild-OCD like me," she smiled back as she left the room.

The rest of the interviews didn't enhance what they already knew. Meghna's alibi was confirmed. They knew her prints did not match the syringe or the wallet. It was quite impossible for her to have done it. If she did, it could only be if she had an accomplice.

ANGELA AND PAUL gathered in Cynthia's office. A bottle of Tylenol sat on her desk and from the looks of it, the pills had not kicked in yet. She massaged the sides of her head for a couple of seconds, then looked up at them with a weak smile. Angela knew it couldn't be easy, what with all the pressure Cynthia was facing. Everyone grilling her daily about why there was no progress on the case. The media, as usual, were relentless, throwing out their own crazy ideas on a regular basis. But Cynthia rarely passed it down to her team, and Angela appreciated her for that.

"Not much of an update on our previous suspect list. But we have a few additions. We are considering the missing girl, Betty."

"Betty Liu? That's interesting."

Angela filled her in on their findings about Betty and their progress with Praveen and Meghna.

"Interesting. Oh, that reminds me, do you have any leads on the threatening letters yet?"

"No, we haven't had time to follow up."

"Well, look what I found the other day while researching some stuff," Cynthia said as she turned her screen towards them.

It was an online flyer for SmartCloudCon held at the Oakland Convention Center from November 13 to 17 the previous year.

Angela's eyes widened.

"So Mark would have been in Oakland that week?"

"Yes, of course. And this guy Praveen was one of the keynote speakers. He would have been there as well."

"Either one of them could have sent the letter. We will question both of them again."

"And is Maya still a suspect?"

"She is, though we don't have a shred of evidence against her. Only reason we haven't ruled her out yet is that she has lied repeatedly. Makes us wonder why she feels the need to hide things."

"Maybe she's a private person and doesn't like to share things unless necessary."

"That's likely. You know, one possibility is that they are all involved. They all had motive to kill him, and they knew each other. They got together and bumped him off."

"What, you mean like *Murder on the Orient Express?*"

"Something like that. Except that in this case there is only one killer. The rest helped plan and facilitate everything."

"That's too fantastic a theory. Only happens in books. Besides, I'm more of a Miss Marple fan."

"I guess you're right. It's just that we have all these potential suspects, but none of it is adding up."

"I feel like I'm standing in front of one of those grand Vegas buffets, hungry and ready to eat, but there's a problem with every dish," chimed in Paul.

Angela smiled. She loved how he was able to lighten her mood even in the most distressing situations. Cynthia couldn't resist smiling either.

"We will talk to Praveen and Mark about the letters."

"Sounds good. Keep me posted. You're doing well, but we need something more to show. People are getting antsy."

MORE QUESTIONS
FEBRUARY 6

The detectives were at Praveen's door a few minutes before 9:00 a.m. After the talk with Cynthia the previous evening, they knew they had to approach the case more aggressively. Part of that was starting the day early. Angela had her finger on the doorbell when her phone buzzed. She checked the message – it was her contact notifying her that Praveen's phone records were ready. About time, she thought. She would get to it after this interview.

Rashmi told them her husband was in the shower, but they could wait if they wanted to. There was no debate about it. They would wait. A delicious aroma had hit them the moment the door opened. Once inside, Paul couldn't resist commenting, "That smells yummy."

Angela tried to suppress her smile. Paul and food. Not surprising at all. But no harm in buttering up Rashmi. Perhaps she would slip up and reveal something. After all, she did look delighted to hear praises for her cooking.

"I am making idli sambhar. It's a traditional South Indian meal."

"What's it made of?" asked Angela, intrigued.

"Idli is rice cakes. You eat it with sambhar, which is a lentil stew with various vegetables and spices. It's Priya's favorite."

"Interesting. Haven't seen that at the Indian restaurants."

"Yeah, most people are only aware of North Indian cuisine. But there are a lot of amazing South Indian joints around."

"I'll be sure to check some out." After a pause, Angela added, "Rashmi, was Praveen really at home all evening?"

The smile on Rashmi's face disappeared. She was quiet for a second. Then she quickly attended to the cooking range, saying, "Oh, the sambhar." She tasted it, turned off the burner and continued, "It's ready. Priya is going to love this. And yes, he was with us the entire time."

Angela was about to follow up when Praveen appeared, a frown clouding his face.

"What is it this time? I have to leave for work."

"We have a few more questions."

He nodded.

"Were you in Oakland on November thirteenth last year?"

He pondered for a moment. "November thirteenth? Hmm ... that was the week we had our conference. Yes, I was there."

"Apart from attending the conference, did you do anything else while you were there?"

"Like what? I didn't have time for anything else."

"You didn't mail any letters?"

"Letters? What kind of letters? No, I attended the conference and that's all."

"Jay received threatening letters in the months before his death. One of the letters was mailed from Oakland on November thirteenth. Quite a coincidence, no?"

"There are plenty of people who could have done that. And what would be the point of it?"

"Yes, anyone could have, but very few people threatened to kill him like you did."

"I can assure you I had nothing to do with those letters."

"You seem familiar with cutting words out of newspapers."

"So? Just simple craft projects for Priya."

"The letters were composed using newspaper cuttings. Another coincidence."

"Look, are you here to waste my time? I didn't do anything."

Angela realized Praveen would not admit to it. And she had no concrete evidence to pin it on him. This wasn't going anywhere. It was time to leave. She hoped they would have more success with Mark.

As they walked out of the apartment towards the stairs, Paul said, "That smelled so delish. I got to get myself some of that Italy sample."

"Umm ... I think she said idli sambhar."

"Oh, what's in a name. All I know is I want to try it."

"Is there a time you are not thinking about food?" she asked in amusement.

"Hey, I had to skip breakfast to get here early this morning. That aroma was driving me nuts. Let's at least grab some coffee on the way."

"Did you notice how she reacted when I asked her about that evening?"

"Yes. It looked suspicious. She was lying. We ..."

"Angela?" asked a voice from behind them.

She turned around to see a tall, blond guy walking towards her with a broad smile.

"It *is* you. Angela White. It's been forever."

"Kyle! What a surprise. What are you doing here?"

"I live here. You crashing here too?"

"No, I'm here on a case. This is my partner, Paul." She turned to Paul and said, "Kyle and I were in college together."

"Let me guess. The Jay Sharma case? Were you here to talk to Praveen?"

"Yes. You know him well?"

"I do. We've been neighbors for a few months now. And before that we worked together at Intelligent Systems. In fact, he's the one who referred me to these apartments."

"Small world."

"Small world indeed. We should catch up sometime."

"Yes, we should. Do you mind if we ask you some questions?"

"Ooh, that sounds scary. Am I a suspect?"

"No, silly. But you have a strong connection to the case. You worked with Jay, and you know Praveen. Could give us some clues."

"Sure. Anything I can do to help. I never interacted with Jay personally, though."

"But do you know anyone who would want to harm him?"

"No way. He was a brilliant man. Of course, you must have heard he was difficult, but if that was reason enough to kill, we would have a lot more murders around here."

"How about Praveen? He had a showdown with Jay and did threaten him."

"Oh, that's why you were talking to him. Nah, not a chance. I have known the guy for a while now. He wouldn't do that. You know, he discussed the row with me once. Told me he felt silly about it. It was so unlike him to threaten someone."

"And the evening of Jay's murder. Do you know if Praveen was home?"

"I was home early that day. There was a Warriors game I wanted to catch. It was around six thirty when I got here. He was leaving his apartment."

"You sure about that?"

"Yes, I remember it well. It's not every day your CEO is found murdered."

"So Praveen was out that evening?"

"I don't know about the entire evening, but I am certain he was going somewhere at that time."

"Interesting. He told us he was in throughout," said Angela, her thoughts going back to the phone records. She couldn't wait to review them.

"Must have slipped his mind."

"You know, this is fascinating. We have been talking to a lot of smart techies, and they all have poor memories. Conveniently forget to tell us important details."

"I hope you don't hold that against all techies," Kyle said with a smile.

Angela laughed.

"No, I can make exceptions for some of them. By the way, do you know Betty Liu?"

"Yes, of course. We work together. Is it about her going missing?"

"You know?"

"What? That she's missing?"

"Yes."

"Yeah. A couple of your detectives came by to ask questions. It's awful. I hope she turns up okay."

"Was she having an affair with Jay?"

"Ah, so you know. That's what it seemed like. But I think they had a falling out."

"Could she kill him over it?"

"Betty? No way! She's one of the sweetest people I know."

"But if she was furious about something? Perhaps then?"

"No, I don't think she could do anything like that."

"Angela, we should talk to Praveen again. Before he leaves," interjected Paul.

"Right. Gotta go, Kyle. Call me sometime. We have a lot to catch up on."

The detectives walked back to Praveen's apartment and got there just as he was stepping out. His nostrils flared when he saw them.

"Oh, not again!"

"Why did you lie to us?"

"What do you mean?"

"You said you were at home the evening of January seventeenth. But you weren't, were you?"

"I don't know what you are talking about."

"We know for a fact that you left the apartment around six thirty p.m."

For a second, it looked like Praveen had been punched in the gut. But he got up well before the count, ready for more.

"Alright, alright. I stepped out for a short while to pick up some dinner. It was hardly thirty minutes."

"You should have told us. Why hide it?"

"I didn't think it mattered. It's not like I had anything to do with the murder."

"All the more reason to be honest with us. Where did you go?"

"An Indian place on El Camino Real. Nowhere near Sunnyvale downtown."

"Anyone who can confirm that?"

"No. I don't think they would remember me there. All I can offer is my credit card statement. That will show you I got the food from there that evening."

"We'll be checking it out. But even if you did pick up there, you could still have gone to Sunnyvale. You have no solid alibi."

"And you have no solid proof. Speculate all you like. The truth is, I didn't do anything. Now, I'm already late for work. Can I leave?"

"Sure, go ahead," replied Angela, knowing there wasn't much more she could do for now.

She watched Praveen walk away. He was right. She didn't have any evidence. But he had become a strong suspect now. They would have to investigate him thoroughly.

AFTER A QUICK STOPOVER at Peet's to quell Paul's worsening hunger, they drove over to SmartCloud. Mark met them in the lobby. They made their way to one of the vacant conference rooms.

"Mark, were you in Oakland on November thirteenth?"

"Yes. In fact, I was there the entire week. We had our annual conference. Big affair."

"Did you mail any letters that day?"

"Letters? No. I didn't have time for anything other than the conference. Why do you ask?"

"Jay received threatening letters before his death. One of the letters was mailed from Oakland that day."

"And you think I did that? How ridiculous. Why would I waste my time on something like that? If I had to whack someone, I would just do it. No games."

Mark paused, realizing he might be misunderstood.

"That's assuming I wanted to whack anyone. I want to make it clear once again – I didn't kill him. Didn't deliver any threats either. A lot of people live and work in Oakland. Anyone could have sent it."

"Possible. But it's interesting that someone who had threatened him was also present in Oakland the day the letter was mailed. What are the odds?"

"And what are the odds you don't have a complete list of people who wanted Jay dead?"

Angela had no answer for that. The detectives left, shoulders drooping. The only way to lift their spirits was to grab some idli sambhar for lunch. Paul was delighted.

PROGRESS
FEBRUARY 7

Angela leaned back in her chair, continuing to twirl the pen in her hand. She had spent the morning reviewing security footage from Vroom for the evening of the seventeenth, and she needed a break. She stopped and inspected the pen, proud that it was still intact. There was a time, not long ago, when she would have gnawed off one end to relieve the stress. For that matter, her nails looked pretty good too. Growing up, she had a nasty habit of nibbling on her nails, especially when nervous. With time that habit had disappeared, only re-emerging briefly during that dark phase after her father's death.

Satisfied, Angela started twirling again, attention back on the case. The video showed Meghna entering the garage a couple of minutes after 7:00 p.m. and leaving around 7:30 p.m. This aligned with what Meghna and her coworkers had told her. That was not enough time to kill a man, drive him to Sunnyvale, dump the body and get back to Milpitas. She could not have done it.

Angela was still lost in thought when Paul walked up to her desk.

"Meghna's alibi checks out," she said, sounding glum.

"I've been examining her phone records," he said. Angela had managed to obtain them in record time. "It confirms there was a text from Jay that evening, but no response from her. And she didn't venture out of the building until nine p.m."

"Anything else of interest?" Angela was quite sure Meghna was a dead end.

"Yes. Lots of calls between her and Mark in the last few months."

"Not incriminating ... unless they worked together on this. But let's see what Meghna has to say about it," she said as she placed the call. Meghna answered at the third ring. Five minutes later Angela hung up.

"She says it was all business. Same as her and Jay. It was all their tech talk – the AI/ML stuff."

"It's possible she is telling the truth. Maybe ..." he trailed off as his phone rang. It was Mark.

"Well, well, look who we have here," said Paul as he accepted the call and put it on speaker.

"Paul, what's this I'm reading about me being a primary suspect in Jay's murder? I mean, I know things looked bad, but I thought you were still investigating."

"You are a person of interest, Mark. You know that. But I can assure you we have not let out any of this information. We wouldn't want to jeopardize the investigation."

"Then why is it all over the place? Someone in the know must have leaked something. It hurts my reputation. And SmartCloud too. Have you seen the stock price lately? If this continues, pretty soon I'll be shown the door."

"The media is blowing things out of proportion as usual. Someone probably found out we talked to you and boom! They have a new story to boost their ratings."

"Well, then, do something about it. Can't have people spreading lies. Bloody fake news!"

"I will see what I can do," replied Paul, trying to calm Mark down. "By the way, we have some more questions for you. Do you mind?"

"Sure, go ahead. Anything if it gets you off my back."

"Do you know Meghna Rao?"

"The CTO at Vroom?"

"Yes, that's the one."

"We have met a few times. And some calls to discuss possibilities for technical collaboration. Why? Is she a suspect too?"

"No. Just something that came up during our investigation."

"Well, then, you should get serious about her. She is a more likely suspect than I am. And I'm not saying this to make my life easier."

"What do you mean?"

"You know they were lovers, right? Jay and Meghna. Until she found out he was conning her. That's when she dumped him and threatened to kill him. Now, that is way more motivation than IP theft."

"How do we know you're telling the truth? She denied having anything more than a professional relationship."

"Of course she didn't tell you. Why would she tell anyone? It's embarrassing. If you don't believe me, ask Maya."

"Maya knew?" asked Angela in surprise.

"You bet she did. It took her a while to find out, but she did. Can't hide this stuff for long."

"How do you know all this?"

"Jay was still at SmartCloud when he first met Meghna. As with all his conquests, he loved sharing the details with me. It boosted his fragile male ego."

"When did Maya find out?"

"Hmm ... I don't remember exactly, but it was after he left SmartCloud."

"How do you know this? I thought you two weren't talking after he left."

"We weren't. But I have my ways. Got to keep tabs on your enemy."

"You were spying on him?"

"Perhaps. Don't forget, we were squabbling a lot. I had to do what I could to get what was due me."

"But you still lost the case."

"Yes, unfortunately I didn't have any leverage."

"How come?"

"Well, I wanted to exploit Jay's weakness and have him admit that he cheated me. I had a private investigator watch him and collect dirt. Something incriminating that he wouldn't want revealed and would force him to concede. One day my detective followed him to Meghna's place and got some compromising pics of them together. He was about to leave once Jay left, when he saw Maya walk up to the door. So he stayed to see what happened. That's when he learned that she knew. And later, when Meghna confronted and threatened Jay, he was there too."

By this time, there was one thought going through Angela's mind. Maya had lied to them. Big time. Maybe Weilin had heard correctly after all. First Betty, now Meghna. Jay's list of affairs grew with every passing day. Wasn't that enough motive for Maya?

"If you had all this dirt on him why didn't you use it?"

"I wanted to. And I tried as well. But that guy's not easy to mess with. He countered with some dirt on me. I had to let it go."

"What did he have on you?"

"That's none of your business."

"You're right. That is none of my business. For now. Now, this detective, does he have a name?"

"Oh, come on. You aren't going to talk to him, are you?"

"This is a murder investigation. It's important we follow every lead thoroughly. If this detective of yours was keeping tabs on Jay, then he may be able to give us some clues. Don't worry, we will be discreet."

"It's Shaun Jacobs. One of the best in the business. Works out of an office in Sunnyvale. You can find his contact info online."

"Thanks, Mark."

"Sorry about my outburst earlier."

Angela and Paul were quiet for a while after hanging up. Both were deep in thought, digesting all this new information. The case was getting complicated. A bunch of suspects, all with sufficient motive to kill Jay. However, there was no strong evidence that would hold up in court. But for now, their next steps were clear. To save time, they decided that Paul would talk to Maya and Angela would interrogate Meghna.

ANGELA MET MEGHNA AT VROOM. She had to wait thirty minutes while Meghna wrapped up her meeting. Then they headed to Taxi Driver conference room.

"So what is it this time?" asked Meghna with an edge in her voice.

"For starters, you keep telling us your discussions with Jay and Mark were related to what you were working on. What is it you discussed?"

"You think I am making it all up?" Meghna's face broke into a wry smile.

"Something like that," replied Angela, mirroring the expression.

"Okay, let me break it down for you. Both SmartCloud and Intelligent Systems offer artificial intelligence/machine learning platforms that can be used by customers for their specific needs. You are probably familiar with these terms – there's been a lot of buzz about it. AI, and its subset ML, enable machines to think and behave like humans, to analyze inputs and take appropriate action. This intelligence is not static. Like with humans, these machines are able to learn from experience and get better at whatever it is they are expected to do. Autonomous cars, at their core, have similar technology. But while the platforms are generic, our software is specialized to focus on the task of driving safely and efficiently. Since the core technology is similar, it opens up opportunities to collaborate, both on a technical level as well as at a business level. We can learn from each other about technical advances, and further down the road, instead of using our custom software, we could use generic platforms for cost efficiency. That's the brief version of it. Of course, there's much more to it, and here at Vroom we have a clear vision of where we are going, but I can't discuss details. Does that make sense?"

"Yes, I think I get the gist. But if that's the agenda, you must have spoken to other companies in this space as well, not just these two, right? Quite a coincidence if you have only been speaking to the two related to this case."

Meghna smirked. "Clutching at straws, are we? The truth is, there isn't any other company worth talking to. There are many other players, but they have a long way to go before they get to where we are. Now, Lumiotech is a strong one and would appear to be an obvious candidate, but they have their hands in everything, including AI/ML and autonomous vehicles. That makes them a direct competitor. It rules them out as an option."

"Fair enough. But we know you lied."

"About what?"

"You and Jay were lovers. You threatened to kill him."

Meghna flinched. "I see you are smarter than I thought. Wonder how you found out. Anyway, it was a long time ago. It's not easy to tell complete strangers that you had an affair with a married man."

She had a point. Angela had to give her that. No, it would be downright embarrassing.

"But you still had an obligation to tell the truth. This concerns a murder investigation."

"I'm sorry I lied. I didn't think it was relevant."

"Let us decide what is relevant and what is not. Now, was that last meeting and text really only professional?"

"Okay, I guess I should come clean. It is true we bumped into each other on the fifteenth. I didn't want to talk to him. But he was so persistent. He literally begged me to have a drink with him for old times' sake, so I obliged. I didn't want to create a scene. We chatted for a short while, and then I left. He wanted to see me again, so I agreed to meet him on the seventeenth. That's why he texted. Of course, I had no intention of actually meeting him. It was an excuse to get away the previous night."

"Quite a coincidence that he sent the text around the time you left the room."

"Yeah, I know. It doesn't look good. But you have to believe me, I did not meet him that night."

"Then why did you leave the room? What did you do? Where did you go?"

"Like I told you last time, I had to inspect something on some of the cars. Regarding an issue we found."

"Did anyone see you there?"

"No, it was kinda late. Why do you keep asking me the same questions over and over?!"

"So it's possible you didn't go to check on the cars. You could have met Jay, murdered him and sneaked back to the room."

"Are you even listening to me? You can speculate and fantasize as much as you like, but you know it was not practically possible. Dead bodies don't transport themselves magically. Even if I did kill him, it is impossible to go from Milpitas to Sunnyvale and back in that short a time, especially at rush hour."

Angela knew Meghna was right. It wasn't adding up. Yet, she had hoped that engaging Meghna in more talk would reveal something. She had to admit, at this point Meghna didn't look like much of a suspect.

PAUL WALKED into the Yummy Tummy lobby and found Maya waiting for him. He had called ahead, and she had confirmed she was available that afternoon. She wasn't back to a full workload yet. In fact, people were surprised she was back to work at all so soon after the tragedy. But she had explained that she needed to keep her mind busy to escape the depressing thoughts. They walked over to one of the vacant conference rooms. Paul spoke once they were seated.

"Maya, do you know Meghna Rao?"

"If you are referring to the Vroom CTO, then yes. I have met her a few times."

"What were these meetings about?"

"May I ask why you need to know?"

"You knew she had an affair with your husband. Yet, you didn't tell us about it."

"What was there to tell? He was involved with a lot of women. Meghna was another one of his conquests. Besides, it was a long time ago."

"You mean to say he was cheating on you the whole time you were married, you knew about it, and you didn't do anything about it?"

"Well, the first one was a shock. The next few were painful. But then I got used to it. I told you earlier. It wasn't a happy marriage."

"Why didn't you tell us about his infidelity earlier?"

"Is it relevant? I doubt he was done in by some angry girlfriend."

"Maya, here's how this works. We ask you questions, you answer truthfully, and we decide what is relevant and what isn't. Got it?"

"Got it."

"Now. Was that what you and Jay fought about on the morning of the seventeenth?"

"Oh, not that silly fight again. I told you before, we did not argue about any affairs that morning."

"But you confronted Meghna when you found out, right?"

Maya flinched. "How do you know?"

"We have our methods. What happened?"

"Well, our mundane married life was drifting along as usual. But at some point, I got this feeling that he was up to no good. It worried me. I had to find out. One night, I managed to get into his phone and read the steamy messages. I was furious. I had to see for myself. What was so special about this woman that he enjoyed her company more than mine? In her last message, she invited him over the following afternoon. I decided to follow him. They spent around an hour in there. He came out beaming. Once he drove off, I got out of my car and went over. The poor woman opened the door looking so happy, sure that Jay was back. You should have seen her face when she realized it was me. The bitch recognized me. All she had on was a negligee. I forced my way inside. It was quite a sight. Her clothes were strewn all over the living room. I could tell they had been having sex. I gave her an earful. She cried, giving me her side of the story. He had cheated her as much as he had cheated me."

"How come?"

"He told her we were getting divorced. Naturally, she had some expectation of marriage further down the road. But our split was nowhere on the horizon, and I told her so."

"How did she react? I expect she was angry?"

"Oh yeah. Livid. Any self-respecting woman would be. Besides, it would be embarrassing to be confronted like that by the woman whose husband you are sleeping with."

"Did she threaten to kill him?"

"She didn't say anything of the sort to me. And I don't think she is the kind of person who could murder anyone."

"You know her that well? Well enough to know whether she could do it?"

"We did meet a few times after that. Chatted on the phone occasionally. I got to know her quite well. In any case, if she was so angry, why would she wait so long?"

"Let me get this straight. You were friendly with that woman? The one your husband had an affair with?" asked Paul, leaving no doubt he wasn't buying that.

"I know it's difficult to believe, but yes. I was furious when I first met her, and I left in a huff. But I bumped into her at a restaurant a couple of days later. She came up to me and apologized. By then I had some time to think things over. Like I said, she didn't know about the situation. If she had, she would never have done it. In some ways this common thread of being cheated by Jay helped us bond. It was fun to talk to someone who knew him as intimately as I did. We could joke about all his quirks, all his flaws. How awful he was in bed."

"So you were close friends after that?"

"I wouldn't say friends, but we got along well."

"And you are still in touch with her?"

"No, I haven't communicated with her in a long time. You know how it is – life gets in the way. With our busy lives it is difficult to stay connected with everyone."

"Did you ever discuss her with Jay?"

"Why would I bother? Our marriage was on the rocks. And it's not like he would have stopped sniffing all over town."

"You sure had a lot of patience, living with a guy like that. You told us earlier he was a real pain to live with. And now you tell us he was cheating on you all the time. I can imagine at some point you must have considered ending the misery. I don't know, maybe divorce is not an option in your culture, but are you telling me you never entertained the thought of doing away with him?"

Maya smirked. "You think killing a man is easier than divorcing him?"

"Certainly a lot more lucrative. You divorce him, you only get half the assets. He dies, you get everything plus the life insurance."

"I know it's been a while since the murder, and you are under pressure to make progress. But this reeks of desperation. You are shooting in the dark. You realize even half the assets is a lot of money? In any case, I earn enough to manage well on my own. Why would I be so stupid? First kill him and then hang for it. My life would be over."

"Not if you planned the perfect murder. You're a smart woman. You could get away with it."

"Come on, Detective. You know there is no such thing as a perfect murder. They always slip up and get caught. Besides, I don't think I could do it. Are you seriously still considering me as a suspect?"

"I do have one more question for you," he replied, ignoring Maya's question.

"Shoot."

"You received a text at seven twenty-five that night. Who was it from?"

"I did? I don't recall."

He showed her the number.

"I don't recognize this. Let me search my contacts."

Maya typed in the number, then continued, "No, nothing. I don't see anything in my text logs either."

"Try to remember. You were in the conference room at the time. One of your coworkers told us you were a bit stressed after that."

"Hmm ... I don't remember being stressed that evening. It was probably one of those annoying spam texts. You know, like get Ray-Ban fifty percent off. Do you get those too?"

"Yeah, I do," replied Paul, sounding disappointed. He had hoped there would be something more substantial. But then again, how could he trust what Maya was saying? She could have made that up. He had already looked up the phone number but had been unable to find an owner. It had been traced to a pay-as-you-go carrier, Bliss-Voice. Paul had subpoenaed their records and found that the purchase had been made six months ago at a mall kiosk in Fresno. The buyer had paid cash. The mall only had surveillance records going back a month. Whoever used the number was determined to stay anonymous. It didn't necessarily mean it was used for criminal activity. Spammers preferred anonymity too.

"One more thing. You told us you were in the conference room until nine o'clock that night."

"That is correct."

"Did you leave the room anytime before that?"

"Yes. For thirty minutes or so. It was getting to be too much. I needed a breath of fresh air."

"What time was this?"

"Sometime after eight, if I recall."

"Couldn't you have waited for the session to be over at nine?"

"I didn't know at the time that we would be done so soon."

"I see. Where did you go?"

"I took a walk in the parking lot. Thankfully, it wasn't raining, or I would have gone crazy."

Paul took a moment to think things through, and decided he was done.

"Maya, that's all the questions I have for you at this time. Thanks again for your time."

"No problem at all. Whatever I can do to help nab the culprit."

He walked out, his head spinning. This was getting way too complicated. He needed some hard evidence. Circumstantial evidence and speculation would only go so far.

THE PRIVATE INVESTIGATOR
FEBRUARY 9

Angela and Paul entered the office of Shaun Jacobs. It was in a small building in a row of businesses along El Camino Real in Sunnyvale. A single worn desk dominated the middle of the room, with the PI ensconced in a chair behind it. In the background stood a wall shelf on which rested a white, marble bust of what appeared to be some ancient Greek philosopher. Angela guessed it was Plato, or was it Socrates? She could never get her philosophers straight. On her side of the desk were two unsteady-looking chairs. Files and papers were strewn all over the place. And there was a musty odor. Not the kind of detective she would have expected someone like Mark to hire. Perhaps Shaun was terrific at his job, and that's what really mattered. Mark did have a high opinion of him.

"What an honor. Real detectives visiting my humble abode. How can I help you?"

Could this guy be any more annoying? thought Angela.

"I see things have improved a lot in the force. Never had such pretty things back in the day," he continued as he ogled her. She glared at him. Before either of them knew what was going on, Paul had reached across the desk and hauled Shaun up by the collar.

"She's the best detective in the department. Show her some respect, you disgusting lowlife! I swear if I catch you looking at her again or making any nasty comments, I will break this little neck of yours!"

Angela was happy to see Paul stand up for her. She only wished he would have the courage to take such action with Shibata as well.

Shaun shuddered, not expecting this hostile reaction. He dared not lock eyes with her, so he gave Paul a meek, apologetic look as he got back into his chair.

"Now, we understand you were engaged by Mark Harrison a few years ago? To watch Jay Sharma," said Paul.

"I can confirm he hired me. But I can't comment on what he hired me for. As a professional, I take client confidentiality seriously."

"He is okay with it. You can call him to confirm. Anyway, we aren't interested in him. We want to know what you found about Jay. He was murdered last month, and we're investigating."

"Ah, yes, I saw that in the papers. I can help you with that. If my memory serves me right, I was to watch Jay for three months and collect any dirt I could. Oh, the stuff I saw. I can tell you, he couldn't keep it in his pants much."

"Yes, that's what we hear too. What did you find?"

"He spent most of his time at work. Nights at home. But in between, he spent a lot of time with women. At Cinebar, in hotel rooms, or their homes. Some were women he knew personally. Others were escorts."

"You documented these encounters?"

"Yes, I have dates, times, also pictures, where possible."

"Anyone he met who would have wanted to murder him?"

"He pissed off a bunch of women, I can tell you that. But no one who would want to kill him. Though, there was this one Indian woman who threatened him. But I don't think she would dare mess with him after what he did to her."

"Who was this woman?"

"Hang on. Let me check my notes," replied Shaun as he fished a set of keys out of his pocket. He used one of the keys to unlock a drawer in the desk and then searched it. Out came a thick diary. He started flipping through it.

"Yes, here she is. Meghna Rao. Incidentally, this is the one where his wife found out. Smart woman followed him there. It was only a matter of time before he was caught in the act."

"What did he do to Meghna?"

"Casanova had told her he was getting a divorce. But she learned from the wife that it was a lie. She was pissed, and invited him over a couple of days later to give him an earful. But it didn't turn out the way she had planned."

"You saw that too?"

"Wouldn't have missed it for the world."

"What happened?"

"She lashed out at him. Called him names, threatened to kill him. Said she never wanted to see him again. He went ballistic and hit her. She fell. He kicked her when she was down, verbally abused her. Then he walked out and slashed her car tires."

"He hit her in front of your eyes, and you didn't do anything?" asked Angela, furious.

"It was all over so fast. I didn't have time to react."

"And she didn't report this abuse?"

"Quite sure she didn't want a scandal. In fact, I don't think she even went to a hospital. She handled it on her own."

"This gives her a much stronger motive to kill him."

"Perhaps. But is it worth the risk of getting caught? I think she's smart enough to know that."

"And the wife? She must have been angry to find out he was cheating. You think she could have done it?"

"Not really. I mean, she was seething going into Meghna's house. But she was calm when she came out. I think she got all the rage out of her system."

"You must have watched Jay when he was home too?"

"Yes, sure I did."

"How was his relationship with his wife?"

"Oh, they fought. Fought a lot. It was like war after this incident. And I don't think they had been intimate in a while. They were living more like roommates."

"Any threats or violence?"

"That night got a little violent. You know, the night she found out. He hit her. She hit him back. She was mad at him for cheating, and he didn't like being accused."

"How did you find out all this?"

"I have my ways. Tricks of the trade."

"Anything else of note?"

"No. My commission ended a few days after that. Mark was delighted with what I got him."

"We appreciate your helping us here, Shaun."

"Glad I could be of help. You suspect the wife?"

"She had motive for sure."

"Nah, I don't think she did it. Not the type. She may have wanted it, but I don't think she could ever follow through."

"Let's hope you're right."

THAT NIGHT

JANUARY 17

It had been a rough day. Mark rose from his office chair, trying to stretch out the tightness in his body. His shoulders felt like rocks. SmartCloud was losing market share to Intelligent Systems. The entire day had been spent in meetings to figure out how to stem the bleeding. It had been the same for the last two days, and he knew it would continue for another few. They needed a winning strategy. Their rival had the momentum after the legal win, and it was not easy to stop them, especially with a ruthless Jay at the top.

Mark checked his watch. It was 6:15 p.m. He decided to pack up for the day and head for dinner. Within a few minutes he was at Sha Sha Shawarma, his body relaxing as he entered his happy place. Jenna and he had been regulars there when they were together. He seated himself, and soon the server was at his table. She was a charming, young woman, and his heart skipped a beat as he scanned her face. Her name was Janine. He couldn't resist flirting with her, nervously fondling his lapel pin like a young schoolboy. She didn't seem to mind, though once she had left with his order he checked himself. What was he thinking? She was young enough to be his daughter. In fact, he guessed his daughter would be about the same age if Jenna hadn't miscarried. Mark was happy to have his two boys, but he always wondered how different life would have been if they hadn't lost the unborn girl. His thoughts were interrupted when Janine placed his order before him. His favorite. Tender chunks of lamb cooked in yogurt and spices. Steaming hot. He mouthed a polite thank you with a smile and dug into the food.

As he ate, Mark looked around him at the packed restaurant. Tables full of people, their radiant faces telling him what a festive time they were having. He glanced across his own table and the empty seat reminded him of Jenna. All the precious moments they had there, enjoying fabulous meals, making lovey-dovey talk, cracking jokes and sharing stories. He missed her so much, and times like these amplified that void.

Janine stopped by to refill his glass. As she left, he checked his watch. 7:30 p.m. This was as good a time as any. He stepped out of the restaurant. Ten minutes later, he was back with a contented smile on his face, and a warmth spreading through his body. Janine returned to clear the table as soon as he had settled down. Yes, he would like some dessert.

A group of young guys eased into the table next to his. He envied them for their youth. Their entire lives ahead of them, so many hopes, so many aspirations. Unlike him, all alone with the love of his life lost to him. Unlike him, with all the stresses and tensions that came with being CEO.

One of the guys turned to him and asked him whether he was Mark Harrison of SmartCloud. Yes, he was. The youth gushingly introduced himself and confessed that he was his role model. Some day he would like to work for SmartCloud. Mark wished him well and returned to his dessert. Life wasn't so bad, was it? He had achieved a lot in life, and it was gratifying to know that people looked up to him, wanted to be him. That thought, and the rich chocolate cake before him, perked him up again. Tomorrow would be a new day. He would bring Intelligent Systems to its knees. Yes, he would.

PRAVEEN STEPPED out of his apartment around 6:30 p.m. He had only gone a few steps when he saw Kyle. They exchanged pleasantries, and then he drove over to the family's favorite Indian restaurant to pick up dinner. Once back in his car, he hesitated about what to do next. The tantalizing aroma of chicken tikka masala and hot naans had pervaded the car, and he was tempted to dig into the food. But then, he was only ten minutes from Sunnyvale downtown. His watch showed it was a few minutes past 7:00 p.m. What he had to do there wouldn't take long. He decided to make the trip. It was best to take care of things before heading back home.

THE SECOND BODY
FEBRUARY 10

The score was tied at 11-11, with less than a minute to go. Paul was determined to add a sixth Super Bowl ring to his impressive collection. After a quick huddle, the players positioned themselves for the next play. Soon the ball was in motion, and he raced down the field the instant he had it in his hands. He was taking a considerable risk with this play, but he was convinced they needed a different approach to seal a win. He ran with the ball, skillfully weaving his way past the Patriots players trying to tackle him. Yard after yard melted away as he sprinted, the roar of the spectators growing with each stride. A few moments later he was in the end zone, slamming the ball into the ground for a historic touchdown. The crowd went berserk. With barely five seconds left on the clock, the Chiefs had pretty much locked in this one. His teammates joined him in celebration. Paul was delirious. His risky play had panned out. He heard a loud, annoying sound. It was so loud that it overpowered the noise from the stands. He wanted it to stop, but it wouldn't. It was his phone.

He tried to ignore it and return to his glorious dream, but it squealed again, four more times in the next two minutes. It was only

7:00 a.m. Why was Angela calling him this early on a Saturday morning?

"Hello," he answered, the word crawling out of his mouth.

"Good morning, Paul. Were you sleeping?" she asked, a hint of excitement in her voice.

"No, I just got back from a twenty-mile hike."

She laughed out loud.

"So you were sleeping. Guess what? Shibata called."

"Shibata called you? Everything okay?"

"Yeah, well, once he got past the usual tawdry talk. Sleeping Beauty. That's how he started off today."

"That doesn't sound tawdry. Corny, yes. But not tawdry."

"Well, it went further downhill from there."

"Sometimes I wanna punch that guy in the face. Hard."

"Only sometimes?"

"Ha! You make an excellent point, Now, why did he call?"

"They found Betty."

"Awesome! Where?"

"In a Sunnyvale home. Dead," replied Angela in a low tone.

"Oh no! That's terrible. Was she murdered?"

"Yes. Her head was bashed in. It appears she was sexually assaulted first. The homeowners returned from a long vacation and noticed there was a break-in. They found the body when they went inside and called 911 immediately. And get this, she was pregnant when she died."

"Jay's baby? Is that what their rift was about?"

"Quite possible. He probably freaked out when she told him. But if Betty is dead, that means she didn't kill him."

"Not necessarily. She could have been attacked after she killed Jay."

"More likely, the killer saw them together and murdered Jay first. Then went for her."

"But then why was Jay's body in the parking lot and her body in the home?"

"Because the killer wanted to assault her first? He needed some privacy."

"Perhaps. Have they found her car yet?"

"No, not yet. You can go back to bed now."

"You think I can sleep after hearing this?"

"If you can't sleep, you should go on that hike for real."

"The kind of shape I'm in, I'll be lucky if I can make it past mile five."

They both laughed, but Paul was grave once he hung up. It was sad, what Betty had gone through. What did this do for their case? Simplified things a bit, with one suspect out of the picture. Which didn't mean much, because the entire investigation was still a huge mess, and they had no idea how to clean it up.

BUNDLES OF JOY
FEBRUARY 11

Maya awoke with a start. Still groggy, it took her a few seconds to recall what had interrupted her sleep. Memories. Bad ones. Hijacking her dreams. She had replayed another conversation with Gauri, this one a few weeks after the one where she had learned the truth about Jay. Maya had called her to apologize for her behavior. Gauri had accepted the apology but had gone on to tell her more about Jay's deviant ways. Her coworker, Martha Jones, had been a strong contender for the CFO position, but she was passed up because she had refused his advances. Instead, he had opted for Sharon Strong, another colleague, one who didn't mind indulging him if it helped her career. It had been another blow to Maya, and strangely, that revelation still rankled. Reliving those memories left her feeling downcast. So, she was only too happy to accept when Anjali called to ask whether she would like to join the Bhatia girls at the park. This was exactly what she needed to get her spirits up.

It was a beautiful Sunday morning, with clear blue skies interspersed with fluffy, white clouds. There was no sign of rain, and people were out in droves to enjoy this respite from the downpour the previous week. Maya and Anjali drove over to nearby Hellyer Park.

Zara and Sara were having a blast, on the swing, on the slide and running around the children's playground, which was a recent addition to the park. Maya loved kids, and with none of her own, she was glad she could spend time with Anjali's little angels.

Suddenly, she felt a burst of sadness. These girls gave her so much joy, but the fact was, they were not hers. She could occasionally spend a few hours with them, but they would not go home with her. She wouldn't read them bedtime stories and tuck them into bed. They wouldn't call her "mama." Had she made a mistake by not starting a family? Her marriage had been a disaster, but perhaps it could have been saved had there been children in the picture? That was the advice she had often heard going around in India when a couple had issues – have kids and it will get better. But she didn't believe that. Children could be a distraction from the real marital issues, but could they solve the problem? She had seen plenty of marriages where it only made the situation worse. And the innocent children were dragged into the mess as well. Seeing their parents fighting constantly, not learning anything about healthy relationships. She hoped it was not too late for her. With Jay gone, there was a chance that someday she would have the family and children she craved.

"Maya aunty, Maya aunty!" she heard Zara calling out to her from the slide. "Look at me," Zara shrieked as she slid down.

She ran over to Maya and gave her a hug. Sara scampered over a few seconds later and joined in. This was nice. This was bliss. It didn't matter that these were not her kids. These girls were bundles of joy, and she was indeed lucky to have them in her life.

***

ANGELA PARKED the car on the street, the wheels almost kissing the curb. She was about to step out, when she saw an SUV drive by and enter Anjali's driveway. Anjali and Maya emerged and eased the twins out of the car seats. Maya planted a soft kiss on the forehead of the girl she was carrying. It brought back fond memories for Angela, memories of her father doing the same to his sweet little angel. She smiled a bittersweet smile as she saw them go inside Anjali's house. What she would give to hug her father one more time. Soon Maya returned, walking towards her own house.

Angela stepped out of the car and called out to her, just as she was unlocking her front door. Maya turned around, curiosity turning to annoyance once she saw who it was.

"What is it?"

"Maya, can we talk? It's about some recent developments."

"Don't you ever take a break? It's Sunday for heaven's sake! Some of us like to relax and recharge for the work week."

"Sorry about that. But we want to resolve this case as soon as possible. I am sure you want the same. It's just that I was in the area and decided this is something I could get done."

"Alright, come in. What do you want to know?"

"When we talked previously, you said you and Jay fought, but there was never any violence. Is it really true?"

"Of course it is. How many times do I have to repeat myself?"

"What about the day you found out about him and Meghna? He didn't hit you?"

Maya sighed.

"Yes, he did. And I hit him back. But that was it. It had never happened before, never happened again."

"Why didn't you tell us about it earlier?"

"Because it is irrelevant. Nothing to do with this case. I can't go around remembering and relaying every little detail about our marriage to perfect strangers."

"Maya, we have told you this before, and I would like to remind you again. This is a murder investigation. Your husband was killed. Details do matter. We keep catching you in a lie over and over. I suspect you are hiding a lot more than what you are letting on. Makes me wonder whether you had anything to do with his death."

"You can think whatever the hell you like! Maybe if you were better at your job, you would have caught the killer by now and wouldn't go around accusing innocent people. I lost my husband and am trying hard to recover. Yet, you come in, trampling over my life every few days, reminding me of my loss. And worse, humiliating me with false accusations."

Maya was in tears now. Angela felt terrible and didn't have the heart to continue the interview. She left Maya alone and drove back home. Some days she hated her job.

JAY

JANUARY 15

Jay sat at the bar at Cinebar, nursing his Zin. It was his favorite place to hang out after work, more so when he was feeling a little gloomy. He didn't drink much, but when he did, he enjoyed a glass of red wine. Cinebar had a vintage movie theme and was tastefully decorated. Various promotional posters of Hollywood blockbusters from the pre-sixties era adorned the walls. His personal favorites were the ones with Humphrey Bogart. Like his beverage preferences, his movie preferences were limited too. He didn't watch a lot of flicks, with only old black-and-white classics making the cut.

His career was thriving, Intelligent Systems was flourishing, he had dodged the SmartCloud crisis, so he should have been happy. Yet, tonight he was miserable on account of his personal life. His marriage was a mess, with an obstinate wife who was always picking fights with him. They didn't have any kids, and likely wouldn't have any, at a time when most guys his age had one or two. He was sick of hearing his mother ask him when she would hear some "good news," and remind him how the clock was ticking. He was sick of his coworkers discussing their children endlessly, talking about school and classes and summer camps. Taking time off for "bonding," whatever that meant. And he was sick of the gloating parents, showing off how their kids were straight-A students, or had aced some science fair or had gotten into MIT. He wanted a child or two, too, so he could shut up those other idiots. With his superior genes his children would outperform them all. But where would these kids come from? Maya, at thirty-six, was probably not capable of giving him any. Not that she wanted to, anyway. She had been distant for a while now, and even the routine intimate moments they used to enjoy earlier were gone. He had to venture outside to satisfy himself. He didn't even find her all that attractive anymore. She was such a beauty when he had first met her. But now she had aged. Yes, it was time to divorce her and find someone young and docile, someone who would give him the children he longed for. Someone who would obey him without question, please him, not have any ambition outside the house. Someone who wouldn't expect him to help with the laundry or dishes or any other household chores. He was made for better things. Such drudgery was a waste of his time. He knew his mother would be happy to hear of it and would be pleased to find him a decent Indian girl.

Jay turned around as a noisy group entered and walked past him to a booth. As he was turning back to his Zin, he noticed a familiar face in the corner booth, right below the fabulous poster of Humphrey Bogart, Peter Lorre and Sydney Greenstreet in *The Maltese Falcon*. It was Meghna, flashing a wide smile at him. Oh, how he missed her. Missed those passionate moments. Now, she was still attractive, though only a couple of years younger than Maya. But she wouldn't make an acceptable wife. Too opinionated, too ambitious. Like Betty. But no harm in having some more fun while he hunted for a new life partner. Meghna had that flirty look in her eyes, the "come, get me, tiger" expression he knew so well. How could he resist?

He walked over to her table and greeted her. She motioned him to sit.

"I thought we weren't talking anymore."

"We weren't. But then I realized how much I missed fucking you."

"Likewise. You stalking me?"

"Kinda. I know how much you love this place."

"What's the plan? Want to go somewhere? Your place, perhaps?"

"I don't have much time today, but how about we walk back to my car, get a little frisky and get together later this week for the main course?"

"Sounds like a plan."

Thirty minutes later, Jay stepped out of Meghna's car, happy and somewhat satisfied. He was looking forward to the full encounter. His plans for Wednesday evening would have to change to accommodate that.

NEW DEVELOPMENTS
FEBRUARY 13

With everything that had been going on, Angela had not had time to review Praveen's phone records. When she finally got around to it, she didn't find anything interesting in the call logs. However, the location data revealed he had lied to them again. He did stop at the Indian restaurant he had indicated, but after that he had driven to Sunnyvale downtown, and had spent considerable time there. She walked over to Paul to discuss her findings.

"This moves Praveen up the list, right?" he asked.

"You bet it does. Why is everyone lying to us if they're all innocent? Let's see what excuse he comes up with this time. I ..." Angela trailed off as her phone rang. She spoke for a few minutes and turned to him with a smile after hanging up.

"What?" he asked, his eyes bright with anticipation.

"That was Officer Garcia from SJPD. They found the guy who robbed Jay."

"Awesome! Did he kill him too?"

"He denied he murdered him. But we have a chance to talk to him. Get some more info, check if he is lying."

"Let's go, then."

A short while later, they were at the police department in down-town San Jose. Officer Garcia greeted them and filled them in on the details.

"His name is Joseph Landry, a homeless guy. Used to hang out in San Jose until they cleaned up the homeless camps. That's when he moved to Sunnyvale."

"Was he in San Jose long?"

"No. Sad story. He was a well-heeled finance professional in San Francisco. Lost his job after the 2008 recession and was unable to land on his feet after that. His wife developed breast cancer. Died soon after. No income, no health insurance and all those medical bills. He went bankrupt, and losing her drove him over the edge. He ended up on the streets."

"Sad indeed. How did you nab him?"

"He was trying to sell off Maya Sharma's jewelry. The jeweler got suspicious and reported it to us. Joseph confessed after his arrest. He stole the Rolex, the wedding ring, cash, and credit cards from Jay. His keys as well. He told us the socks and sneakers he was wearing were Jay's. Maya's address was obtained from the driver's license. That's how he knew where to go, and he was able to waltz in there."

"You mean to say this guy broke into her home?"

"Yes. You didn't know that?"

"No, she never told us."

"When did this happen?"

"The night of January twenty-first."

"A few days after Jay's death. Interesting. Did Joseph murder Jay?"

"He says he found the body, but he didn't kill him. But then, we didn't press him much on that. We were more interested in the break-in. You can interrogate him about the murder."

"Thanks, we appreciate that."

The detectives were shown into the interrogation room. Joseph was seated at the table. So much hair, was Angela's first thought. The long, unkempt locks, full mustache and beard. The hairless parts of his face were covered in patches of grime. It took her a few moments to recover from the odors and continue.

"Joseph, what were you doing in Sunnyvale downtown that evening?"

"I go there often. Some of the restaurant workers are thoughtful enough to hand me leftover food at the end of the night. I was there to get some."

"Tell us what happened."

"I was walking over to the restaurants when I saw the body. He seemed quite dead, so I got his shoes. Perfect fit. You see, I had been barefoot for a long time, ever since my last pair went to pieces. It was cold that evening, so I figured, let's get the socks too. I put them on, and was about to walk away, when I noticed the Rolex. I grabbed it. And then I thought, might as well check his wallet. I'm glad I did, because he was loaded. I took his cash and cards. Then I got greedy. I thought, this is a rich guy, I can do better. I checked his other pockets and found his keys. He owned a Tesla. Cool, I thought. Now, if I had his address, I could find some more riches in his house. I had barely read the address off his license when I heard a sound and saw this woman looking straight at me. I panicked and ran away."

Angela's heart skipped a beat. The woman again. Could this be the break they needed?

"This woman, what did she look like?" she asked.

"I didn't get much of a look. I was so scared. I didn't want to get caught stealing, or worse, be accused of killing that guy. All I remember is, she was tall, blonde, and had a red coat on."

It was quite generic, but this matched the description of the woman Andy had seen with the body. But if Jay was dead when she came by, she couldn't have killed him. Angela still wasn't sure what all this meant.

"Did you murder him?"

"No! I told you – I found him dead."

"And what time was it that you saw the body?"

"I remember the Rolex showed it was almost nine o'clock."

"And where were you before that? Specifically, between seven p.m. and eight p.m.?"

"Oh, just walking around town."

"So no alibi?"

"I wish I did."

"You realize this makes you a murder suspect?"

"Yes, I do. But who cares what a homeless man like me does with his time? There is no one to vouch for me. All I can tell you is, I did not kill him. I stole from him. I don't deny that. But I did not kill him."

"Did you take his cell phone too?"

"No. I searched him but didn't find one."

"Interesting." Angela wondered whether the killer took it. "Have you ever been arrested before?"

"No. I have lived an honest life. Well, at least until now, that is."

This meant it was unlikely his prints would be on file anywhere. She made a mental note to run his prints against the ones they had found on the evidence.

"Do you own syringes? A lot of homeless people do drugs."

"No. Not anymore. I did experiment a long time back. Those were dark days. But I was able to kick the habit. So no, I don't own any."

There was not much more Angela could do at this point. The detectives exited the room for a discussion with Officer Garcia.

"Officer, did you search Joseph's belongings?"

"Yes, we got everything. A shopping cart full of random stuff. Didn't find anything interesting."

"No drugs or syringes?"

"No, nothing of the sort. He's clean. You think he did it?"

"We don't have any evidence. He claims to have been with the body a while after our murder window. Quite likely, he didn't have anything to do with it, but we will look into it. Thanks for notifying us. By the way, did you take his prints?"

"Yes, we did."

"Great. We need to run those against the ones we found at the scene."

"Sure. By the way, these two murders your department is investigating – Jay Sharma and Betty Liu – we may have something more for you."

"What do you mean?"

"There's this woman, Margaret Lane. Lives in San Jose. She claims she has visions. Visions of dead people that she sees a while before they die. She has come to us in the past with all kinds of crazy stories. But this last time was different. She reported visions of two deaths. As usual, we laughed it off, but once we heard about Jay's and Betty's murders, we realized it matched her descriptions. This was a few days before they died."

"Interesting. Can you give us her contact information?"

"I'll get it for you."

Angela noted the details. They drove back in silence until the car stopped at a light. Paul peered out the window and spotted a man in shabby clothes standing at the intersection. He had a sign saying, "Homeless and hungry please anything helps." People in some of the cars ahead of them were rolling down their windows and handing him money. It was a sight Paul had observed many times since he had moved to California.

"How did it come to this?" he asked.

"What do you mean?"

"So much poverty, so many homeless people. Everywhere I turn I see people starving and begging for food. People living on the streets or in filthy tents, with only a shopping cart full of possessions. Sometimes not even that. I hear that a significant number of school and college students sleep hungry every night, and don't have a place to call home. All this in one of the richest places in the country – the world, in fact – where so many have so much. People driving flashy cars, living in homes that cost over a million dollars. People splurging on ten-course meals at fancy restaurants. So much disparity in one small region. We hear about such stuff happening in third-world countries, but I am shocked to see it here in my own country. How did this come about? How can people let it happen? I haven't seen anything like this back in Wichita."

"I understand what you're saying. It is painful to watch. But it wasn't always like this. Things have gotten worse in the last few years. It has everybody's attention, but progress will take time."

The man stopped at their car. Paul rolled down the window and handed him five dollars. The man thanked him and walked over to the next car.

"Sad. Very sad. The rich get richer. The poor get poorer. Sometimes I wonder why we are wasting our time and taxpayer money to figure out who killed another rich guy."

"You aren't serious, are you? What about law and order? We can't have people going around killing others without any consequences."

"Oh, don't mind me. I'm just ranting. It's frustrating sometimes, not being able to do anything about it."

"Well, you are not alone. A lot of people feel the same way and are trying to do whatever they can to help."

"Clearly, it's not enough."

"That fiver you gave him - you know he'll use it to get high."

"Nah. I don't think so. Quite sure he'll buy himself a Big Mac."

Angela smiled. How could the conversation not lead to food?

"Speaking of Big Macs, I'm craving one."

This time she laughed. "Sure, let's get you one. Wouldn't want you to pass out on me."

Paul chuckled, the woes of the homeless forgotten. The light turned green and they drove off.

THE EXCITEMENT for the day did not end there. Back at the station, Wilson stopped by Paul's desk to give him the latest on the Betty Liu case. Paul, in turn, invited Angela over so she wouldn't miss out on the scoop. She walked over reluctantly, not surprised to see

Wilson get uncomfortable in her presence. He was the youngest detective on the force. She liked him. And he liked her too. But things had gotten awkward for him after that night a couple of years ago when they had casually hooked up. He had ended up in an embarrassing situation. She was fine with it. She understood that stuff happened. But Wilson couldn't get over it. Angela hated the awkwardness. As a rule, she never got involved with anyone at work, but this one time she had stumbled, unable to resist his charms. She had resolved to never let it happen again.

"What's the scoop?" she asked, looking at Paul.

"Wilson," he turned to Wilson, indicating he should begin.

"We found Betty's killer," replied Wilson, avoiding eye-contact with Angela.

"Awesome! Who is it?"

"A registered sex offender, Jeff Blake. He confessed. He told us he had been wandering around Sunnyvale downtown that evening looking for women. When he saw Betty, he drugged her and stuffed her in her car. Then he drove the car to a home which he knew was vacant for a few weeks. He assaulted her multiple times. He said he didn't want to kill her, but at some point she regained consciousness and started screaming, threatening to report him if he didn't stop. That's when he panicked and smashed her head with a table lamp. Then he took off in her car."

"Poor Betty," said Angela with a tinge of sadness in her voice.

"How did you find him?"

"He was incredibly stupid. He left his fingerprints all over the place, including the lamp. You can see him clearly on the surveillance camera, entering with Betty and leaving alone. Bless those home-owners for installing that system, it makes our life so much easier. As if this was not enough, her car was sitting right outside his home. We got him good."

"Stupid indeed," chuckled Paul.

"Did he kill Jay too?" asked Angela.

"He said he didn't know anything about Jay. When he found Betty, she was alone."

"And where was it that he found her?"

"Your favorite spot. The Sha Sha parking lot," replied Wilson, a little less awkward now.

"And what time was this?"

"He doesn't recall. But the surveillance footage shows him entering the house around eight forty p.m."

"How far is the home from Sha Sha?"

"Not far. At that time of night, ten to fifteen minutes tops."

"This fits in with the info we got from her location history earlier. So she could have killed Jay first, before Jeff got her."

"It's possible."

"The question is, how do we prove it," said Angela before she got lost in deep thought.

YET ANOTHER CHAT
FEBRUARY 14

"This had better be productive. I can't believe we are talking to Mr. Rudeness again," Paul complained to Angela as they climbed up the stairs to Praveen's apartment.

"Well, if he did it, then it will all have been worth it."

"So. Valentine's Day. Got a hot date tonight?"

"Nah. It's only me and my wonderful job. How about you?"

"Me and a box of delicious truffles I will pick up on the way home."

"Don't finish it all. Leave some for me."

"I'll try, but don't get your hopes up."

Angela rang the doorbell. She was met with the familiar sight of Rashmi in the doorway. This time Praveen was peering at them from further in the distance. Angela silently high-fived herself. His pissed off expression was just as she had pictured it. Rashmi managed a faint smile, conflicted between being a gracious host and expressing resentment towards these unwelcome visitors.

"What now?!" barked Praveen. It was Paul's turn to high-five himself. These were the exact words he had expected, and the tone was accurate too. He stepped inside with his partner.

"You lied again. Not anymore. We want the truth this time. Or you leave with us."

"I didn't lie about anything."

"Really? You sure you came right back home after picking up dinner that night?"

"Of course, I did. How many times do I have to repeat myself?"

"So no detour to Sunnyvale downtown? A full thirty minutes there. No?"

Praveen's face fell. Rashmi's lips trembled.

"How did you find out?"

"As a techie, we thought you would know better. Your cell phone let you down."

"Well, for what it's worth, that trip didn't have anything to do with Jay."

"Then why did you lie?"

"I didn't think it was important. The more I say, the more you talk. Wasting my time, that's all."

"How many times do we have to repeat ourselves? You give us the facts. Let us decide what is important and what is not," said Paul in a firm, even tone. "Now, tell us what really happened."

"Nothing relevant to your investigation. Rashmi's birthday was coming up, and I wanted to surprise her with a nice gift. It seemed like a convenient time to buy one, so I went to Macy's in downtown."

"So you went to Macy's, picked up her gift, and drove back home?"

"Yes."

"Quite convenient that you happened to be so close to the man you hated around the time he was murdered."

"You know, if I had known he was going to die there that night, I would have stayed away from the area. I didn't do it. You must believe me!"

"And why should we? Since the first time we met, all you have done is lie, lie, lie."

"He is telling the truth. He was shopping," interjected Rashmi.

"And how can you be so sure? Did he give you the gift that night?"

"No. He gave it to me on my birthday."

"Then how do you know when he bought it?"

"I ... I ... don't. I just ... just ... assumed," Rashmi replied, looking apologetically at Praveen.

"Exactly! We can't go around assuming things. We need facts. And concrete evidence. Now, maybe he did go to Macy's. But how do you know that's all he did? It hardly takes five to ten minutes to buy something. That still leaves a full twenty minutes where he could have walked over to Sha Sha and killed Jay."

"The saleswoman. She will remember me. You can ask her. She helped me pick out the gift."

"How convenient. Perhaps you planned it that way. Spend some time at Macy's, chat up the saleswoman, so she can vouch for you, and then you slip away to do what you really went there for. But we will talk to her."

FIFTEEN MINUTES LATER, Angela and Paul were at the Macy's in Sunnyvale. After asking around, Angela learned that Janet was the saleswoman working in the jewelry department on the night of January 17. They were in luck. She was working today as well. While Angela gave her the context, Paul searched online using his phone and found Praveen's picture. It was from Praveen's LinkedIn profile, the subject dressed in a sharp suit, looking every bit the successful professional that he was. Paul showed Janet the picture.

She did indeed remember the charming, young man who had bought his wife a beautiful set of diamond earrings, a set that Janet herself had her eye on but could not afford. She confirmed he had been there a long time, long enough that he could not have had time to kill Jay. Yet, something about it all nagged Angela. She was not convinced he was innocent.

DOUBLE VISION
FEBRUARY 15

Angela was intrigued about the woman with the visions and decided to pay her a visit. Perhaps she could shed some light on the murders. The detectives were at the door a few minutes after 10:00 a.m. A hand-written note stated that the doorbell was busted. Angela knocked. It was answered immediately by Margaret, dressed in a snug tank top and leggings.

"Margaret Lane? I am Detective Angela White, and this is my partner, Paul Conley, from Sunnyvale DPS. Hope we aren't interrupting anything. We have some questions for you."

"Do come in. I was getting started with my yoga session, but it can wait. You must be Don's girl," replied Margaret with a smile that indicated she was delighted to see her.

"How ...?" Angela began to ask in amazement.

"There's a strong resemblance. And I see a bit of Diane in you, too. You are so lovely, a perfect mix of your parents. Oh, you're wondering how I know them. Don and I were college sweethearts before your mother whisked him away from me," continued Margaret, maintaining her pleasant demeanor.

"Ah, I don't think he ever mentioned you. I guess you didn't keep in touch after college?" Angela replied as she studied her, curious about this woman who claimed to have been so close to her father. It was a rather unremarkable face, but one that exuded calm. Nowhere as pretty as her mother, she thought. But then, age played dirty tricks. She had to admit that Margaret was in excellent shape for her age. In any case, Angela knew her father valued character and personality over appearance, so this woman probably had some remarkable qualities.

"Something like that. Now, how can I help you today? Is it about my vision about your case?"

"Yes. Officer Garcia told us you had visions about Jay Sharma's death. And Betty Liu's too."

"I did. Strangest thing. I don't get them often, but that week I had three."

"Three? Who was the third?"

"My neighbor. Poor Brenda. You want to know what I saw? Well, the first one was three days before it happened. I saw legs wearing jeans, and bare feet. Lying on asphalt. The legs were long, so I figured it would be someone tall. I could tell it was going to happen within the week. The second one was the following night. I saw a woman, naked from the waist down, lying partially on a white rug and partially on a dark hardwood floor. She looked petite."

"Matches what we found. But that's all you see in your visions? Can't identify who it is, right?"

"Most of the time, yes. That's the most frustrating part. But I still feel an obligation to warn people."

Margaret continued with more details about her visions, ensuring they understood how it all worked. Angela nodded as she tried to absorb it all. She had never known anyone with such gifts before, so it fascinated her.

"Margaret, where were you that night? The night of January seventeenth," asked Paul, once Margaret was done explaining.

"I was in Santa Cruz all day. Didn't get back until late."

"How late?"

"Tough to say. It's been a while. We did have an early dinner there, so I would say we were back around nine p.m."

"And what were you doing in Santa Cruz? Work?"

"No, I retired last year. This was a pleasure trip."

"What work did you do?" asked Angela.

"I was a software engineer. Like every third person around here," replied Margaret with a twinkle in her blue eyes.

"Can anyone vouch for you?" asked Paul, trying to ensure his line of questioning stayed on track.

"Vouch for me?"

"I mean, can anyone confirm you were in Santa Cruz the entire day?"

"I was with my date. You can talk to him. Why all these questions? You think I had something to do with it? I didn't know either of them."

"Just routine. Now, if you can give us his contact information."

"Whose information?"

"Your date," replied Paul, beginning to get frustrated with all the return queries.

"Oh, yes, of course."

He noted the information and stepped out, with Angela following after him.

"YOU THINK she had something to do with it?" asked Angela, as they walked back to the car.

"I don't buy any of that nonsense about the visions. Don't tell me you believed her."

"I'm not sure yet. But if she did it, why draw attention to herself by going to the cops with those stories?"

"Maybe she was trying to deflect suspicion. People would think she couldn't have done it, since she is the one who reported the visions. Or she is playing games. She drops these hints about who she is going to kill next, and then she goes ahead and does it. Daring the cops to figure it out and stop her in time."

"So she's a crazy serial killer playing cat and mouse with us? That only happens in the movies."

"Okay, I guess that's going too far, but I still have my money on her. Now, let's talk to this date."

A SHORT WHILE LATER, the detectives were sitting in the San Jose living room of Margaret's date, Arthur Bentley. All three held steaming cups of green tea. Arthur had insisted, and they had been unable to refuse. Angela studied him as she sipped the soothing beverage and felt the cold melting away. He was in reasonable shape for someone in his sixties. But the oversized glasses resting on his nose made him appear older.

Paul was doing some studying of his own. His attention, however, was not on his host. He looked around furtively to figure out where he could dump the tea at the first opportunity. Years ago, he had a revolting introduction to this insipid concoction. He dared not make the same mistake again.

"So what do you want to know about Margaret?" asked Arthur.

"She told us the two of you were in Santa Cruz the entire day. January seventeenth. Can you confirm that?" asked Angela.

"Yes, yes, we did go there last month. Left around ten a.m. and didn't get back until after dinner."

"Do you recall what time you returned?"

"It was around nine o'clock when I dropped her off. I remember, because I was worried I was late for my pills. And it took another fifteen minutes for me to get back home."

"And you are sure it was the seventeenth?"

"Oh. I don't know. I will have to check my calendar," he replied as he got up and walked towards the kitchen.

Paul grasped his chance and emptied his cup into Angela's with an impish grin. She responded with an amused smile, then turned her attention back to Arthur. He was standing before a wall calendar which had a captivating shot of Yosemite Valley blanketed in snow. He turned the page to January, which revealed another snowy capture of some place Angela could not recognize. Funny, she thought. She had assumed he would refer to the calendar on his phone. This old-school method was charming.

"Yes, here it is. The seventeenth. 'Margaret Santa Cruz', it says. You can see for yourself."

"Thank you, Arthur. That won't be necessary."

"May I ask what this is about?" he asked as he returned to his chair and took another sip of his tea.

"It's for a homicide investigation."

Arthur's eyes widened. "You suspect her?"

"It was a possibility. But you confirmed she wasn't anywhere near the victim that day. Did she warn you we were coming?"

"No. We haven't spoken in over a week. What I told you is the absolute truth."

"That long?" asked Angela, not buying that one bit.

Arthur shifted in his seat. "You see, the thing is ..." he started, then hesitated. "You won't tell her any of this, will you?"

"I assure you we won't."

"I don't think it's working out. I want to end it, you see."

"You're dumping her?"

"Dump is too harsh a word. She is an amazing woman. But the fact is, sometimes she creeps me out."

"What do you mean? Is this because of her visions?"

"Visions? What visions?"

"Never mind. What do you mean she creeps you out?"

"It's just the way she looks at me, especially when she doesn't agree with something I do or say."

"Isn't that what all women do?" Paul said with a smile. "My ex gave me the stare all the time."

Arthur maintained his serious expression. "I've been married before, so I know what you are talking about. But this is different. It's just so sinister. It's like she is plotting my demise. And after our last meeting, I'm convinced this has to end."

"Why is that?"

"She was here at my place. Turned up uninvited. We got talking, and at one point I suggested we should give each other some space. She just exploded."

"Seems like a natural reaction."

"Well, I have broken up with women before. And women have broken up with me. It's never been so dramatic. Sure, I know some people don't take it well, but this was nuts. She grabbed a knife and held it at my throat."

"Oh. That's extreme. What happened next?"

"I was so scared. I just talked my way out of it."

"So you haven't broken it off then?"

"I don't know how to. I've just been avoiding her. I'm a lot more careful when opening the door, just in case it's her."

"You think she could kill someone?"

Arthur's eyes widened again. "I don't know about that, and I don't want to find out the hard way. All I know is, she had me terrified that day."

"But you are sure she was with you all day January seventeenth?"

"Yes, that I am sure of."

"Well, thank you, Arthur. You have been most helpful."

The detectives departed, convinced that Margaret was not involved in Jay's death.

MORE VISIONS
FEBRUARY 16

Angela and Paul were busy at work, discussing the case. Joseph Landry's prints did not match any of the prints found at the crime scene, except those on Jay's wallet and driver's license. But Angela wasn't ready to rule him out as a suspect yet. Her phone buzzed. It was Margaret, and she wanted Angela to come over right away to discuss her latest vision. Paul wasn't interested in talking to that "crazy woman," as he put it, so Angela decided to go alone. What Arthur had shared was disconcerting, but was well within the realm of behavior one could expect from a dumpee. She figured there was no point bringing it up with Margaret.

Margaret welcomed her with a smile.

"So Margaret, what is this vision about? Anything to do with my case?"

"I don't know if it's related. But it was a strong one, so I expect this will happen soon, probably less than a week."

"What did you see?"

"I saw a lifeless hand resting on a nightstand. There was an open bottle of pills sitting next to the hand, toppled over. I couldn't see the name on the bottle, only that it started with an 'M'."

"Was it a man or a woman?"

"I couldn't tell for sure, but if I were to guess, it was a man."

"And what does this have to do with my case?"

"Nothing. At least, I don't see any relation."

"Then why call me?" asked Angela, quite irritated that Margaret had wasted her time.

"To be honest, I needed to tell someone. But the cops and others, they never believe me. They see me as a joke. But after talking to you the other day, I got this feeling that you would understand. I was hoping you would help me figure this one out."

"Margaret, you will have to give me more. Based on what you have told me, there's nothing to go on. I appreciate that you trust me, but I'm sorry, I can't do much here. Besides, Officer Garcia mentioned that after your visions about Jay and Betty, he may have become a believer. You should report it to him, though I am not sure he will be able to help either."

"It's okay. I understand."

Angela had started to walk away when Margaret said, "Don't do it, Angela."

Angela turned around, looking confused. "Don't do what?"

"It's this other vision I had. About you."

"Don't do what?" asked Angela, quite intrigued now.

"Don't join the FBI."

"How ... how do you know I want to?"

"I had a vision of you, you years from now. In FBI gear, lying dead in the woods with a bullet wound in your chest. So, you see, if you join the FBI, you will die."

Angela recalled her dream about Dirty Dan. Was it possible ...?

"I thought you couldn't tell who died," she said, cutting off her own thoughts.

"Sometimes the visions do reveal more."

"I don't believe you."

"Don didn't either. You know that didn't end well."

"What do you mean?"

BAREFOOT IN THE PARKING LOT 147

"A few days before your father died, I saw him in a vision. He was in uniform, lying in a pool of blood. I was so devastated when I saw that, since I knew it was only a matter of days. I called him to warn him about it, but he laughed it off. He never took my visions seriously."

Angela teared up. Her father's death was something she tried not to think about. And now this woman was saying it could have been avoided.

"I don't believe you. You made that up, didn't you?" said Angela, the emotions building up inside her. "Last time you told me you and my dad were in a relationship. Why didn't that work out? If you two were so close, why didn't I ever hear about you?"

"I wish you would believe me. Don would be alive today if he had only listened. I don't want to see you die too. We were crazy in love. But these visions troubled me a lot. At one point, I was obsessed with them. He always thought I was making it up. That this stuff wasn't real. In the end, it placed a strain on our relationship. This was around the time your mother came into his life. She was such a beautiful and caring woman, so full of life. I don't blame him for drifting towards her. We still kept in touch for a while, but Diane didn't like it. Quite understandable, given our history. Gradually, I fell out of their life."

"I will think about it. You were right about Jay's and Betty's deaths. Let's see if this new 'M' vision comes true as well."

Back at the station, Angela recounted to Paul what Margaret had told her. As expected, he laughed it off. This was not something he would be wasting his time on.

ANGELA

Angela had been awake a while when the alarm hummed at 6:00 a.m. She had spent the night tossing and turning, Margaret's words echoing in her head. But she ignored her aching body, pulled herself out of bed and laced up for her daily run. The day wasn't complete without that six-mile loop. It helped clear her mind, and the health benefits were a bonus.

As she sprinted through the streets of Sunnyvale, her eyes welled up. Images of her father flashed before her eyes. They had spent so much time together here. So many fond memories. She pictured him at the ice-cream shop, where he had treated her countless times over the years. The store where he bought her her first bicycle. The park where he taught her how to ride that bike.

Angela remembered the day he had fallen, killed by a hail of bullets when answering a domestic abuse call. Sixteen years had passed, but it seemed like yesterday. She was just twenty and was in class when she was notified. Her sobbing mother barely managed to ask her to hurry home. She made no mention of what had happened. Angela had rushed home, worried. She was shattered once she learned that her father was no more. The horrific way he had died made it worse. He must have endured so much pain during those last few moments.

Mother and daughter had spent the next few days in shock and grief. Angela soon recovered, trying not to think about it, but her mother never did. She spiraled into depression and passed away two years later, leaving Angela all alone. It had been a rough few years for Angela, but she had made it through. She had accepted her father's death, knowing it was something that was always a possibility in his profession. But now, after hearing from Margaret, she felt angry. It could have been avoided. If only her father had listened to Margaret, he would still be alive. He would still be with her, perhaps her mother too.

The rage rising inside her fueled Angela to run harder. Her lungs burned up as she flew past block after block. Once she was done, she checked her watch: thirty-eight minutes. Two minutes faster than usual. That cheered her up a bit. But she still felt alone. It was times like this when she wished she had someone in her life. Friends were great, but this needed a life partner. But it was slim pickings. Most of the guys she had dated had turned out to be frogs. Her thoughts drifted to Paul. He was a nice guy, and they got along well. Too bad he was still not over his ex. Besides, she was a health freak and couldn't stand Paul's poor eating habits and sedentary lifestyle. Now, Kyle was a different story. She was glad she had bumped into him. She had always liked him, and he enjoyed her company too. For some reason, their relationship had never progressed beyond the friend stage, and they had lost touch after graduation. He had helped her through the dismal period after her father's death. It was about time she called him.

HANGING OUT
FEBRUARY 18

The stress from the case was driving Angela and Paul crazy. For a change, they had decided to take a break and relax on the weekend. It also helped Angela to take her mind off her dad and the encounter with Margaret. Not that they could completely escape case-talk. The news had broken that Mark was taking a leave of absence from SmartCloud for health reasons. Paul wondered whether it was because of Mark's pre-existing depression issues or stress induced by the murder investigation. Angela was of the opinion that health was an excuse, and he had been pushed out by the board, just as he had predicted.

Once the latest development had been discussed, Paul suggested they attend a screening of *Dial M for Murder* at the Stanford Theatre. He was a huge movie buff and favored the oldies. Angela, not so much, but she did love Hitchcock. Besides, she had never been there, even though she had spent her entire life ten minutes away.

"Oh, that ceiling! Those walls!" exclaimed Angela in delight as they stepped out of the theatre. "It was so beautiful. So ornate."

"And that curtain. All that red velvet creeping up the screen. Grand."

"I enjoyed the organ."

"Yeah, that was cool."

"But I think I am done with movies about murders for a while."

"Why? I thought you loved the stuff."

"I do, but it reminds me too much of work. I need something that takes my mind off homicide."

"I know what you mean. But watching Grace Kelly takes my mind off everything."

"I bet it does," said Angela with a laugh.

Paul chuckled and looked at her. He considered himself lucky to have such a good friend and coworker. It had been difficult adjusting to life in Silicon Valley. Wichita was not a small town, but life here was so fast-paced, and people were rushing constantly. The traffic, the cost of living, everything was so depressing. Perhaps the only positive was the weather. And Angela.

They went over to Angela's and settled on the couch, beers in hand, sampling the variety of snacks she had laid out. She was dressed in blue jeans and a red sweater and looked quite fetching. It was different from the smart and professional look she carried at work, wearing a suit every day.

"Nice place you have here," remarked Paul, as he munched on some cheese and crackers. It was the first time he had visited. Angela lived in a comfortable single-family home in Sunnyvale, complete with a backyard. That was a luxury he couldn't afford.

"Thanks. I was lucky I inherited. For sure, I couldn't manage it on my income. Can you believe this place is worth around two million bucks? Back in the day, my parents bought it for fifty thousand dollars, and it's fully paid off now."

Paul let out a whistle. "Back in the day, fifty grand was a lot of money. But I guess back then working stiffs like us could still afford it. Not anymore."

"So, tell me more about your secret life in Kansas. I have never been there."

"My secret life?"

"Well, you never talk about it much."

"Ha ha, very funny. You won't believe me, but it was pretty awesome out there. I had a wonderful childhood, amazing friends and family. You know, I was an aspiring football star. Thought I would play for the Chiefs some day."

"What happened?"

"Busted my knee in a college game. Never recovered enough to compete at a professional level. I hadn't given anything other than football a thought. So I had some career choices to make. Decided to become a cop."

"Injury sucks. But you ended up picking the right career."

"I guess. Brigette was by my side throughout. We got married when I was twenty-three."

"That's sweet. What went wrong?"

"Well, one day she told me she was leaving. She had met someone else. I was so angry. But then I realized, it wasn't a surprise she walked away. I never had time for her. Always busy working."

"Any kids?"

"Nope. We tried. Turns out I can't have any."

"Oh. But there are options."

"Too expensive. And painful. We figured it was better not to. I think deep down we knew it wasn't going to last. Why bring children into the picture? Though I do wish I had put more effort into the marriage. I think I was disappointed with myself. Couldn't get over the fact that I wasn't a pro-football player. So I overcompensated by grinding myself down as a cop."

"You cannot define who you are by your job. There is so much more to us than our work."

"I know. I know. But it took a long time for me to understand that."

"Well, the important thing is you are able to see where you went wrong. Gives you a chance to fix things and be prepared when the right woman comes along."

"I guess. Though I am still slogging away at work."

"That's true. Hopefully that will change once you're in a relationship. By the way, what do you feel like for dinner? I haven't cooked, so we could order in. That Yummy Tummy app works out quite well."

"Ah. Maya's app. How about we do some Thai?"

"Sure, that sounds good." She placed the order. "Should be here in thirty minutes. Better whip up an appetite quick."

"Oh, I always have an appetite. You know that."

"You bet I do," she replied, eyeing his belly which was more prominent than usual. At work the suit helped to hide it some. But today his t-shirt couldn't do much.

"Hey, it wasn't always like this. I was quite fit until recently. Just let myself go after she left. Gotta get back into shape now."

"You had better, if you want to impress any cool California women. Met anyone yet?"

"You mean other than you? Nah. Haven't had time to go on any dates. You know how it is."

"I see. Just checking. That's another thing you never talk about."

The conversation continued until the food arrived. The aroma of Thai cuisine wafted in as Angela returned with the grub.

"The delivery girl was cute. I should have introduced you to her."

"Darn it, missed opportunity," said Paul, feigning disappointment as he walked towards the goodies. "They still have people delivering? I was told it would be robots and autonomous cars by now."

"They are experimenting with robots and cars for some stuff. Pretty sure soon they'll be delivering food as well. You know, I saw something funny the other day. Vroom had this thing about the various applications for autonomous cars. There was the usual story about better traffic flow, delivery, etc., but there was one blurb about autonomous hearses."

"You're kidding me."

"Nope, I'm serious. You know that joke about the hearse driver, chugging along with a coffin in the back, almost frightened to death when he hears a knock on the glass behind him? Well, that's one of the things they fear, that someone gets out of the coffin to say 'Hi'."

"Oh, come on, that can't be the reason they want it."

"No, of course not. It's more about the economics of it. Don't need a hearse driver anymore. Saves them a lot of money. So cool though, dead bodies driving themselves around. Oh ..." Angela froze, deep in thought, like she'd had a revelation.

"What happened?"

"Those cars can move dead people, too. What if ..."

"I'm not sure I understand what you're getting at, Angela."

"Remember that guy, what was his name? Josh something? It was in the news recently. He said he was nearly hit by a Vroom car. So close to Mark's work. It was that same night. He saw a man asleep in the passenger seat. What if that man was Jay?"

"Whoa, whoa! That's quite a wild idea. You are telling me he saw a dead Jay being driven to where we found him?"

"Yes, but driven by no one. The car was driving itself. Remember, Meghna was gone between seven and seven thirty. That would be enough time for her to kill Jay and stuff him in the car. She has easy access to the cars and knows how to use one. She sends the car across town to her accomplice, my guess is Mark, who disposes of the body appropriately."

"Wow, that's complicated, but possible. Meghna gets her alibi. But Mark is exposed – too much risk for him since he doesn't have an alibi," pondered Paul.

"Well, maybe it wasn't Mark. Some other accomplice, perhaps. But the key is, it wasn't supposed to happen this way. No one was supposed to notice the car."

Angela picked up her laptop and searched for "Josh Vroom." It brought up several links about Josh Green and his near miss with the Vroom car. Most of the articles included the picture he had clicked. It showed the rear of a car with a Vroom logo and license plate VRM32. This was the lead they had to follow.

"I think we have some work to do at Vroom tomorrow," declared Angela as she closed her laptop.

VROOM VROOM
FEBRUARY 19

Angela and Paul were at Vroom early the next morning. Karen Davis, who was in charge of Vroom's fleet of self-driving cars, walked them over to a conference room. This time it was Raging Bull. Paul couldn't help but smile a bit in approval – he loved that movie. Angela explained why they were there and began the interview.

"Karen, how many cars do you have?"

"We try to maintain around twenty."

"And what kind of information do you have about these cars?"

"Oh, everything there is to know. There's the basics like the make, mileage, registration info, etc., and we also log all the activity, like when the car was checked out, where it went, when it got back, all details about the ride, like what it saw, how it reacted to each situation. In short, everything we need to determine that it's functioning the way it should."

"Great. We are particularly interested in the car with license plate VRM32."

"VRM32? Oh, is this about that fake accident report? What's his name ... some Green guy, I think. The case was dismissed."

Paul's mind strayed again. Green guy. The Hulk. He stifled a laugh.

"Yes, that's the one, Josh Green. But it is not directly related to that incident. We need information about that car's activity that evening."

"So January seventeenth? I told everyone when we investigated the case – the car did not leave the building all day. I checked and rechecked the logs myself. That kid was lying."

"Any chance the logs are missing something?"

Karen gave Angela a hard stare. "I designed and implemented that system myself. In all these years we haven't had any issues with the logging. Whatever bugs we had were quashed within the first year of operation."

"I'm sorry, that's not what I meant. Could someone have deleted a log entry?"

Karen was all set to defend herself again, almost replying before the question was complete. Then she paused.

"Yes, that is possible. It's something left over from the early days when we needed a way to delete erroneous entries. But no one uses that feature anymore."

Angela wondered whether the car had been moved, and Meghna deleted the log later.

"Can you tell if an entry was deleted?"

"No, that's not possible. We had considered an audit logging feature, but no one uses that option either, so we never got around to it."

"Can we inspect the car?" asked Paul.

"Too late for that. The car was retired a couple of weeks ago. It's routine practice once a car hits two hundred thousand miles."

"You're not using it anymore, but I assume it's still sitting around somewhere, right?"

"Sorry to disappoint you. The cars are destroyed once we're done with them. There's not much market value for a car with that much mileage, and it's not worth it for us to strip the car of the equipment. We don't want our IP in the wrong hands."

"Oh," Angela grimaced.

"One last question. Who has access to delete logs?"

"Only a handful of people. Me and Ann in this department, and Meghna Rao, our CTO, since she was also involved in the early implementation."

Paul and Angela exchanged glances, convinced that Meghna did have something to hide.

"We had another car out that evening in the same area. But the license plate was VRM31. You sure that's not the one you are looking for?" added Karen. She had been searching for more data.

"The picture we saw clearly shows VRM32. Can't be VRM31. Was anyone in the car?"

"We always have someone in the driver's seat. In case something goes wrong."

"Who was in the car that night?"

"One of our interns, Jessica Langley."

"This problem reported by Josh Green – it just went away? Vroom is in the clear now?"

"Yes. It's not often that government organizations move fast, but they did on this one. We got a clean chit from the NTSB. Not surprising, since there was no problem to begin with. As you can see, we have no record of that car leaving the building. And it's not like anyone believes Josh. The case was dismissed as soon as the truth about him was out."

"What do you mean?"

"Have you seen the guy's Facebook page? He's a conspiracy theorist. Crazy guy with all kinds of weird ideas. This was not the first time he's made such allegations against a prominent firm. Quite likely, he took some random pic and photoshopped it to look like it was one of our cars."

Angela hadn't gotten that far in her research the previous night. She realized she had no idea about Josh's past or his reputation.

"Interesting. Karen, can we talk to Jessica as well?"

"Sure, let me call her."

Jessica walked in a few minutes later.

"Jessica, we have a few questions about the evening of January seventeenth. We believe you took one of the cars out for a test drive?"

"I do that most days. Not sure I would remember a specific day."

"I see. Do you always take the cars in the evening?"

"No, I usually go during the day. But I did do a couple of night drives recently."

"We are interested in the night drives. When was the last one?"

"A few days ago."

"And the first one?"

"That was last month."

"Can you tell us about that one?"

"Let me check the records."

Jessica returned in a few minutes.

"It was on January seventeenth. We were told we didn't have enough nighttime testing hours for the cars, so we had to get that started. I took the car at around six forty-five p.m. and got back around nine p.m."

"Which car did you take?"

"It was VRM31."

"And not VRM32?"

"No."

"Did you notice whether VRM32 was in the garage?"

"No. But I remember the garage was full. Quite sure mine was the only one out."

"If Vroom was behind on nighttime hours, wouldn't there be a lot more cars out in the evening?"

"Well, they wanted to do limited nighttime test runs for a couple of days before expanding."

"Was anyone else in the car with you?"

"No, only me."

"What route did you take?"

"I did some neighborhoods in Milpitas, then some in Sunnyvale. Went all the way up to Mountain View and then back to Sunnyvale again."

"Who made the request?"

"Not sure. I believe it was from discussions the technical team had with Meghna."

"And who set the route?"

"I don't know. Probably Meghna again."

"And did you see her that evening?"

"Yes, I did."

"What time was that?"

"When I got back, around nine."

"Did she see you?"

"No, I don't think so. I had parked the car but hadn't stepped out. I figured I would start working on my report in there. And my boyfriend was texting me, so I stayed in. That's when she entered."

"What did she do?"

"She went over to one of the cars and inspected it. Then she went over to the console and worked on that. After that she went back to the workshop and was in there for a while."

"Which car did she inspect?"

"Can't say."

"Could it have been VRM32?"

"It's possible. But like I said, I couldn't tell from where I was."

"Anything unusual about what she did?"

"No."

"Did she look nervous?"

"Not that I could tell. I don't think I have ever seen her nervous."

"Thanks, Jessica. Do call us if you remember anything else that could be important."

Angela turned back to Karen. "Thank you, Karen. We will get back to you if we have any further questions."

They followed Karen out. As soon as she was out of earshot, Angela said, "Meghna is devious. She picked a car that was going to be destroyed, so there would be no evidence to examine. She used the car and then deleted the logs."

"But how do we prove any of this? At this point it's all speculation. Without the car or any eyewitness, we have nothing. For all you know, this had nothing to do with the murder, and she only cleared the logs because of the near-accident. And that's assuming any of this happened at all."

"Well, I think it's time we talk to Josh Green."

"You think it's worth our time? You heard what she said. The guy can't be trusted. He made it all up."

"I don't know. I have a feeling about this. Let's at least talk to him once."

"Okay, let's find him."

JOSH GREEN
FEBRUARY 19

The detectives waited for Josh as he completed his shift and walked out of the Target store on Coleman Avenue. It was 4:00 p.m. Paul had found his contact information and called him as they were leaving Vroom. Josh seemed eager to talk to them. He was a young guy of twenty years. Angela hoped this would be worth their time. Needing a place to sit, they went back inside and grabbed some coffee at Starbucks.

"Josh, you claimed a Vroom car hit you in Sunnyvale on the evening of January seventeenth. Can you tell us what happened that night?"

"Sure. I was meeting some friends for dinner at Sha Sha that evening. Decided to ditch the car and walk over. I started down Mathilda Avenue, and then I had to cross the street. I stopped at the intersection, since I saw the Vroom car coming. It slowed down, so I thought it was stopping for me. But as soon as I stepped into the intersection, it sped up like it never saw me. If not for my quick reflexes, I would have been flattened."

"So it didn't hit you?"

"No, like I said, it *would* have. These cars are a menace."

"What more can you tell us about the incident?"

"It all happened so fast. I was all shook up, didn't know what to do. But I did manage to click a picture with my phone as the car drove away. Got the license plate."

"VRM32?"

"Yes, that's the one."

"Did you see who was in the car?"

"Like I said, it all happened so fast. I know I saw a guy in the passenger seat."

"Can you describe this guy?"

"Didn't get a good look, but I think he had a mustache. Seemed tall. The seat was reclined, so he was all laid back. Sleeping, perhaps."

"Do you remember what he was wearing?"

"Um ... seemed like it was a dress shirt. Long sleeves."

Jay was tall. Jay had a mustache. Jay was wearing a dress shirt that evening. Maybe Josh was telling the truth. Then again, this was quite a generic description. Were they shooting in the dark?

"What about the driver?"

"No idea. Sorry."

"And what time did this happen?"

"This was at seven thirty-seven p.m."

"Gee, that's precise."

"Oh, that was easy. I checked the time on that pic I clicked."

"Can we see the pic?"

"Sure, here you go."

It was the same one they had seen online.

"What time did you get to Sha Sha?"

"Around seven forty-five."

"Josh, don't take this the wrong way, but did this really happen? The case was dismissed immediately. People claim none of this occurred. You have a history of making false claims against corporations. Quite the conspiracy theorist."

"Hey, if you came all this way to tell me I am a liar, then I don't know what to say. You got me there. I admit I have done some stupid things in the past. I have made allegations without having all the facts. Some of it to boost my following on social media, some simply out of sheer immaturity. But you have got to believe me – this did happen. I am not lying. I wouldn't be surprised if Vroom coughed up loads of money to make this go away. A lot of big shots have invested in that company. They would want to protect their investment."

Somehow, Angela did not find that believable. He sounded earnest, but his track record didn't inspire confidence. On a hunch, she dug out her phone and showed him a pic of Mark Harrison.

"Did you see this guy at Sha Sha?"

Josh chuckled. "Mark Harrison? Yeah, he was at the next table. I spoke to him."

"You know him?" she asked in amazement, not expecting that.

"Well, not personally. I mean, he's the SmartCloud CEO. I hope to work there someday, once I graduate. Just tried to sneak in a good word about myself, maybe snag an internship. Why are you asking about him? Did he do something?"

"No, it's something else."

"Do you remember what time he left?"

"A short while after that. Slightly after eight, I think."

"You sure?"

"Yeah. Got any more questions for me? I have tons of homework."

"Which school are you at?"

"San Jose State. Computer Engineering."

"Cool. Good luck with that. Thanks for your time. Do call us if you remember anything else. And ... stay out of trouble."

"No problem. Thanks for the coffee."

Angela turned to Paul as soon as Josh had left.

"So that confirms Mark was at Sha Sha until eight. If he did it, he could still have disappeared for a few minutes without anyone notic- ing. And if he helped Meghna do it, it still gives him enough time to meet the car and dump the body before it was found."

"Yeah, let's first confirm what time he got there."

"You know, we should have done this a long time ago."

"Yes. Just got distracted by the growing list of suspects. Well, better late than never."

THEY DROVE over to Sha Sha to confirm Mark's alibi. Angela found the manager on duty, Delilah. It was easy to get her attention since it was still early, before the evening flood of patrons rushed in. Angela gave her the details. Delilah checked her records and confirmed he had indeed come in at 6:30 p.m. She pointed out the table where he had dined. The server was Janine.

"Can we talk to her?" asked Paul.

"Well, you're in luck. She's working tonight. Why don't you take that booth in the corner, and I will bring her over."

The detectives slid into the booth. The aroma of delicious food had hit Paul as soon as they had walked in, and now that he was seated, he was ravenous. But there was work to do first. Janine joined them in the seat opposite after a few minutes.

"Thanks for talking to us, Janine. We have some questions about the evening of January seventeenth. We know it's been a long time, but whatever you can recall might help us."

"Sure, I will try my best."

Angela showed her a picture of Mark.

"Do you recognize this man? He was here that evening."

"Oh yes, I remember him. He sat there," she indicated the correct booth, to Angela's surprise.

"How do you remember it so well? You must attend to a lot of customers here."

"Oh, but you don't forget customers like this one."

"Why is that?"

"For starters, he came in alone. Most people come here in groups. He was super friendly, talked a lot, almost flirting at times. And he left me a huge tip. Now, that is something one doesn't forget easily."

"How much did he leave?"

"A hundred bucks. And his bill was only forty-two dollars."

"Wow. Why do you think he left you so much?"

"I don't know. I think he liked me. Maybe he was trying to impress me. To be honest, he was too old for me, but, hey, who am I to complain? I would have to serve a lot of tables to make that much in tips."

Or perhaps, he did it to ensure you remembered him. That would give him a strong alibi, thought Angela.

"Do you remember if he left his seat at any time during the evening?"

"I can say for sure, every time I came by, he was in his seat. But I can't say whether he moved when I wasn't there."

"What was the longest time you were away?"

"Five, maybe ten minutes, max. I was attending to other tables as well, so I passed by often enough."

"Anything else you recall that might be of help?"

"No. What is this about?"

"A homicide investigation."

"You think that sweet man could have killed someone?" asked Janine, a concerned expression on her face.

"In our line of work we are open to all possibilities. If you only knew how many sweet people do rotten things. Now, can we order something? We are starving."

She smiled and brought them the menus. They ordered and went back to discussing the case.

"So, where do we stand with Mark? That didn't help much, did it?"

"Well, it didn't help with any post-eight p.m. activities. But for the time that he was here, we're down to a maximum ten-minute window. That is still plenty of time for him to rush over to the parking lot, attack Jay and get back."

"But how did he know Jay would be there at precisely that time?

Did they plan to meet? Did Jay call him once he got there? We didn't see anything in the phone records. This doesn't make any sense."

"Perhaps he didn't do it after all."

"But if he didn't, then who did? Almost everyone else has an alibi. Unless we go back to the two-person theory."

The detectives spent the next few minutes in deep thought. Then the food arrived, and they attacked it right away. There was silence as they enjoyed the meal. Shop-talk could wait.

ONCE THEY HAD DINED, Angela called Meghna. As expected, it didn't yield anything useful, but at least she had tried. Meghna admitted that she had gone back to the garage that evening around 9:00 p.m., but it was for routine work. She hadn't seen anyone there, and she had left after a few minutes once her work there was done. And that was that.

SUICIDE
FEBRUARY 20

Paul put the phone down with a grim face. Angela waited expectantly. They had been discussing the case when he received a call.

"Who was that?"

"My buddy from Los Gatos PD. Bad news."

"What happened?"

"Mark Harrison killed himself."

"What?! When did this happen?"

"Sunday night. They found the body yesterday, after he didn't show up for work."

"Work? Wasn't he on leave?"

"Apparently, he was to have a meeting with the interim CEO to transition stuff."

"So you mean to tell me, he was already dead while we were at Sha Sha verifying his alibi?"

"Yes."

"Are they sure it was suicide?"

"Yes. He took a full bottle of sleeping pills. Left a note in his handwriting."

"What did it say?"

"Among other things, he swears he is innocent. You can't argue with a dead man. We were wrong."

"Oh no! Did we drive him over the edge?"

"I don't know. We may have contributed. We know he was already depressed. From what I hear, his wife's departure hit him hard. And his loss to Jay didn't help either. This murder investigation could have been one problem too many."

"And he was forced out of his job because of this investigation. What else did the note say?"

"I don't know. It was addressed to his ex. They gave her a copy."

"Should we talk to her? Or is it too soon?"

"Well, she is his *ex*. And she left him a year ago. I don't think she'll be too torn up over his death. We must get to the bottom of this right away."

"Let's go, then."

A SHORT WHILE LATER, Angela was driving through a swanky Los Gatos neighborhood, with mansions on either side of beautiful, tree-lined streets. She stopped in front of Jenna Harrison's home. This was once Mark's home too, before he had moved out. It was imposing from the outside. They had barely reached the front door when it opened, and a couple of cops entered into view. Los Gatos PD. Jenna was standing behind the officers, looking moist-eyed. So she had been crying. Angela felt guilty about bothering her so soon, more so since Jenna had already spent time with the other cops. But now that they were there, might as well get down to business.

Angela made the introductions and Jenna ushered them in. She was an elegant woman and appeared to be in excellent shape. As they made their way through the house, Paul detected a strong scent of cinnamon. It reminded him of Cinnabon, and he suddenly felt famished. But once he got to the living room, he noticed a scented candle burning and realized that's where the fragrance originated. He was both disappointed and relieved. Jenna directed them to the couch. The back wall of the room was all glass and brought in considerable natural light. Through it, Angela could see an enormous swimming pool. Two young men in their early twenties were seated poolside, looking glum. Must be the sons, she thought.

"Jenna, we are so sorry about Mark. And sorry for intruding at this time."

"Let's get it over with. First you hounded him, and now you are here so soon after his death. Can't expect much better from you two."

So she knew they were on the Jay Sharma case. And she did blame them for at least some of Mark's troubles.

"We realize now, we may have been wrong about Mark. But we are just trying to solve a murder. You can help."

"Well, if it does anything to clear his name. He was no angel, but I know for a fact he could never murder anyone. What do you need to know?"

"We hear he left a note. Do you mind if we take a look?"

"I have it right here. It was certainly written by him."

Angela took the note from her. She read it, and was quite convinced of Mark's innocence.

Dear Jenna,

You are a wonderful woman and an even better mother. You were an amazing wife to me, the best a man could ask for. I truly am sorry I hurt you so much. I wish I could have done things differently. I wish I had not made the mistakes I made. I miss you and the boys so much. Life is so empty without you. Please tell the boys they make me proud every day. They have grown up to be such thoughtful, responsible men. I am sure they will be better men than I ever was. I wish them a bright future. I ask them to forgive me for any pain I may have caused them.

I am leaving the world today with a heavy heart. I tried to go on, but I can't do this anymore. I do want to make one thing clear – I did not have anything to do with Jay's death. I hated his guts after what he did to me, but I could never take someone else's life, or help anyone do

it. You know that. Hopefully, I will be proven innocent and my name
will be cleared.

Always yours,
Mark

Angela handed the letter back to Jenna. They were all quiet for
some time. Then Angela broke the silence and asked, "Jenna, may we
know why you left him? He mentions some mistakes."

"We had been married twenty-five years, and over time we had
drifted apart. Don't get me wrong, we still loved each other. But the
spark was gone. We were always so busy, between our careers and
raising the boys. Once the boys moved out for college, it was just the
two of us. You would think that would be a positive. It would give us
a chance to reconnect. But we realized we had both changed over
time, and we didn't have much to talk about anymore. Then he
cheated on me. That pushed things over the edge. He said he was
sorry, that it was the first and last time. I tried to forgive him, tried to
get things back to normal, but I couldn't trust him anymore. Finally, I
decided it was over. He was heartbroken, but he had only himself to
blame."

"How did you find out he cheated? He confessed?"

"No, I found out by chance. I was at the Santa Clara Marriott
one evening, meeting a friend who was here on a business trip. We
were chatting in the lobby when I noticed Mark walk by. He hadn't
seen me. That morning he had told me he would be working late, so I
was curious. Since he hadn't met Kathy before, I asked her to ride up
in the elevator with him, and let me know which room he went to. I
joined her once he was inside. We waited an entire hour before he
stepped out. I knocked on the door once he was gone. It was opened
by this blonde tart. She probably thought he had forgotten something
and was back, because she was shocked to see me. I pushed my way
inside and grilled her. She confessed she was an escort, and Mark was
her client. She swore it was the first time she had seen him. He was
referred to her by Jay, who was a regular. I always knew that man was
a bad influence. I hated him. And, before you ask, no, I did not kill

Jay. I believe in karma, and he got what was coming to him. I didn't even have to lift a finger."

"Did Mark ever cheat again?"

"Not that I know of. I think he was genuinely sorry. But that tart didn't stop, did she? Messing up more lives. Who cares, as long as the money keeps rolling in."

"What do you mean?"

"Oh, this woman, she's the one who was in the news a while back. You know, the one who was caught with that exec, big court case accusing her of killing him with a drug overdose. Too bad she went free."

"Ah, I remember. Candy something. Candy Cane?"

"Yes, that's the one. But it was Floss. Candy Floss. Rich executives seem to be her thing."

"Interesting. Did you talk to Mark after you split?"

"Occasionally, yes. We hoped we would still be friends. Plus, there were times I felt awful about leaving him alone like that. Every time I talked to him, I could hear that pain in his voice. He didn't take the separation well. I was worried he would go into depression. It finally drove him to suicide."

"You feel responsible?"

"The thought did occur to me. But like I said before, he only had himself to blame. I am trying to get it out of my head and carry on. And then this murder investigation. He couldn't tolerate the fact that people thought he had something to do with Jay's death. He was afraid if people started digging, they would find out why I left him. All his life achievements would forever be tainted. He wanted to be remembered as a visionary tech leader, not some two-timing murderer. You know, he called me that night. The night that Jay died."

"Oh. What time was this?"

"I don't remember. He told me he was eating at Sha Sha and was missing me. Poor sod. We used to eat there often. We have wonderful memories of that place."

"How did he sound?"

"Sad. But I think I cheered him up. He sounded a lot better by the time we were done."

"How long did you talk?"

"I don't know. Five, maybe ten minutes."

"And he called from inside the restaurant?"

"No. He said he had stepped out to make the call. Too noisy in there."

"Jenna, we really appreciate you talking to us at a time like this. Do call us if you remember anything else that might help."

"Sure. And forget what I said earlier. Don't beat yourself up about accusing Mark. You were doing your job."

"Oh, one more thing, if you don't mind. His letter said he missed the boys. Why is that? Weren't they on talking terms?"

Jenna sighed.

"They were, until they learned about his infidelity. Overheard us arguing about it. I didn't want them to find out, since he was such an excellent father to them. They hated him after that. I think that's what hurt him the most. But I can see that his death has hit them hard. Somewhere in there, they still had a soft spot for him."

"Sorry to hear that, Jenna."

They walked back to the car and got in, Paul taking one last glimpse of the mansion he could never dream of affording.

"So, what do you think? Rules out Mark?" he asked.

"Yeah, I'm pretty sure now he didn't have anything to do with it. I was thinking ... should we talk to this Candy Floss woman? Could she have something to do with it? I mean, she was there when that exec died, syringe as murder weapon, same as Jay. Sounds like she saw Jay regularly as well. Could the same thing have happened here?"

"It would be stupid of her to do something like that so soon after the previous incident. But I think it's worth a shot. She might give us some clues about Jay."

CANDY FLOSS
FEBRUARY 21

Angela had spent the previous night researching Candy Floss. She knew a lot about her from the news, but she decided some more detail wouldn't hurt. Candy had been working as an escort for a long time. She advertised her services on a website called Escorts Forever, which catered to the high end of the market. There were over a hundred listings in the Bay Area alone. Angela was always amazed by how this illegal profession promoted itself so openly. Of course, all that the women on there offered was different forms of "companion-ship," but it was clear from the explicit pictures and the provocative verbiage that the services included a lot more than mere talk and time together.

Candy's page had a brief bio about her, including some physical stats. There were roughly twenty professionally shot images of her in various stages of undress. Angela noted that Candy was gorgeous, even sexy. How could anyone resist? What caught her eye were the outrageous prices quoted for the services. People were crazy enough to pay that much? It was no wonder women like Candy had no interest in making an honest living. This was easy money.

Angela moved on to researching the incident that made Candy

famous. Famous, that is, outside of the Escorts Forever domain. Lumiotech was one of the largest tech companies in the world and was headquartered in San Francisco. One of their top executives had succumbed to a drug overdose a couple of years earlier. Candy was with him when he died. It was alleged that she was the one who had supplied him with the drugs and the one who had administered the fatal dose. She had panicked and fled the scene. She was arrested soon after, but she had claimed innocence. According to her, he had seen her website and called to book an appointment. When she showed up, the cocaine was already present, and at one point he had injected himself one last time. In a surprise decision, the jury found her not guilty. She had been released shortly before Christmas.

IT WAS a few minutes after 9:30 a.m. when the detectives reached Candy's apartment in Mountain View. Her address was easy to find, and they were quite confident she would be home that early in the morning. Angela rang the doorbell and surveyed the surroundings as she waited. It was one of the shabbier complexes in town, not many of which remained. With the booming economy and skyrocketing rents, everyone was trying to rebuild or upgrade to cash in while the going was good.

The door opened to reveal a tall, attractive woman with blonde hair. It took Angela a few moments to recognize Candy. She looked quite different without the makeup, and it appeared she had been awoken from a deep sleep. It was possible she had been crying, too. She had on a bright, pink sweatshirt with a purple, glittery unicorn pattern on it, and bubblegum pink pajama pants with dark red lips printed all over. Pink overload, thought Angela. But Paul couldn't take his eyes off the stunning face, ruffled hair notwithstanding.

"What do you want?"

"Candy?" he asked as the acidic voice jolted him out of his reverie.

"Call me Rebecca. Candy Floss is my professional name. Who are you?"

"Rebecca, I am Detective Paul Conley, and this is my partner, Angela White. Can we talk to you?"

"About what? I ain't interested in talking to no cops today."

"We are investigating the murder of Jay Sharma. We believe you knew him?"

Candy bit her lips, and for a few seconds it appeared her mind was occupied somewhere else. Then she said, "Oh, that jerk. Come on in."

"Amazing how almost everyone we talk to thinks he was a jerk. But from what we hear, you got along well with him," remarked Angela as she entered the apartment.

"I wouldn't say that. Our relationship was strictly professional. He helped pay the bills. But I couldn't stand him. He treated me like I was an object. I know, I know, in my line of work that shouldn't be a surprise, but he could at least have treated me nice."

"How long had you known him?"

"A few years now. We met a few times a year. But I hadn't seen him since my incident. I assume you know about that?"

"The Lumiotech case? Yes, we do. Why did you stop seeing him?"

"I didn't. That scandal scared everyone away. It's been a pain trying to rack up any business. That's how I landed in this dump of an apartment. I am hopeful with time people will forget."

"Where did you usually meet him?"

"Different hotels. Whatever was convenient."

"And did he ever talk about himself?"

"He didn't share much. But he did tell me once that he was in a bad marriage, and his wife was a real bitch."

Candy giggled as she said the last word. Her expression turned serious when she realized no one else was amused.

"Any drugs during your sessions?"

"Oh no. He was dead against that stuff. Oops, sorry. Pun not intended. I mean, he hated drugs. Told me he didn't even smoke. Didn't drink much either."

"Rebecca, where were you on the evening of January seventeenth?"

"How the heck do I remember that? That was a while ago."

"Try to remember, this is important for your own good," said Angela, a threat lurking somewhere in her voice.

"Well, let me see ... I dunno. Ah, let me check my calendar."

Candy took a minute to browse.

"Here it is. I was out with some friends for dinner that night."

"Where did you go?"

"A Thai place. The one in Sunnyvale downtown."

Angela tried to keep her excitement in check. This couldn't be a coincidence.

"What time did you get there?"

"Well, let's see. I got there around six thirty."

"What time did you leave?"

"We were at the restaurant for around an hour. Then we went over to that pub for a quick drink. I wanted to stick around and party some more, but my friends had to work early the next day. So we left. It was around nine, I think."

"These friends, what are their names?"

"Katie, Cheryl and Laura. My besties," replied Candy with a smile.

"And they can confirm these times?" asked Angela. She didn't give much weight to testimony from a suspect's friends, but they would have to check.

"Yeah, sure. Ask them yourself."

"Oh, we will. Give us their contact information."

Angela continued with the questioning once Paul had noted the information.

"Did you go anywhere near Sha Sha?"

"Sha Sha? Oh, I love that place. Well, yeah, I was parked there.

Couldn't find parking any other place. You know how busy it gets around there."

"Did you see or meet anyone before or after?"

"No. I parked and went straight to the restaurant. And from the pub I ... I went straight to my car." Candy reddened as she said this.

"Rebecca, what were you wearing that night?"

"What kinda question is that? Why do you care what I was wearing?"

"Just answer the damn question!"

"Okay, okay! No need to get mad! Let's see. I think I might have some pictures from the night. We girls love our selfies."

She searched through her iPhone again.

"Ah, here are some."

Angela leaned over as Candy showed the three pics. The first two were the famous selfies, with four beautiful women pouting for the camera, decked up for a night out on the town. Angela noticed Candy was wearing a white blouse with an unbuttoned red jacket on top. The third one was a full-length shot of Candy with one of the other girls. She had on a pink skirt.

Paul and Angela exchanged glances. Were they onto something here?

"Rebecca, are you sure you went straight to your car? Didn't meet anybody?"

Candy was biting her lips again. "I ... I ... yes, straight to my car ... I told you already!"

"You're lying. We have eyewitnesses who claim they saw you bent over the dead body of Jay Sharma. You killed him!"

"No, no, I did not kill him! I ... I was walking to my car when I saw this body. There was a man hunched over it. He scooted when he saw me. The body wasn't moving, so I went over to check. He looked dead. And then a bunch of guys were staring at me, so I panicked and ran."

Angela felt her pulse quickening. This was their mystery woman, the one they had been searching for all along. So far, her account fit in with what they had heard from Andy and Joseph.

"This man who ran away, what did he look like?"

"I only caught a glimpse, but he was short ... and shabby."

That sounded like Joseph. Their stories still gelled.

"Why did you lie to us if you didn't do anything?"

"For the same reason I ran. I'm always in some kind of mess or other, even if I don't do anything. I assumed you'd think I did it. But I didn't do it, please believe me. I just got out of one problem, why would I do this? I don't want any more trouble."

"We will have to search your apartment."

"What for? I told you I didn't do anything."

By now Candy was having difficulty breathing. Angela noticed she was clenching and unclenching her fists over and over.

"You claim you didn't kill him. Then let us confirm it. You shouldn't have anything to fear."

"You can't do this! Do you have a search warrant?"

"We don't. But it will be easy to get one real quick. It's better if you cooperate with us now. In fact, we would like to search your car as well."

"My car too?"

"Yes, your car too."

Candy gave in reluctantly. Angela ensured she had the consent for both searches on record, in case Candy backtracked later. She put on her gloves and kicked off the search, as Paul led Candy out of the apartment. He would be searching the car. Angela didn't have to cover much ground. It was a small, one-bedroom apartment, and it was sparsely furnished. Soon she had a find – a few sachets of cocaine and some syringes buried under clothes in a dresser drawer. She bagged the evidence. Then she resumed her search. Before long, she uncovered a Taser in Candy's purse. It joined the other evidence. Angela realized this was going a lot better than expected. Once she was done, she let in Paul and Candy.

"Find anything?" she asked him.

"Nothing. You?"

She showed him the bag.

"Awesome!"

"You taking that with you?" asked Candy.

"Yes. It's evidence. Don't worry, you'll get a receipt."

"What am I supposed to do without my stuff?"

"Don't know, don't care. You realize Jay was poisoned using a cocaine mixture that was injected in his neck? And now we find this in your apartment."

"Just because I have that stuff doesn't mean I did it."

"Then what do you have all this for? I don't think you do drugs yourself. You seem smart enough to know it's bad for you."

"Yes, but ..."

"What? You keep it for your clients? Worried we'll get you on drug charges if you tell us? Not telling is worse. Remember, this is a murder investigation."

"Okay, yeah. I do take some coke for my clients. Makes me a lot more money."

"But in the Lumiotech case you said you didn't bring the drugs, right?"

"Because it was the first time I was seeing him. I never carry the drugs for a first session. Never know who you are going to get. It's only for my regulars."

"And what about the Taser? What's that doing here? Is this what you used on Jay that night?"

"I told you I didn't meet him that night. Did you forget what I do for a living? The Taser is for my protection. There's all kinds of crazy out there."

"I also found a can of pepper spray in your purse. Isn't that enough protection?"

"When it comes to my safety, I don't take chances. Always better to have a couple of options."

The evidence was promising, but it wasn't enough. Angela knew that. She would have to figure out the next steps.

"FIRST, we should check her prints. See if they match the syringe. Then we talk to her friends." Paul outlined his thoughts as they walked back to the car.

"Sure, though one thing concerns me. What if she is telling the truth? Jay died sometime between seven and eight. So her being there at nine doesn't implicate her. Maybe she really did stumble upon the body."

"Or she killed him earlier and then remembered she had forgotten something. The syringe, for example."

"That makes sense. I think we should have someone watch her. She might panic and do something incriminating."

"Sounds like a plan."

THE FRIENDS
FEBRUARY 22

It was time to talk to Candy's friends. She was a top suspect now, and it was important that the detectives learn everything they could about her activities that evening.

First up was Laura. She owned a hair salon in Santa Clara, imaginatively named Laura's Hair. They got there a few minutes after 11:00 a.m. It was a small place, with only four stations, but it was neat and clean. A customer was getting her hair done at the first one. Other than that, the place was empty. Angela heard a woman laughing somewhere in the rear.

"Laura here?" she asked the hairdresser, who pointed to the back of the place. They walked to the opposite end of the salon and turned into a cramped area which had a desk and a couple of chairs. Angela recognized Laura from the pictures Candy had shown them. She was lounging in one of the chairs, eyes glued to her phone, guffawing away. Gabriel Iglesias had that effect on most people. Especially when he was doing his "The Fat and the Furious" routine, no matter how many times you had seen it. She paused the video once she saw them, her face turning grim.

"You must be the detectives who talked to my girl."

"If you mean Candy, then yes. And you must be Laura. We have some questions for you."

"That's me. Let me tell you right away, she didn't do anything. She wouldn't hurt a fly."

"Let us figure that out, okay? Please cooperate and answer our questions. Truthfully."

Laura nodded her assent.

"Tell us about that evening. What time you came, what time you left, where you went. All of it."

"We girls had plans to meet. Rebecca was initially in, then out, and then she texted us the day before to say she could make it after all."

"Did she say why her plans changed?"

"She said one of her regulars wanted to hook up, and she didn't want to miss out on the money. But then he cancelled. She was real bummed about it. So we all met at six thirty at Thai Basil down on Murphy."

"Who was in the group?"

"Other than me and Rebecca, it was Cheryl and Katie. We are all besties."

"And everyone was on time?"

"Yes, give or take five minutes."

"How long were you there?"

"We left the restaurant around seven thirty. I remember, because that's when I called the sitter to check on my daughter. Then we went over to Lilly Mac's for some drinks. Left there around nine."

"And was Candy with you throughout?"

"Pretty much."

"So there were periods where she wasn't with you?"

"I don't recall anyone leaving the table while we were at the restaurant."

"And how about Lilly Mac's?"

"Oh, I don't remember much of that. You know how it is after a few beers."

"Try to remember," urged Angela.

"It's been a long time. I don't recall."

"After the pub, did you walk back together?"

"No, she was parked way over at Sha Sha's. We were all on the other side, so she walked back alone."

"Was she drunk?"

"Nah, a bit buzzed, but not drunk."

"How did she seem?"

"Happy, I guess. Yeah, very happy. After all that crap she had to go through, she looked forward to our girls' night out."

"So she didn't seem nervous?"

"Nervous? No. Why would she be nervous?"

"And did she say what she was going to do later?"

"It was nine p.m. What do you expect? Go home and sleep, I guess."

"You didn't talk to her again that night?"

"Nope. I had an early start the next morning. Crashed as soon as I got home."

"Thanks, Laura. Call us if you remember anything else."

They had started to walk out when Angela turned back to Laura. "I love your hair."

"Oh, thanks. That's what we do here. You want anything done?"

"Yeah, I was thinking something shorter. Maybe get some color too."

"I can help you with that."

Paul motioned to Angela that they should leave. She gestured back that she needed a couple of minutes. He rolled his eyes and stormed out, muttering under his breath, "Women!"

Five minutes later, she walked out with a wide grin.

"That was quick. Decided what you want?"

"Yeah."

"Must have made an appointment, too?"

"Appointment? No way. That would be too unprofessional. I

tried to get her to talk. Sometimes it's easier when you are just another woman, or potential customer, and not a cop."

"And did she talk?"

"For sure her memory got sharper. She thinks Candy and Cheryl were gone for around fifteen minutes when they were at Lilly Mac's."

"Gone where?"

"The ladies room, she thought. At least that's what Candy told her once she got back. Apparently, she felt a bit nauseous."

"Interesting. And what time was this?"

"Would have been around eight."

"So, close enough to our window. She could have done it."

"Yes, she could have. Now let's see what Katie has to say."

FIFTEEN MINUTES LATER, Angela was parking in a lot off Castro Street in Mountain View. Katie worked as a receptionist at one of the tech startups there. She was on her way to lunch when they walked into the lobby.

"I only have an hour for lunch, so make it quick," she said with an edge in her voice. Angela deduced she was not happy about this delay.

"We do appreciate your talking to us at short notice. We promise we won't take too much of your time."

"What do you want to know?"

"We want to confirm Candy's movements on the evening of January seventeenth. She told us you had a girls' night out."

"Yes, she was with us the entire evening. From six thirty to nine."

"And she was never out of your sight?"

"Maybe for a few minutes, when we were at Lilly Mac's."

"But she was with you the whole time at the restaurant?"

"I guess. I'm not sure I remember."

"At Lilly Mac's, how long was she gone for?"

"Not long, I think. Maybe five minutes?"

"You sure about that?"

"It's not like I timed it, but it wasn't long."

"Long enough to walk over to Sha Sha, kill someone, and walk back?"

"Oh."

Katie let the question sink in for a moment.

"No, I don't think so. She wasn't getting anywhere fast in those heels."

"Did she go alone?"

"I don't remember."

"So Cheryl did not go with her?"

"Maybe she did. Sorry, it's been a long time. And honestly, I was more interested in the guy checking me out. The only reason I even remember Rebecca leaving, is that she told me he was cute before she left."

"Did she look stressed or nervous?"

"Quite the contrary. She was so cheerful and wanted to party hard. She went through hell with that murder case. It was heartening to see her back to normal. Too bad she's in this mess again. But she'll get through it. I'm sure of it. She's not a killer. You hear that?" Katie gave them a hard stare.

"Well, Katie, thanks for your time. We will get back to you if we have any more questions. Enjoy your lunch."

"Whatever is left of it," she shot back.

They stepped out into the cold, gloomy afternoon. So far, Candy's friends seemed to think she could not have done it. But that wasn't surprising. Friends and family rarely believe one can do bad things. One thing was clear. Candy was away for a few minutes, so she did have the opportunity.

Cheryl was up next. She resided in Mountain View, a block away from Castro. Like Candy, she too worked as an escort. The detectives walked over to her apartment and knocked. The apartments were newly constructed, and the complex had a clean, fresh feel to it. Much better than where Candy lived. The door opened just as Paul was about to knock again. There stood a stunning blonde, slightly taller than him. Judging from the makeup and the way she was dressed, she was going somewhere. He thought it was stupid of her to be wearing such a short skirt in chilly weather, but then realized she might be meeting a client. In any case, he didn't mind the view one bit.

"Cheryl Andrews? Detectives Paul Conley and Angela White with Sunnyvale DPS. We have some questions about your friend Candy."

"Come on in, but make it quick. I have an appointment in Palo Alto in an hour. Gotta leave soon."

"January seventeenth. Was she with you all evening?"

"Yes, we met at six thirty and left around nine. We were together throughout."

"Not even apart for a few minutes?"

"No."

"How about Laura and Katie? You and Candy were with them the entire time?"

"Yes."

"That's not what your friends told us. They said Candy was away for a while. And she went with you."

Cheryl paused for a moment and looked down at her hands. Then she turned to Paul and replied, "They probably don't remember. I am sure she never went anywhere. I didn't go anywhere either. Anything else you want to know?"

Her face was defiant.

"You sure you want to lie to us? It's great that you want to protect your friend, but be careful. You could get into a lot of trouble."

"But I ain't lying, am I? By the way, come see me sometime when you're off-duty. Special discount for coppers." Cheryl winked at Paul.

"You disgust me," he sneered. Internally, he felt a bit guilty. Had she caught him staring at her legs?

"You should come too. All genders are welcome in my paradise."

This one directed at Angela, who decided not to engage. No point arguing with this woman.

"Coming back to the point. You were never out of sight of the others that evening? Not even to go to the restroom?" continued Angela.

"What, am I a suspect now?"

"Just answer the question."

"No. I stuck close to them all evening."

Angela figured they wouldn't get much more out of Cheryl. But it didn't matter. They had enough from Laura and Katie.

"CAN you believe the nerve of that woman!" barked Paul, zipping up his jacket as the cold hit him hard.

"Let it go, Paul. The fact that Cheryl is covering for Candy, it tells us something. Put that together with what Laura and Katie told us, and we know Candy was out of sight for a short while and could have done it."

"Even if she did do it, the question is, where? It couldn't have been where we found Jay, because then the body would have been spotted much earlier. A lot of people pass through that place at that hour. She must have done it somewhere else and stashed the body. Then she moved it later. It's possible that's what she was doing when those guys saw her. She was placing the body there."

"But moving it from where? And how did she manage that alone? And don't forget Joseph. He was with the body when she arrived."

"She must have had help. Cheryl for example. Together they could have pulled it off. Or maybe Joseph and Candy were in it together? Candy's car was nearby. They could have stashed the body in there."

"But why put it in the alley? They could have dumped it some- where else. Some place no one would see them do it."

"Yeah, not sure about that one. Maybe they were trying to secure alibis by dumping it before nine?"

"Possible. I get this feeling that we are so close, yet so far. There's a lot of evidence that points to Candy. We just have to put it all together. Something that will stand up in court."

"We have to keep at it. We'll get there. For starters, let's pull the phone records for these women. At least confirm they're clean."

"Right, I'll work on that. We got lucky when we talked to Jenna. Otherwise, we might have never found the woman in the pink skirt."

"That reminds me. Remember the grainy surveillance video we saw? The one with the pink skirt. We should review it again. It may make a lot more sense now that we know what we're looking for."

"Good idea. I'll do that first thing tomorrow morning."

IT'S A MATCH!
FEBRUARY 23

Angela had an early start to the day. She retrieved the copy of the surveillance video from Lilly Mac's and played it, scrolling to a few minutes before 7:30 p.m. This was one of the three they had collected during the initial stages of the investigation in their hunt for the woman in the pink skirt. Since the video quality was average, it had not helped with identification and had been forgotten. At 7:28 p.m., Angela noticed the blob of pink entering the bar along with three other women. This must have been Candy and her friends. Now that Candy had shown her the photographs, Angela was able to locate Cheryl in her yellow jacket.

For the next fifteen minutes there was no interesting activity, at which point she observed the pink and yellow blobs exit. They didn't return until after 8:00 p.m. This confirmed that Candy and Cheryl had left the bar for that duration. And this period fell within the window of Jay's death. The footage wasn't clear enough as concrete evidence, but at least it was something they could ask Candy about.

Angela paused the video when her phone buzzed. Great news. Candy's fingerprints had matched the ones on the syringe. An hour later, the detectives were with their latest suspect. As expected, she had a simple explanation.

"Of course it had my prints. I saw it halfway out of his pocket and picked it up."

"And why would you do something stupid like that?"

"I dunno. I just did, okay. I was a bit drunk and didn't know what I was doing. And when those guys came, I got scared and dropped it."

"There's another detail you missed."

Angela had saved her trump card for last.

"What's that?" asked Candy, as her jaw tensed, and she looked from Paul to Angela and back.

"Jay's phone logs show you called him on the tenth, and he called you back on the fourteenth. There was another call from him on the sixteenth. You didn't tell us about that."

Candy went pale.

"I thought it wasn't important. It was just a call, and it's not like we met up or anything."

"All the more reason to not hide it, right? Why did you call him? And what did you talk about?"

"It had been a while since we had hooked up. And with my scandal, business was slow. So I started reaching out to my regulars, hoping to make some money. He didn't answer that day. But he called a few days later. Said he had been busy. Asked how I was doing. He wanted to meet."

"And did you meet?"

"No, I told you, we didn't."

"But there was a plan to meet?"

"We ... we had planned for the seventeenth. But he cancelled a day before, said something had come up."

"Oh, come on Candy ... er ... Rebecca. Now you're messing with us. Out with the truth. You met on the seventeenth, and you killed him."

"No, we didn't meet! And why would I kill him? I made a lot of money off him."

"Maybe you had a fight over something and you lost it."

"How many times do I have to repeat this? I did not do it! Please believe me!"

"Here's the thing. You keep lying to us. That's what makes it hard to trust you. Now, I am curious. When we were here to interview you earlier, your eyes were red. What were you crying about? Guilty about what you did?"

"No! It was nothing like that. I was sad."

"About what?"

"Mark Harrison. He died."

"Yes, we know. No tears for Jay but sobbing over Mark?"

"I told you, Jay was a jerk. But Mark was nice. Real nice."

"Did you see him often?"

"No, only twice."

"When was this?"

"The first time was a few years back. We had a terrific time, but after we were done he told me he felt guilty about cheating on his wife. And guess what? As soon as he left, she barged in and yelled at me. I never heard from him again until some months ago."

"That's when you met him the second time?"

"Yes."

"What happened in this meeting?"

"This time he called me to his apartment. He said we had nothing to worry about, since he was single now. I undressed, but then he didn't want to do anything. He cried and told me he missed his wife. He asked if I could stay the night. Asked me to wear this pajama set. It was his wife's. Then we cuddled and slept. I felt bad for him. He was so sad. Next morning, he made me breakfast and gave me ten thousand dollars. Can you believe it? All that money, and I didn't even have to do anything. He told me I should stop doing this dirty work and study something, get a decent job. I wish I had listened to him. And now he's gone."

Candy started sobbing. Angela handed her a box of tissues and waited for her to calm down.

"I could have been somebody, you know," Candy said as she wiped off the last of her tears.

"What, you coulda been a contender?" Paul could barely control his laughter.

"You mocking me? I know that line, it's from that old movie. How dare you? I'm serious. I could have made something of my life. But I got unlucky, made a few mistakes. You know, I was a straight-A student in school. All you see is a dumb, blonde hooker."

"Sorry, Rebecca. What went wrong?" Paul decided to indulge her a bit. If she relaxed, perhaps she would slip up and tell them something important.

"My dad died when I was seven. My mom worked hard to make sure I stayed on the right track. She was my rock. But she passed away when I was in sophomore year. Died in a hit-and-run. So unfair. I couldn't handle it and fell apart. Dropped out of college, got into bad company. Without my mom's income, I ran out of money real quick. Then one day my friend Cheryl called. We grew up together in Knoxville, but she had moved to California after high school. Told me she was doing great, and I should come, too. So I did. She got me into this business. I was so messed up at the time that I went along with it. Over the years I told myself it was only temporary, that I was just doing it for the money. Once I had enough, I would go to law school. But this life was so easy. I couldn't get out of it."

"You're telling me you wanted to be a lawyer?"

"Yep. Can't believe that? Ever since I saw Marisa Tomei in *My Cousin Vinny*, that's what I wanted to be. She was so smart and funny, I wanted to be just like her. Just as smart, but with a law degree. My mom and I would watch that movie so many times. It was one of her favorites."

Tears streamed down Candy's face. Tissues were piling up. Paul watched her, not knowing what to say. Once she had calmed down, Angela asked, "One last question, Rebecca. Did Mark ever talk about Jay?"

"No, he only talked about his wife and kids."

Angela decided it was time to bring up the video.

"Rebecca, where did you and Cheryl go from Lilly Mac's?"

"I already told you. We went to our cars."

"Not at nine p.m. This is around seven forty-five, while the others were still inside."

"I don't remember stepping outside."

"You did. You were gone for around fifteen minutes. We have it all on the surveillance video."

"Oh. Yeah, I remember now. I was craving a smoke. So we went out to share a cig."

"Really? That's all? You didn't walk up to Sha Sha and murder Jay? The timing is suspicious."

Candy shrugged her shoulders in response. Do I have to repeat myself again? she seemed to be saying.

Angela wasn't surprised by the denial. They had their work cut out for them.

"Well, Candy, it's only a matter of time before we have some solid evidence. And when we do, we will be back to get you," Paul added.

"Rebecca! It's Rebecca, not Candy!" cried Candy, reaching for the tissues again as the detectives stepped out of the apartment.

"YOU KNOW, I'm beginning to like her a bit," said Paul.

"Why, because she got your Marlon Brando reference? Or because of her sad story?"

"Oh, the Brando reference for sure. Didn't have her pegged as someone who liked the oldies. But this was a very revealing conversation. It tells us we shouldn't underestimate her. She has the smarts to plan and execute a murder like this."

"Very true."

"One thing I don't understand. Candy was arrested before. Her prints should have been in the database. Yet, we didn't find a match when we searched for the prints from the syringe."

"I checked on that. Whoever took her prints back then did a poor job. They were smeared. Would have saved us a lot of time and effort if we had found her earlier."

"Well, better late than never. She was seen at the crime scene. We have her prints on the murder weapon. Time to make an arrest?"

"I think Cynthia would want more evidence. Let's see what else we can find."

LATER THAT NIGHT, Angela received a phone call from Officer Bennett. He had been watching Candy and had followed her to a storage unit in San Jose. If she had a unit, it would have to be searched. Angela made a mental note to request a search warrant first thing the next morning. In the meantime, he would continue to monitor Candy.

THE SEARCH
FEBRUARY 26

The search warrant was ready early Monday morning. Angela and Paul raced over to San Jose, not wanting to waste any more time.

It was a spacious storage unit, and it was packed with a variety of items. Angela guessed Candy had shifted all her belongings here when she had been forced to downsize from her own home to the crummy little apartment. There were couches, dressers, chairs, a bed, and even a treadmill. Interspersed with these were an array of packing boxes. She sighed. They would have to search through all of it.

Four hours later, they had scanned every box and every drawer but had not found anything incriminating. Disappointed and exhausted, Angela sank into one of the couches. Paul joined her on the other one. They sat in silence for a few minutes.

"This is a lot of stuff. And expensive. She must have had a large home. Must be sad to lose everything," she remarked.

"Yeah. But I'm not shedding any tears for her. She earned that money doing immoral and illegal things. She had it coming."

"Well, she still worked hard for it. A lot of people get away with much worse."

"That's no excuse. Now, what next?"

"Did you look behind that dresser?"

"No. Why?"

"I noticed there's a significant gap between it and the wall. We should check."

Angela walked over to the dresser and peered behind it. There were stacks of little boxes, but it was too dark to tell what they contained. She turned on her flashlight and pointed it at the target.

"What on earth is she doing with all this?" she wondered out loud as she picked up a box and opened it. She had to confirm that the contents matched the label.

Seeing her reaction, Paul hurried over and looked over the dresser, then inside the box.

"So many e-cigs," said Angela.

"Perhaps this is what we've been looking for."

"What do you mean?"

"Liquid nicotine."

"Oh. There's so much of it here. Enough to experiment and come up with a potent mixture to kill Jay."

"We have her, don't we?"

"Yes, I think we do!"

ANGELA AND PAUL huddled in Cynthia's office to discuss their next move.

"What do we have?" asked Cynthia.

"All the evidence points to Candy. She didn't like Jay. She was near Sha Sha that night and had sufficient time to do it. Her prints are on the murder weapon. We found syringes and raw material for the poison in her possession. A Taser too. Only wrinkle is, how did she hide and move the body. Our hunch is she had help from Cheryl."

"What about her friends? You were checking their phone records."

"All clean. No suspicious calls or texts. Location data also confirms what they told us."

"Have you ruled out that homeless guy, Joseph?"

"His prints matched the ones on the wallet and license. Nothing other than that."

"But he could be an accomplice?"

"It's a remote possibility. At this point we need Candy to cooperate and spill the beans. We're hoping she'll cave once we arrest her, and she starts feeling the pressure."

"What about Mark and Praveen?"

"They did threaten Jay, and they were both in the area around the time he died. But we don't have anything concrete like we have with Candy. Yes, Praveen did lie to us, but he was just scared."

"But with Mark, you did find his Purdue pin."

"Which he could have dropped at any time. I know it's a coincidence he lost it that same week, but he did step out to call his ex-wife that evening. And then there's his suicide note."

"Yes. Tragic. It's not like we can arrest a dead man, anyway. The Meghna Rao angle you were exploring – I assume that's gone too?"

"We were quite confident she had something to do with it. But there is no evidence, and she has a strong alibi. We even scrutinized her call records going back a few months, but we didn't find anything suspicious. Maybe she had an accomplice as well, but the same question – who? Nothing fits. We were counting on the autonomous car to transport the body, but there is no evidence around that either. We come right back to Candy."

"To be honest, that autonomous car theory was too far-fetched. No one was going to buy that. Not the jury for sure. That stuff is still far beyond what the average person can comprehend. To them, it only happens in sci-fi movies set in the 2050s."

"Well, if I was going for the 2050s, I would have worked in something about flying cars," quipped Angela.

"Now that would be cool," said Paul.

"People, let's focus here. We have enough for probable cause against Candy. Get cracking on that arrest warrant. Great work both of you!"

THE ARREST
FEBRUARY 27

Arrest warrant in hand, Angela and Paul went over to Candy's.

"It's not looking good, Rebecca," he started.

"What now?" asked Candy in a cautious tone.

"We searched your storage unit. Guess what we found? Vapes, tons of them. That's enough nicotine to down a few more of your clients."

"I told you. I didn't kill anybody."

"Then what do you have all that for?"

"Those are for me."

"You going to smoke all those e-cigs? A bit much, no?"

"I stocked up. You know how they're saying vapes might be banned soon. I love that stuff. And, might as well tell you. I figured that after the ban I could make a lot of money selling it at a premium. You won't believe how crazy kids are about it. I desperately need the cash, you know."

"You're a smart cookie. You have an answer for everything. But you have got to come up with something more convincing. We aren't buying any of this nonsense. You were there that night, your prints are on the syringe, and you have everything needed to murder him.

And to top it all, you didn't like the guy because he didn't treat you right. We have motive and all the evidence we need. You aren't going to make it out of this one."

The detectives arrested Candy, ignoring her protests. She still maintained she was innocent. But it didn't matter. They had enough to prove she was guilty.

ANGELA VISITED Maya one last time. As a courtesy, she would be informing her they had found the killer.

"You're looking better today," Angela said as she walked in the door.

"Yes, I do feel better. I have been taking it day by day, trying to get over it. Getting back to work helped quite a bit. Took my mind off things. And the cremation brought some closure. Like I finally said goodbye to him. But I know it will be difficult to move on completely."

"It is a huge loss. I remember how devastated I was when my father passed away. I can only imagine what you are going through."

"Thank you for your kind words. What brings you here today? More questions?" Maya asked quite plainly, without the usual irritation.

"No, not this time. I am here to tell you that we have the killer. We haven't announced it publicly yet, so please keep this news to yourself."

"Oh, who is it?"

"An escort who goes by the name Candy Floss. Jay was a regular."

"He was? I knew he had affairs and harassed women, but I never imagined he could stoop any lower. Visiting prostitutes. Disgusting!"

"Sorry, we thought you knew."

"Never mind. It's all over now. So she confessed?"

"She claims innocence, but we have overwhelming evidence that she did it."

"Why did she do it?"

"We don't know for sure yet. But quite likely because he used to mistreat her."

"Her too," said Maya, shaking her head. "Was she the one who mailed the threatening letters?"

"We don't know who sent them. We had some leads, but nothing concrete."

"I guess it doesn't matter anymore."

"Right. What do you plan to do now?"

"A trip to India with his ashes. Spend some time with my family."

"I wish you the best."

"Thank you. What happens next?"

"I have to warn you, it will be a lengthy affair. The prosecutor will build a case. Then there's the whole jury selection process and pretrial hearings. The trial itself can last a long time. Could be more than a year before it's all over. But we're confident that justice will be served."

"Thank you so much for all the hard work you put in. It couldn't have been easy."

"It rarely is, but it's part of the job. I should be going now."

Maya saw Angela out. She heaved a sigh of relief once the door was closed. It was all over.

THE ARRAIGNMENT
MARCH 2

Angela walked into the courtroom with Paul by her side, a spring in her step now that she had another criminal behind bars. The court was a lot fuller than she had expected, but she realized that, by now, Candy was a celebrity. If the Lumiotech trial had made the country aware of Candy, this case had magnified her notoriety. Angela recognized a number of familiar faces, all journalists eager to snag a scoop, flashing broad smiles. In the front row she saw some more faces she knew, these not so welcoming. Cheryl and Katie were there to support their friend, and they did not look happy. The cold, piercing stares they gave Angela could have burned holes through her. But she didn't care. She had apprehended a lot of criminals in her career, and she was used to such behavior from the accused's supporters. Maya was nowhere to be found. It was not surprising. Such proceedings were often hard on the victim's kin.

She noticed Candy had hired Francis Dern as her attorney. This was as expected, since he had successfully defended her in the previous trial. He was one of the best attorneys in town, and Angela admired him for it, though she disliked the fact that he mostly represented criminals. Winning a case against him would be challenging. She hoped the prosecution had enough to deliver the goods.

Everyone rose as the judge, Terence Ngo, entered. Candy followed soon after, dressed in her Sunday best. She was the picture of virtue. No one could have guessed what she did for a living, or why she was on trial. Before she sat down, she glared at Angela.

The proceedings were quick. As expected, the defendant pleaded "not guilty." But Angela was shocked when Judge Ngo granted bail. It was set at a steep five hundred thousand dollars, but at least it was an option. Murder in the county was a non-bailable offense, and rarely had she seen a murder suspect get out on bail. Francis Dern had worked his magic. So far, he was worth every penny Candy was spending on him.

REUNITED

MARCH 9

It was a few minutes past 2:00 p.m. when Meghna entered the Fairmont Hotel in downtown San Jose, a spring in her step. A delightful weekend lay ahead. The elevator took her to the twentieth floor. Once inside her room, she dropped her bag at the entrance and dashed to the bed, where the object of her desire was reading a book. Their eyes met. Meghna locked lips with her lover.

"I missed you."

"I missed you, too."

Tender words that followed the luscious kiss and led into a frenzied rush to undress. Their naked bodies connected and let loose unbridled passion that had been caged for so long. So many months since they had last laid eyes on each other, had touched each other. Now every caress brought pure ecstasy, and before long they lay side by side, their faces emanating bliss. Minutes passed. Meghna got out of bed and walked over to the table. Her lover watched her, taking in every inch of that beautiful body.

"Come back to bed."

"Soon, my darling."

"I want you."

"You just had me."

"I need more."

"I am yours all weekend. And beyond. Now, let's celebrate."

The lover smiled at the thought. Yes. Meghna forever. Meghna opened the bottle of champagne and poured two glasses. She walked back and handed one to her lover. They clinked and drank up.

"We did it!"

"We pulled it off!"

The lips met again, and Meghna pinned her lover to the bed as she worked kisses down the body. Then it was Meghna's turn to lie back and be pampered. Satisfied once again, they lay there in silence, still trying to let their success sink in. The time apart was crucial to their plan. It had to appear that they were no longer in touch, or suspicions would be aroused. This was the only way they could build on the strength of their alibis and get away with murder.

Lying there, Meghna recalled her first time with Jay. It was their second meeting. He had tried to impress, wooing her with dinner at the Plumed Horse in Saratoga. They had enjoyed an intimate and delectable meal. She had noticed he was not wearing his wedding ring, and she couldn't decide whether it was a good sign or a bad one. After the repast they had driven over to her place and had spent an hour making love. It had been a disappointing encounter – she had had a lot better. But there was more to Jay than that. She found him to be a charming and brilliant man, someone who could articulate his thoughts effectively. These qualities, in addition to his looks, were quite a turn-on, and a little deficiency in bed was not going to keep her away from him. Who would have thought she would murder this man a few years later?

THE IDEA TO murder Jay had appeared out of the blue. Maya was at Meghna's one April night the previous year. He was out of town on a business trip, so they had planned a sleepover. Maya arrived after work, and they plopped on the couch, polishing off a large pizza and two bottles of wine. They were watching *Thelma and Louise*, a movie they both loved. As the protagonists plunged to their deaths, Meghna had said:

"I hate Brad Pitt."

"I thought you adored him. He was so hot in this one."

"Yes, but look what he did to Thelma. Someone should kill him. And their asshole husbands, too. Come to think of it, someone should kill all men."

"Isn't that going too far?"

"Yeah. But we should at least kill Jay. He is the real asshole."

Maya giggled, the way she did when she was a bit tipsy. She was sure Meghna was drunk too.

"That would be cool."

"Yes, it would be," replied Meghna.

Nothing else was said after that. They staggered back to the bedroom and crashed into bed, Maya with her head on Meghna's chest, holding her tight. They had slept content and peaceful.

The next morning Maya had stepped out of the room to an appetizing aroma emanating from the kitchen. Meghna had cooked some upma and omelets. The popular Indian semolina dish was Maya's favorite.

"Ooh, this looks delicious. A breakfast feast!"

"I couldn't decide what to make. So I made both. Let's eat, I am starving."

Maya was savoring the first spoonful when Meghna had asked, "So, how should we do it?"

"Do what?" asked Maya with a blank expression as she scarfed down the upma.

"What we discussed last night. You know."

"The trip to Europe?"

"No, silly. Killing Jay," replied Meghna, moving her finger across her neck in throat-slitting fashion.

"Oh, I remember. You were serious?"

"Yes, of course. I wouldn't joke about something like that."

"I have wished him dead several times. Have even imagined myself doing the deed. But doing it for real? I don't know. That's wrong."

"Is it? He is an awful man who has done nasty things to so many women, including you and me, and there have been no consequences. He must be punished. Or he will go on hurting others. And you, too."

"So we take the law into our hands? Dish out vigilante justice?"

"Yes, something like that."

"But, how do we do it? I don't even think I have it in me to take a life. What if we get caught?"

"We won't if we are smart. We have to plan it impeccably and execute to plan. Not a lot different from any of our software projects. In fact, this will have more chances of succeeding than any software project," added Meghna with a smile.

"Now you are being facetious."

"Trying to lighten the mood. You went all serious on me."

"Well, this is serious stuff. And you sprung it on me."

"In my defense, I did give you a heads-up last night."

"When we were both drunk bigly. That doesn't count."

"Bigly? Is that officially a word now?"

"Apparently it is. Blessed by the high and mighty."

"So, what do you say?"

"I can't do it, Meghna. It's not like killing him will solve any problem. Others will continue doing stuff like this. If we could make it public, get to him legally, that would still have some impact."

"You know that will not work. He will get away, while all the accusers, and you, will be humiliated. Besides, do you think you have it in you to take that step? Or at least divorce him?"

"You are right. It will not work. As for the divorce, you know I can't do that. My parents will disown me if I do. Even if we murder him, it will still not help us get together. They won't like that either."

"But if he dies, you have their sympathy. They might be more accepting if they see you as the grieving widow, the woman who was true to her marriage and stood by her husband through everything."

"You mean I should emotionally manipulate them? That's not right."

"And it's right when they do it to you? Isn't that what they do? Burdening you with their outdated baggage. Tradition this, society that. When do you get to live your life the way you want to?"

"You are lucky, Meghna. Your parents have a liberal outlook. They support you in whatever you do, accept you as you are. But I still love my parents, even the way they are. I wouldn't feel right doing this."

Meghna gave up. She understood she wasn't getting through to Maya. Maybe it just needed time. Keep bringing it up periodically, and Maya might change her mind.

And that was what happened. As time passed and things got worse, Maya realized Meghna was right. Jay had to go. Her fights with him got more frequent. He was sleeping around a lot more and didn't even care to hide it anymore. One day she caught him leering at Anjali. Anjali had noticed and was uncomfortable. Maya knew it was only a matter of time before he would make a pass at Anjali, and she didn't want her friend to endure any more harassment from Jay.

Meghna was glad to hear Maya had come around. She had not wasted time while she waited. In the interim, Meghna had completed some of the research and planning, and was ready with the proposal. She discussed it with Maya.

Jay liked to frequent Cinebar for after-work drinks. Meghna would show up there one evening while he was there and ensure that he saw her. Old memories would be rekindled, and he would want to get into her pants right away. She would play hard to get at first. Eventually, she would agree to meet him a few nights later. All he would know is that she would pick him up from work and drive him over to her place to spend a couple of passionate hours in bed.

"That's good. But how do we kill him? Shooting, stabbing, whacking him on the head – all sounds messy. Poison?" asked Maya.

"You read my thoughts. And it has to be done in a way that neither of us is suspected, especially you, since the spouse always tops the suspect list. We must have airtight alibis."

"So I guess, first we have to pick a poison. It can't be something in his food or drink, or they will suspect me. We will have to find something we can inject and is easy to obtain."

"Right. I have some ideas about that. And we will have to figure out where to do it. Outside the home would be better, unless we can get you a strong alibi."

"If it's outdoors then we should do it at night to reduce the chances of being seen by someone."

The discussion had gone on, and finally they had the key points nailed down. Over the next few weeks, they had worked out the details and finalized the plan. One critical decision was that they would break off all visible contact a few months before D-Day. They would only meet if absolutely necessary, and the meetings would be discreet. All communication would be through burner phones, which they would destroy as soon as they were done. Another idea was to plant a story that Jay was receiving death threats. This would distract the cops and have them probe elsewhere. They didn't have to go through the trouble of sending all the letters, just provide some evidence such missives existed. For that, Maya had put together one and clicked a picture as proof. She had then mailed it from Oakland and preserved the envelope, while the letter was destroyed once it arrived.

Meghna had researched poisons and had decided that a concentrated mixture of cocaine in liquid nicotine would be ideal. It was well known that a cocaine overdose could be fatal, especially for someone who had never done drugs. She had also come across some cases of murderers using liquid nicotine. To play it safe, she decided to combine them. The nicotine would be easy to extract from the variety of vaping products available. Of course, she would have to pick the right ones since the nicotine concentration could vary a lot. Obtaining the cocaine took more effort, but she did manage to locate a supplier. All purchases were made in cash. For her research, she was careful to only use library computers and to clear her search history so that this was not easily traceable back to her.

Next, they needed strong alibis. Multiple people vouching for them would be most effective to rule out suspicion of anyone lying. Maya suggested using coworkers. Arranging late work meetings that entire week was straightforward, since they both had software releases coming up anyway. It was important to split the work and the locations for killing and dumping the body so that neither of them would be away from their coworkers long enough. For the same reason, it was necessary to dump it somewhere it would be found while they were still in the office. Maya had spent considerable time scouting locations and checking for security cameras, so they knew which places to avoid. The last thing they wanted was to pull off a spectacular crime but be caught on camera.

Finally, they worked out their stories for when they would be interrogated by the cops. They were certain Maya would be on the radar, and they figured it would only be a matter of time before the investigators would learn about Meghna. It was crucial to throw in some truths along with the lies to sound authentic and minimize suspicion. For that reason, Maya decided she would reveal some facts about the state of her marriage. They were confident they had prepared well. Would there be curveballs? Yes. But they would have to figure those out as they came.

Then they waited patiently for D-Day.

D-DAY

JANUARY 17

Maya woke up in a sweat, her stomach tied in knots. A lot more nervous than she had expected. The big day had arrived. It was time to follow through and execute the meticulous plans made in the last few months. Jay was up already, probably on one of his early morning business calls. She hopped into the shower. It calmed her. For a few minutes she enjoyed the soothing flow of hot water on her body. Once done, she went downstairs for breakfast. She had just put down her bowl of oatmeal when he stormed into the kitchen, nostrils flaring. He was holding something up in his hand. She went numb when she realized what it was.

"Look what I found."

It was the burner phone. How could she have been so careless? Had he discovered the plot? Maya had a sinking feeling in her stomach.

"What are you hiding from me? You use this to talk to your boyfriends?" Jay continued as he moved towards her, bringing his face menacingly close to hers.

So he thought she was having an affair? Well, not entirely untrue. But if that was all he knew, then he was probably unaware of the plan. She had to be brave and stand up to him like she had done before.

"Sadly, no boyfriends for me. I am not as attractive as you."

"Then why do you have this secret phone?"

"It's none of your business. I don't ask you about your girlfriends."

She saw the anger bubbling over in his eyes. It seemed any moment now he would hit her, hard. But better sense prevailed, and he stepped back. He snapped the phone in two and smashed it to the ground.

"Why did you do that?!" screamed Maya. This would ruin the plan. How would she communicate safely with Meghna without the burner?

"You know why. You can't cheat on me and get away with it."

"Me cheating? You are the big fucking cheat. How dare you accuse me? And you know what? Not only are you a cheat, you are a creepy pervert, preying on defenseless women. Guys like you should be put behind bars," she continued. The phone was destroyed. What did it matter now? She just wanted to let out all her pent-up frustrations while she still had the chance.

She had never seen Jay so angry before. He picked up a knife, and for a moment she feared for her life. He brought it down hard through the box of oatmeal sitting on the counter. Raising his eyes from the box, he glared at her, his eyes still menacing, and said, "Next time this will go through your face, you bitch!" and stormed out. A couple of minutes later, he drove off.

By now Maya was shuddering. She slid down to the floor and sat there for a while, trying to compose herself. Jay was dangerous. She was convinced now that the decision to kill him was correct and timely. Then she worried about how they would continue without the phone. Would they have to abort the mission because of this one setback? Maybe they could take some risks. Meghna could text her on her main cell instead of the burner. Maya would have to be careful not to initiate anything to Meghna from her own phone. But how would Meghna know about the change in plan? Maya did a quick search online for pay phones and found a couple near home. She would call Meghna's burner from one and give her the update.

She cleared up the mess from the burner and packed it up to toss somewhere on her way to work. It would be a disaster if it was found in her trash. The day had not started well at all. Still anxious, she hoped fervently nothing else would go wrong.

MEGHNA GOT in to work early, since there were some things she had to take care of in preparation for the task ahead. She had barely finished when she received a call on her burner phone from an unknown number. She picked up and waited for the caller to speak. It was Maya, brief and to the point. Then she hung up. Meghna was a bit concerned, but decided they were still in business. For the rest of the day it was difficult to concentrate, but she managed to get through it. In the evening, the team huddled together in the conference room. Catered dinner came in around 6:00 p.m., and soon the room broke out in chatter and laughter. Nothing like free food to keep them happy and working.

At 7:00 p.m., Meghna excused herself and walked over to the garage. She could see that VRM31 was out. She checked out VRM32 and got in. A text from Jay. He was waiting for her at his work entrance. She replied, then got out of the car and left her phone on the desk. This way if anyone tried to trace her location, it would appear she had never exited the building. She got back in the car and donned her gloves. It was a little chilly outside, so he would not be suspicious about the gloves. She took the loaded syringe and the Taser from her purse and taped them separately to the rear of the passenger seat. The handcuffs and the scarf came next, placed in the cup holder. Things could get messy, so she had brought along a bag with paper towels and cleaning supplies which she kept in the rear. Then she drove off. Within five minutes she was at Intelligent

Systems, beaming at Jay as he got in next to her with a wide grin of his own. It screamed "I can't wait to grab you." She noted with relief that he wasn't wearing a jacket in spite of the cold. That would make it easier for her.

"Sweet ride," he said as he got in.

"Thought I would show off our superior technology."

"Ha, can't be better than ours."

"Aren't you cold without a jacket?"

"You are so hot. Why would I need a jacket?"

Still got the cheesy lines, thought Meghna. She eased the car to a more secluded area of the parking lot, stopped and turned off the engine.

"I thought we were going to your place."

"Shouldn't we have some appetizers first?" she replied with a wink.

Jay moved in for a kiss. She kissed him back as she grabbed the syringe and plunged it into his neck, dispensing the poison into him. He fell back in shock, clutching his neck. Once he saw the needle in her hand, he realized it was an attack. He lunged at her. Meghna pushed him back with all her might and reached for the Taser. As he came back for her, she stunned him with it. While he was incapacitated, she cuffed him behind his back and gagged him with the scarf. Within a few seconds he was stirring again. She hoped the poison would start working soon, but until then he had to be kept under control. It was already fifteen minutes since she had left the conference room. She had to act fast now. She wiped the syringe and slipped it into Jay's shirt pocket. Maya, cautious as always, had wanted the syringe destroyed. But Meghna wanted to leave it as a signature for their well-planned murder. There was no risk if they took all the precautions. As with most of their discussions, Meghna had prevailed.

She switched off his cell and put it in her pocket. This would prevent the cops from tracking his movements from the phone records. And with no device to search, they would be unable to extract any potential evidence. By now he had stopped struggling, and it looked like he would pass out at any moment. She figured the restraints were not required anymore. The handcuffs and the scarf came off and went into the bag. She reclined his seat and sped off to her office. Before exiting, she programmed the car to go to Yummy Tummy. A quick text to Maya from the burner to let her know the car was on the way. Then she went inside and picked up her cell phone from the garage. In thirty minutes flat, Meghna was back in the conference room. Some of her colleagues were still huddled over their laptops, others were busy with a second round of the leftover food. She was confident no one would think she had been out for more than twenty minutes.

Around 9:00 p.m., everyone was done for the day. The car was back. Meghna went to the garage and scanned it one last time to ensure it was clean. She logged into the console and deleted the history for VRM32 for the evening. Meghna had arranged for a second Vroom car to be in the vicinity, in case people reported seeing one. She spotted Jessica sitting in VRM31 but acted as if she had not seen her. The logs confirmed that the car had indeed traveled through Milpitas and Sunnyvale around the right times. The workshop was behind the garage, and no one was present there. She went in, smashed the Taser, the burner and Jay's phone, and put the pieces into a bag. These would be disposed of on her way home.

AT 7:25 P.M., Maya received the text she had been dreading all day. The next few minutes were difficult. The car was sitting in the parking lot with a dead Jay in it. She was worried what would happen if someone found the car before she got to it. She felt this was one of the weak links in the plan, but Meghna had dismissed her fears.

Time to act. At 8:15 p.m., she excused herself and went down to the Vroom car, stopping at her desk first to leave her cell phone there. Once in the car, it took her a full minute to collect herself as she viewed Jay's lifeless body lying next to her. He was a terrible man and an awful husband, but had she done the right thing? Too late for second thoughts. She felt his pulse and was convinced he was dead. He had vomited due to the poison. She grabbed the supplies from the back and cleaned him up. Then she drove off to Sunnyvale downtown, which was less than five minutes away. In the darkness of one of the alleys, she unloaded him from the car and checked that the syringe was still in his pocket. For a moment, she had this feeling that she was being watched, but she didn't see a soul when she scanned her surroundings. She was still shaking when she sped off. Once at work, she inspected the car one last time, scrubbing carefully to leave no trace of anyone having been in the car that night. She programmed the car to return to Vroom and exited with the cleaning supplies. The car headed back to Meghna. On her way back to the meeting, Maya stopped at her desk to pick up her cell phone and drop off the bag. Within twenty-five minutes she was back in the conference room, her heart ready to explode.

At around 9:15 p.m., everyone dispersed for the day. Maya left too, after picking up the bag from her desk. On her way home, she stopped in a McDonald's parking lot to trash the bag. She still couldn't get Jay's image out of her head. There was an element of guilt which gnawed at her, but each time, she overpowered it with every justification for why he had to go. All she could do now was to get home and play the part of a concerned wife. And wait patiently for the body to be found.

BRENDA WAS HAVING A BLAST. She was at Sha Sha, drinking and dining with some of her closest friends. Jason had offered to watch the kids so she could have a girls' night out, the first in a long, long time. She needed the break. In fact, she was sure she deserved it for all the hard work she had been putting in, both at work and at home. At around 8:30 p.m., she felt a strong urge to smoke. She had quit when she had learned she was pregnant with Jacob, but now that the kids were older, she treated herself to the occasional cigarette. Bumming one off Shannon, she stepped out the rear entrance of the restaurant, into the shadows by the door. She was about to light up, when a car crawled past and stopped a few feet away. A figure emerged. Even in the darkness she could tell it was Maya Sharma, a coworker at her previous job. Brenda would have rushed over to say "Hi," but something about Maya's demeanor held her back. She was looking around furtively. Brenda decided to stay back in the shadows. She watched in horror as Maya opened the passenger door, pulled out a body and left it by the side of the car. She waited for Maya to leave, and only then did she dare move. It didn't make any sense. Could Maya have murdered someone? That was not the Maya she knew. She was tempted to walk over and see who it was, but the thought gave her the shudders. For a moment, she contemplated calling 911, but then dismissed the thought. Too much trouble. She tossed the unlit cigarette and went back inside, deeply distressed by what she had witnessed.

BETTY FOLLOWED Jay down to the Intelligent Systems lobby, only to see him step out the front door of the building. By the time she exited the building, she could see him getting into a car. She spotted a woman at the wheel. Who was this woman? His new girl-friend? She felt a pang of jealousy. And rage. Instead of leaving the parking lot, the car moved to an empty area. Betty got into her own car to do a casual drive-by and check on what was going on. The other vehicle started moving as soon as she started her Civic. It was heading towards the exit. She followed it all the way into the Vroom parking lot. There, she saw the woman get out.

A minute later, the car left again, this time heading onto 237-W. She followed as it exited in Sunnyvale and stopped in the Yummy Tummy parking lot. Betty waited a few minutes for something to happen. Anything. But no one stepped out of the car. She had seen the woman leave the car earlier, so was Jay all alone in there? What was he doing? She crept over to the car and peered inside. As expected, it was empty except for him. Strangely, he was fast asleep. Why? She tapped on the window. No response. She tapped harder. Again, no response. She didn't want to draw too much attention by making any more noise, so she decided to call him on his cell. But her phone was dead. She knew she had a charger somewhere in her car. It took her a few minutes to find it and plug it in. That's when she saw a woman walk towards the car and get in. She knew this one. It was Maya.

The car took off within a minute. Betty followed again, and this time it stopped in the parking lot of Sha Sha Shawarma. She saw Maya emerge and go over to the other side of the car. Betty stepped out to take a better look. It was a shocking sight. Jay, the father of the child growing inside her, was gone! Had Maya murdered him? She rushed back to her car to grab her phone. She was about to place the emergency call when someone grabbed her from behind and placed a wet cloth over her mouth. The grip was strong, and her efforts to break free were fruitless. She tried to scream for help, but the sound barely registered. Soon she was pushed into the back seat of her car. A few minutes later, all was darkness.

A MURDER
APRIL 4

Angela opened her eyes. The clock showed 7:00 a.m., and she could tell the sun was shining bright. She recalled hitting the snooze button an hour earlier and again a while later. For some reason, she didn't want to leave the bed today. And then she remembered why. The previous day, she had learned that Candy was working on an autobiography. It was something that had been in the works during the Lumiotech trial and would be published soon. As it is, Angela was pissed that Candy was out on bail. Now this news that Candy was going on with her life and could end up making a ton of money enraged her. Of course, Candy was still on trial for Jay's murder, but she should already have been rotting in jail.

Angela flushed these negative thoughts from her head and dragged herself out of bed. A couple of hours later, she was at work. Paul appeared before she had a chance to sit down. She could tell he had important news.

"You won't believe what happened."

"Enlighten me."

"They found a sixty-five-year-old man, an Adam Newman, dead at his home last night. Guess how he died."

"Not in the mood for guessing games."

"Somebody's grumpy today. Still mad about Candy's book?"

"Yep. Aren't you?"

"Yes. But what does it matter? We'll get her in court."

"That we will. So, how did he die?"

"He was Tasered and injected with a lethal dose of nicotine and cocaine. Sound familiar?"

"Oh. You think it's a copycat killer?"

"Either that, or Candy struck again."

"You think she's stupid enough to do that again? While she's awaiting trial for another murder? No. I feel this is someone inspired by Jay's murder."

"Well, don't forget she was stupid enough to kill soon after getting out of the previous charges."

"That's true. Do we have this one?"

"Cynthia assigned Wilson and Shibata."

"That's a relief. I think I have had my fill of syringes and Tasers. Do they have any leads yet?"

"No. The odd thing about this one is that Newman was found naked on the floor with the syringe in his hand. It was like the killer was trying to make some kind of statement."

"What do you mean?"

"His body was laid out in an X formation. Arms and legs spread out above and below him. The syringe was in his right hand, between his index and middle fingers, like he was smoking a cigarette."

"Interesting. Who found the body?"

"His wife. She was out for the evening with her bowling group. Quite a shock for her."

"I would imagine. Why are they suspecting murder? If he had the syringe in his hand, could it be suicide?"

"Don't forget the Taser. Besides, why would anyone committing suicide stage his body like that?"

"Beats me. Well, I hope they're able to solve this one."

"Yep, I hope so too," replied Paul as he walked away.

While Angela had admitted relief that she was not on this case, somewhere deep inside she knew she would have loved to dig into another one like this. The problem-solver in her couldn't resist it.

HAVING MISSED HER MORNING RUN, Angela wanted to make up for it in the evening. It was past 8:00 p.m. and beginning to get dark when she laced up and stepped outside the house. She started down the street, taking her regular route. The tension began to melt away as she breathed in the fresh air and her heart revved up. Suddenly, she had the feeling she was being followed. Out of the corner of her eye, she saw a vehicle inching in the same direction as her. She figured it was someone searching for a specific address. But then her instincts kicked in, and she decided to verify that assumption. At the next intersection, she took a sharp left turn and ran into the side street. At the same time, she attempted to get a better look at the vehicle, determined not to let the occupant realize she was aware of his presence.

It was a black SUV with tinted windows. That would make it hard to see who was inside. She hoped it would continue on, but it turned down the same street. Now she was convinced she was being followed. This was cause for worry. She preferred to run light, so she never carried her phone or her gun when out running. One option was to stop at one of the houses alongside and get help. But she didn't want to risk anyone's life in case the person following her was armed. Her best alternative was to get back home. At the next corner she turned right, immediately crossed the street and started running in that direction. Within this time, she had managed to confirm that the SUV was a Cadillac Escalade with the license plate covered. This added to her suspicions. As she ran, she heard it making a sharp turn. She recalled she had noticed this vehicle parked across from her house when she had started the run. So he had been watching and waiting. She picked up speed and raced home.

As soon as she entered, she grabbed her phone and got away from the windows, in case there was any shooting. Then she got her gun from the safe. She tried to peek outside to get a handle on the situation, as she began dialing for help. Before she could complete the call, she heard a couple of thumps followed by the sound of glass shattering. It was her living room window. Through the broken shards she saw the Escalade speeding away. She rushed toward the door, ready to shoot if necessary. But by the time she made it outside, the SUV was too far away. Dejected, she turned to see her neighbor, Ron, standing in his front yard. She lowered the gun. He was a widower in his eighties and lived alone but was still active and mentally agile. Angela enjoyed the occasional chess game with him.

"Punks," he said in disgust.

"There was more than one?"

"I saw two before they rolled up the window and flew away. One driving, and the other shooting."

"Did you see their faces?"

"Nah. They had on black masks, couldn't see anything. Even their clothes looked black."

"Oh. Anything else you noticed in the car?"

"Sorry, missy. That's all I could get. Good luck with that," said Ron, pointing to the front of her house, as he returned to his.

Her heart still racing, she turned around to inspect the damage. There were a few paint splatters on the exterior wall of her home, which she concluded were shot with a paintball gun. Her window was shattered. She wondered why anyone would want to do this. She stepped inside the house to check what had broken the glass. It turned out to be another paintball. Who were these people? Was someone trying to send her a message, trying to threaten her? It did not look like a random attack. If these people wanted to hurt her, or worse, kill her, they could have done so easily. But they didn't. She contemplated notifying the authorities, but then decided against it. This seemed personal, and she would find her way out of it on her own.

While Angela cleaned the paint off and patched the window, she considered her next steps. Her only clue was the Escalade, and it would be painful to locate without the license plate. At least she could tell it was a current year model. Also, the fact that Escalades didn't sell anywhere near as much as, say Toyotas, upped her spirits a bit. It would be difficult, but not impossible. She was not one to walk away from a challenge.

I KNOW
APRIL 7

Maya woke up with a start. She had dreamed Jay was still alive, and she had stabbed him brutally until he had bled to death. This was one of her recurring nightmares, and it always left her feeling weary and guilty. But today she was able to handle it, with Meghna by her side. There was a sense of security and comfort, and she hoped things would get better now that they were together. What she had done was necessary. There was still some guilt about Candy and having an innocent person pay the price for her actions. But she erased it from her mind. That woman had it coming, what with the immoral life she led.

Lying there with Meghna, it reminded her of her time as a child, those carefree days without the burdens that came with adulthood. No difficult decisions to make, and her mother always there to comfort her when she was down. It was so ironic that back then, she couldn't wait to grow up and live her life as an independent adult. And now as a grownup, she often longed for that carefree childhood period again.

Maya's thoughts rolled back to those early days with her partner. The first time they met, how angry Maya had been. Then the chance meeting, with Meghna offering an apology. How their friendship had flourished after that. They would meet over coffee or dinner and take day trips to nearby places. One evening, Maya was at Meghna's. They were in the kitchen, cooking. Meghna had taken her hand and caressed it. That simple touch had ignited something in Maya. Soon they were kissing, and they ended up on the floor, making love. Maya had never known anything like it, and she hoped she would get to experience those sensations again. She confessed it was her first time with anyone other than Jay. Meghna admitted she had experimented with women before. They realized they were in love, and they craved a life together. A few nights later, when they were in bed, Meghna had disclosed that she had lied. She had not trusted Jay when he told her about the divorce, but she had been unable to resist his charms. She wasn't proud of it. Maya had replied that she wasn't surprised, but she forgave her. It was not like Meghna had wrecked the marriage. It was already on the rocks, and it was not the first time Jay had cheated. All Maya requested was that, moving forward, they would be honest with each other. Meghna had agreed, and they had sealed the agreement with a passionate kiss.

Meghna was still asleep. Maya decided to whip up some pancakes and surprise her in bed. Except for the guilty feelings, the last few months had been amazing. Living together, sharing their lives, it was all lovely. They hadn't told their parents yet. Soon they would have to, since they wanted to get married. Besides that, Yummy Tummy was preparing for an IPO, and Vroom had started making money after gaining the requisite approvals for sales in Arizona. Financially and career-wise, they felt accomplished.

Sometimes Maya missed her old home and neighborhood, and the Bhatias in particular. But it was important for her to move out. With Jay gone, it had been difficult. There wasn't a room in the house which didn't trigger a negative memory. The kitchen reminded her of the first time he had hit her. The living room flashed images of the time she had caught him watching an objectionable video on his laptop. A visit to the guest bedroom brought back memories of all those times she had gone in there for a cathartic cry, away from his prying eyes. Her bed reminded her of all the arguments they had there, and the umpteen occasions when she had cringed while satisfying his carnal desires. And then there was the homeless intruder she couldn't get out of her head. Even weeks after the incident, the slightest sound at night would give rise to fears that someone had broken in, and she found it impossible to go back to sleep. Once they had decided to live together, figuring out who would move was an easy decision. It was necessary for her sanity.

Maya prepared the batter and got the pan ready. Before starting to cook, she headed to the front door to grab the newspaper. She was about to step out when she spotted a square, red envelope tucked under the welcome mat. There was no stamp, and the envelope only said "To M & M" on a printed label. Intrigued, she ripped it open and found a plain, white sheet of paper. She unfolded it, and one glimpse chilled her to the bone. It had characters pasted from a newspaper. It read:

"I know what you did. Get ready to pay up or I talk. You will hear from me soon."

AN OLD FRIEND
APRIL 10

John Robbins put down his fork. One more meal he had plodded through, dining all alone. It was at times like this that he regretted never marrying. It would have been swell to have a family – a loving wife, children, grandchildren. He had never been adept at making friends, and apart from a couple of close chums and the array of women he had dated, he never had much of a social life. Now they were gone, and he was at an age where he didn't have the energy to seek out new relationships. Senior facilities were ruled out, since he feared losing his independence. He had decided to stay put.

He placed the plate in the kitchen sink and moved over to the couch. Like most nights, he would entertain himself with whatever Netflix had to offer. He had made it as far as the main menu when he heard the doorbell. That was odd. He rarely had any visitors, and never at this hour. He cracked open the door to find a stranger standing there. Not a complete stranger, though. There was something vaguely familiar about that face. The introduction from the visitor confirmed it. This was an old friend he hadn't seen in a long, long time. That history brought back some pleasant memories, and an unpleasant one from the last time they had met. For a few moments, he debated whether he should let his guest in. Then he stepped aside and led the way back to the living room. He realized he was grateful for the company.

Once inside, they got talking and catching up on their lives, like old friends usually do. There was no mention of the long, awkward pause in their relationship. At some point John got up to bring over some wine for his guest, his offer for a drink having been graciously accepted. He placed the bottle on the counter and was reaching for the corkscrew when his body started cramping painfully. He fell to the floor, paralyzed. For a moment, he thought he was having a stroke. He was sure his friend would call for help. Or so he thought. A sudden fear gripped him as he saw the visitor walk over, Taser in hand. He had been attacked! He was going to die! He wanted to fight back, but he was helpless. The friend placed the weapon on the counter and returned with a syringe. John could faintly hear something about revenge as the needle moved towards him and pierced his skin. Soon its contents were emptied into him. He was in acute discomfort and knew he didn't have much time. The words continued and grew fainter as the minutes passed. The menacing smile on the visitor's face faded away as well. In the end, death came as a relief, and his last thought was that of gratitude, as he accepted this way out of his miserable, lonely life.

SEARCHING FOR ANSWERS
APRIL 13

Angela sat at her desk, staring at the stack of papers. It was from her contact at the DMV. A list of names, addresses and phone numbers of everyone who had registered the latest model Cadillac Escalade in California. This might not provide the answer she needed, but at least it was a starting point. The attackers might not own the SUV and might only have rented it. Or they could have been driving an out-of-state vehicle. These were all possibilities. But she could not let such an attack go unanswered. She had to know who was responsible and mete out justice.

The list contained nearly five thousand names. A daunting number. The fact that she was only searching for black cars would make it somewhat easier, but she would still have to scan all the entries to filter it. She decided to start with people who lived in the Bay Area. If she was lucky, the attackers would be in or around Sunnyvale.

Two hours later, she was still poring over the list. She had to stop a few times to jog her memory. Some names seemed familiar but led nowhere. She was about to take a stretch break, when she spotted a name she was sure about. Mark Harrison. He had purchased the vehicle a couple of months before he had died. But it didn't make any sense. He couldn't have come back from the dead to torment her. Unless someone else was using it now. Ron had seen two people in the car. What if it was Mark's sons, blaming her for their father's death and aching for revenge?

Angela called her DMV contact to inquire about the car. She learned that it was registered in Jenna's name now, and she had specified the PNO option. Planned Non-Operation was used if the owner intended to store the vehicle and not drive it during the coming year. If that was the case, then this was not the Escalade she was looking for. But she had her doubts and wanted to confirm it herself.

Thirty minutes later, she was in Los Gatos, parked across from Jenna's luxurious mansion. The driveway was clear, and all the garage doors were closed. The house had a two-car garage next to a single-car garage. Angela had not spotted any Escalades on the street, so she assumed it was in one of the garages. While she pondered her next move, she saw the larger door open. A sexy red Corvette backed out. She glimpsed Jenna in it as the car drove away. The door closed on an empty space. That left the single unit as the only option.

Angela had driven over on a whim and didn't have much of a plan. Now she debated whether she should locate the Escalade and search it. It was illegal, of course, but she needed to know. Besides, sometimes the real thrill came from such escapades rather than her regular job, which she mostly conducted by the book.

But how would she enter? She recalled from her previous visit that the house had a security system. Could she count on Jenna not arming it? Perhaps. This was a low-crime neighborhood and Angela estimated most residents had only installed their systems as a deterrent and never used them. She would still have to break in, though. Unless Jenna was careless enough to leave a door unlocked. The next question was, should she risk this in broad daylight or wait until dark. Nighttime would give her some cover, but it was likely Jenna would be home.

She started the car and parked it further down the street. No one should remember seeing the car so close to the house in case things went south. Selecting a couple of tools from the trunk, she walked back to the house. She went around the back and tried the door. Locked. Within five minutes, she had picked the lock and entered. No alarm. She went to the front door and saw the bowl of keys by the entrance. It had been there the last time too. The key to the Escalade was at the bottom. Key in hand, she strode over and opened the door leading to the garage. Yes! The SUV was there. She unlocked it and got into the driver's seat. The air inside was stale. Angela pressed the start button. Nothing. She tried again. Nothing. The battery was dead. It appeared it had not been driven for months. To be thorough, she climbed into the rear and performed a quick search. Empty and spotless. No signs of use, and no evidence of any paint or paintball equipment. This was not the one.

Disappointed, she figured it was time to lock up and leave. But she heard a car drive up, followed by the sound of a garage door opening. It was not the one she was in. Jenna must be back, she thought as her heart skipped a beat. She decided to wait until Jenna got inside and started closing the door. That's when Angela would open her garage door a crack and sneak out. The sound of one moving door would mask the other one, and Jenna would not realize there was a problem. If she did notice the slightly open door later, she would likely think she had been careless. Angela got out of the SUV and found the garage door switch. She placed her finger on it, ready to press it as soon as she heard the other one opening. Then it hit her. She still had the Escalade key. It had to go back in the bowl. Or did it? The car had been untouched for ages. No one would miss the key. But she felt guilty about breaking in and didn't want the guilt of absconding with the key as well.

Angela re-entered the house and raced to the main door. She placed the key in the bowl. The front door was a better exit option now. She waited to hear the garage door closing to ensure Jenna would not see her leaving. But she didn't hear it. What she heard instead was the faint strains of "Dark Necessities" by Red Hot Chili Peppers coming from somewhere close.

"Shit," muttered Angela under her breath as she realized she didn't have her cell. If she could still hear her ringtone, it could only mean one thing. She had dropped the phone in the garage. The ringing stopped. She heard the garage door closing. There wasn't much time. She sprinted to the garage and entered, just as Jenna stepped into the house. The phone rang again. Angela spotted it next to the driver-side door, grabbed it and muted it in one swift action. The relief was short-lived because the door through which she had entered opened again. She dashed behind the Escalade. Jenna must have heard the phone. The next few seconds felt like an eternity. Angela dared not move, her heart pounding. She was tempted to see what Jenna was doing, but that would be risky. There would be trouble if Jenna spotted her. Her hope was that Jenna would not conduct a thorough search of the garage. And she lucked out. The door closed. Jenna was gone.

Angela breathed a sigh of relief. But it was not over yet. She still had to get out of there without being seen. Trying to go back into the house was not an option, since Jenna could be there. She could slip out the garage door, but Jenna would be alerted. What if Jenna called the cops out of fear? And what if they decided to check for prints? It was a remote possibility, but not something that could be ruled out. But it was a risk Angela would have to take. As a precaution, she wiped down all the surfaces she remembered touching, on the car and in the garage. Inside the car was not an option anymore. She pushed her elbow against the garage door switch and made a dash for it. Two minutes later, she was in the safety of her car. She turned around to check if anyone had followed her. No one. She gently drove off, trying to attract as little attention as possible. It had been a close call, and she knew she had been uncharacteristically sloppy. But, boy, what a thrill that was, she thought. It took her back to her days as a patrol officer, when she was often in dangerous situations, adrenaline pumping. Life had changed quite a bit after she had become a detective. It brought different challenges and was satisfying in its own way, but she missed the action. Perhaps it was for the better, she thought, thinking about how her father had died. The memory filled her with sadness, the thrills forgotten. She wiped her moist eyes before stepping out and going back into the station.

ANOTHER BODY

APRIL 13

Angela spotted Paul walking up to her when she was halfway to her desk. Right, she remembered. He was the one who had called while she was at Jenna's. She wondered what was so urgent. He was grinning and seemed excited to share some news with her.

"What is it this time, Paul?"

"There's a second one."

"A second what?"

"A second murder. Taser and syringe containing nicotine and cocaine."

"Who's the victim?"

"A seventy-one-year-old man, John Robbins."

"Clothes?"

"No clothes on. Syringe in hand. The body was placed the same way as that Adam Newman guy."

"Oh. Do we have a serial killer here?"

"Quite possible. Though other than the murder weapons, there is no similarity to the Jay Sharma case."

"Yes. That's why I think this is a different killer using the same weapons. Probably inspired by that murder but trying to leave his own mark with his own series. Who found the body?"

"Robbins was single and lived alone. A neighbor noticed newspapers piled up outside, and no sign of him in two days. She called the cops. They had to break down the door."

"I see."

"It gets even more interesting. Your loony friend had reported this one a couple of weeks ago."

"My loony friend ...? Oh. I've told you several times, don't call her that! So, Margaret had a vision about this?"

"Yes, and as usual, we ignored it. I think she made it up. I'm telling you, there is something not right about that woman. Even Arthur agrees."

"Be nice, and don't call her a loon, okay? She has had a tough life."

"I'll try."

"It appears this killer is targeting older males. Wonder what the motive would be."

"No idea. I'm glad I don't fit the profile," replied Paul with a grin.

"You don't?" she asked, feigning confusion.

"Hey, what are you trying to say? I'm a long way from old."

"Just kidding. I'm sure you can defend yourself a lot better than either of those guys."

"That's true. It's nice you have confidence in me."

The detectives laughed. A few jokes later, they got back to work. Angela tried, but couldn't get the deaths out of her head. One question nagged her – why use the same weapons that were used on Jay?

THE SERIAL KILLER didn't stop there. There was another murder the next week and one more in the week after that. Both men, sixty-year-old Miguel Santoro and sixty-two-year-old Ted Brown, had been found dead by their wives, naked, Tasered and poisoned by a nicotine and cocaine cocktail administered to them using a syringe. Their bodies and the syringe were placed in an identical manner to the previous murders. Once again, the detectives had no concrete leads. There was no clear motive for any of the killings. The men had lived simple lives and had been likable members of society. No one could identify any enemies. Wilson and Shibata were frustrated and disappointed. Margaret had notified them in advance about another vision, which had turned out to be Miguel. They questioned whether they could have done anything to prevent his murder, but as with most of her visions, there wasn't much to go on.

Meanwhile, Angela continued to be intrigued by these crimes. Who was this killer? Why was he using the same technique used to kill Jay? Was there any link between the deaths at all? In her spare time, she tried to understand the details of this new string of murders, but like the case detectives, she hit a dead end as well. She hoped the killer would slip up and give them the break they needed. She was confident that, if the slayings continued, it was only a matter of time before a mistake would be made. The question was, how many innocent lives would be lost before they were able to put an end to it?

SOME DEMANDS
APRIL 14

Maya sat in her wedding finery, both nervous and excited. The much-awaited day had arrived. It had been an exhausting week, with various ceremonies and celebrations on a daily basis leading up to the main event. But it had been fun as well, with her family and closest friends present to join in the festivities. All those late nights, laughing and singing and dancing together. It was, in the truest sense, a big, fat, traditional Punjabi wedding. Of course, Maya would have preferred a quick, simple ceremony, but both families and, surprisingly, Jay as well, had wanted the works, so she had no choice but to cave in. Soon, she was in the banquet hall, advancing towards Jay. One glance at him, and all her exhaustion melted away. She saw the delight on his face, and she couldn't resist a smile. The ceremony began and before she knew it, they were a couple.

It was 4:00 a.m. by the time they got to Jay's home and were done with the post-wedding games. Both Jay and Maya, were spent. Once inside their room, they barely mustered enough energy to undress and go to bed. Any thoughts of intimacy remained just thoughts. They would be flying to Kerala the next evening for their honeymoon and a chance to come closer. She closed her eyes and fell into deep sleep, dreaming about what that would be like.

The sound of the doorbell pierced the quiet and shook Maya awake. Still foggy, she was relieved to find she was not in wedding finery, and it was not Jay lying next to her. It was weird that she had dreamed about her nuptials. She had been so happy that day, not knowing what was to come. What if she could go back in time and change it all and not marry him? How different, and how much better would her life have been? If only it were so easy. Coming back to reality, she wondered who was at the door this early in the morning.

There was no one. A red envelope was sticking out from under the mat. Bad news, without a doubt. She had waited in fear for a couple of days after receiving the first letter. But when nothing happened, she had convinced herself it was someone playing a prank, and she had forgotten about it. But this second missive looked ominous. With heart pounding, and a sinking feeling in her stomach, she walked back to the dining table and sat down. She opened the envelope, and what she saw shocked her. It was a picture of her and Meghna at the Fairmont, in the throes of passion. Accompanying it was a note prepared the same way as the previous one. It simply read:

"I will call you at 9am"

AN HOUR LATER, Maya and Meghna waited nervously at the dining table. Maya had roused Meghna as soon as she had read the note. They had spent the time wondering who could have taken the photograph, and why this was only coming up now, weeks after it had happened. If this were to get out, it would be humiliating. The phone buzzed and Maya answered, putting it on speakerphone. It was a male voice.

"Hello, ladies. I assume you got my message?"

There was something in that voice that made Maya's hair stand on end. Slimy, she thought.

"We did. Who is this?"

"Did you like the fine touch I gave the letters? Inspired by you."

"Who is this?" continued Maya, ignoring the comment. How did this man know about the threatening letters to Jay?

"That's not important. What is important is that I have ten photographs of this nature, which I am willing to sell to you for a reasonable price. What can I say, I am a very reasonable man."

"So you are blackmailing us?"

"Now, now, let's not call names. It's just a simple transaction. Five hundred thousand dollars. That is all I ask. A fair deal, you will agree. I want it delivered to me tomorrow in hundred-dollar bills. In exchange, I will hand over all these photographs."

"Five hundred thousand! That's a lot of money. How do we arrange it so quick?"

"Do you take me for a fool? I know how well off you are. That amount is easy for you. You drop it off tomorrow before ten a.m. on the Lower Wildcat Trail at Rancho San Antonio. Leave the bag in the bushes by the third hairpin bend going up. I know Maya is quite familiar with that trail and will have no trouble figuring it out. Once you place the money, leave. No funny business. I will have the photographs delivered to you by the end of the day."

The mention of the trail made Maya shudder. She loved hiking there. Had this creep been following her everywhere?

"How do we know you will give us the pics? And what if there are more copies?"

"The simple answer is, you have to trust me. I assure you that you will get all the photographs in my possession. But remember – the money should be in place by ten a.m. tomorrow. And one more thing – don't even think of calling the cops, or you can imagine what I will do."

MAYA AND MEGHNA thought it over. They ran the risk of humiliation if they did not pay up. There wasn't much of a choice. They hurried to their banks and withdrew the cash. By evening the bag was ready. Maya was unable to sleep all night, hoping this ordeal would be over soon.

THE TRANSACTION
APRIL 15

At 8:00 a.m., Maya and Meghna left for Rancho San Antonio Park with the money. By the time they had parked, it was 8:45. It took them another thirty minutes to get to the drop point. As usual, the park was busy with hikers, runners and families out for a stroll, but they didn't see anyone on the designated trail. As planned, Maya hid the bag in the bushes, and then they split up. Maya took up a position further up, and Meghna went downhill. They were curious to see who was blackmailing them.

Several minutes passed. The occasional hiker went past them. Maya even saw a couple of deer trundle by, but there was no sign of their target. Finally, at 10:05 a.m., she spotted a hunched-over man approach the drop. He was bundled up in thick clothing, and his head was covered, making it difficult to see his face. He took the bag and started walking down the trail. Maya and Meghna followed, being careful to stay out of sight. They were with him until Deer Hollow Farm, but they lost him in the crowds. Desperate, they scanned the area, but to no avail. He was nowhere to be found. They trudged back to the parking lot in silence and got into the car. To their surprise, they saw an envelope on the dash.

"What the ...!" exclaimed Maya.

"How did this get here? You locked the car, right?" asked Meghna, just as shocked as Maya.

"I'm sure I did."

Meghna opened the envelope and was relieved to see all the photographs. She still couldn't get over the fact that someone had watched them in that vulnerable state. Each and every picture was explicit and didn't leave much to the imagination. Who was this person? she wondered.

Once they were home, Maya turned on the fireplace and tossed the pics in. She sat down, relieved, though there was still the lingering doubt whether there were more copies. She had no choice but to wait and see.

THERE WAS a knock on the door shortly after 5:00 p.m. that evening. Meghna peeked out and spotted a familiar, red envelope on the ground. Bleak news, she thought, as she joined Maya in the living room. She opened the envelope. There were two photographs. If the previous set of pics had shocked her, this set almost stopped her heart. The first one showed Meghna attacking Jay in the car. The second one had Maya dragging Jay's body out of the car. How was this possible? Who was this man who had captured so much about them? The accompanying note was consistent with the earlier ones in style. It simply read:

"We will talk again at 9pm"

Meghna's mouth went dry. The nude pics were one thing, but this was way more serious. If these got out, they could spend the rest of their lives in prison. She wondered what he would demand this time. The wait until 9:00 p.m. was excruciating. And then the phone pleaded for attention.

"Hello again, ladies. I assume you received my latest missive?"

"Yes, we did. What do you want?"

"I must say, I'm very disappointed in you."

"Why is that?"

"I explicitly specified, no tricks. Yet, you followed me. Of course, it was quite easy to shake you off, but I prefer not to play such games."

"We are sorry. We were curious, that's all."

"Your curiosity could cost you. I will let it go this time. But let me warn you. You do anything like this again, the deal is off."

"What do you want this time?"

"You have seen two of my wonderful samples. I have ten such photographs. Since I am a reasonable man, I request only one million dollars. All hundred-dollar bills as before, to be delivered to me a week from today. I'll finalize the location in a few days."

The figure was a massive blow. How were they going to manage it, and so quickly?

"That is too much. We can't handle that."

"Ladies. I think we have known each other long enough now. Do you think I'm that stupid? I know you are good for it. No more games. You get me the money next week, or I deliver these pics to sweet Angela."

"We'll try, but if we can get some more time ..."

"One week is all you get."

"How long have you had all these pictures?"

"A long time. I took them all. It wasn't easy, but it's so worth it now."

"Why did you wait this long?" Meghna's curiosity got the better of her, and she decided to ask the question that had been nagging her.

"Good question. The money was tempting, but I was looking for more than that. Back then, you ladies were so stressed out, it wasn't much fun playing this game. But now that you two are so happy together, it gives me such a rush to see you squirm."

"You are one sick bastard!"

"Now, now, watch your language. I am not someone you want to piss off. One million dollars, a week from today. Don't forget. And if you can't get it all, I could give you a discount if both of you come over and satisfy me. If you know what I mean."

Meghna was furious. The temerity of that man! But she resisted the urge to respond in anger. The situation was delicate, and she did not want to take any chances. She was sure if he had been in front of her, she would have smashed his head in rage. Instead, she gave a resigned reply, "We will get you the money."

The last thing she heard was the man chuckling to himself before he hung up.

THE SEARCH CONTINUES

APRIL 16

Angela got back to the DMV list. It was another thirty minutes before she found another familiar name. This one was a much stronger suspect. Cheryl Andrews. She and Candy could have been in the Escalade that night. They had strong reasons to be enraged at Angela. And they seemed like people who would do something like that.

Now the question was, how to confirm it was them? Angela would have to search the car. But how? If Cheryl still lived in the apartment complex, her car would be parked out in the open in one of the resident parking spots. Trying to break into it there would attract attention. Angela had broken into cars before, but those had been older models. She hadn't kept up with the latest advances in car security technology. The last thing she wanted was to set off the alarm and have some passerby nab her. She would need the key. But after her experience at Jenna's, she wasn't keen on breaking into Cheryl's apartment to get it. And in this case, if the car was home, Cheryl would be home too. This required some thought.

An hour later, she had come up with a solution. She picked up the phone and made the call. In another twenty minutes, she got a call back. It would happen at 9:00 p.m., in two days.

SECRETS

APRIL 17

Candy maneuvered herself off her client, relieved that it was done. He had booked her for the night, so she still had to tolerate him for a lot longer, but at least she got a brief break. If it was not for the money, she would have rejected him outright. The guy was a twisted beast and she feared him.

She walked over to the table and poured him another glass, hoping this one would do the trick and knock him out for the night. He was already quite sloshed. She had never seen him drink so much, but she deduced he was celebrating something. All that alcohol had made him extra chatty, and he started telling her things, things he would have been wise enough not to talk about when sober.

She handed him the whisky and settled next to him on the bed. As he caressed her naked body, he told her he would be coming into loads of money soon. He had pictures of some women killing and disposing of Jay Sharma, and they had agreed to pay up. The mention of Jay caught her attention. So this man had evidence of her innocence, but never presented it to the cops? He let her suffer all this time. The swine! And now he was going to profit from her misfortune. The thought made her furious, and she was tempted to smash the whisky bottle on his head.

That was not all. He confessed to killing a woman named Brenda. Brenda had seen Maya dispose of the body, and he was worried she would spill the beans. So he pushed her onto the tracks, and watched her get crushed by a train. The thought repulsed Candy. But he was so proud of it. Everyone thought it was an accident, and he managed to get away with it. She viewed him with disgust, as he droned on about how awesome he was, and about all his amazing accomplishments. Soon he drifted into sleep and lay motionless.

Candy got up and scanned the room for something to put on. But all her clothes were on the bed, under the swine. She didn't want to risk waking him up, so she got up and walked across the room. There was a full-length mirror resting against the wall. She admired her bare figure. Not bad at all. She was still in great shape. But for how long? Time would catch up with her soon, and that tight, perky body would sag. Her face was already beginning to age. The stress from her legal troubles didn't help. In her profession, she had to look amazing. The money would dry up if guys didn't find her attractive. She needed that income, what with all the expenses she had incurred fighting for her freedom. Attorneys like Francis Dern didn't come cheap. No wonder she had to tolerate clients like this one. He paid well, and that's the only reason she never refused him. What a fall she had had in life. Only two years ago, she was rolling in wealth, turning down assholes like him. She eyed the bruise on her waist and the red blotch on her thigh, all courtesy of this creep. No. This could not continue. She had to find a way to get rich again. She hoped the book deal would make her a ton of dough. But she feared it would not be enough.

Candy could feel the stress building up again. She picked up the almost empty bottle of Chivas and put it to her lips, downing it all. The liquid warmed her up and brought a much-desired calm. She could think clearly now, an idea germinating in her head. She turned off the light and moved to the other room. The swine had revealed a lot of useful information. Now she had to figure out how to use it. It was time to talk things over with someone she could trust.

MORE THRILLS
APRIL 18

Angela eased the car into a visitor parking space of the apartment complex in West San Jose. The spot was near the entrance, so it would be easy to catch the Escalade when it entered. It was only 8:50 p.m. That gave her some time. She had contacted Doug Jones, one-time criminal who had turned over a new leaf, and was now living a clean, respectable life. They knew each other professionally from that old life, and he owed her some favors. He might not be a felon anymore, but he still had his weaknesses. One of which was his need for hookers. She had exploited this craving by asking him to book Cheryl for an hour. Once Cheryl was in his bedroom, he would text Angela. Angela could then sneak into the apartment and grab the key. A one-hour session would give her enough time to search the car and return the key.

At 8:58 p.m., she spotted the Escalade. She emerged from the car and started walking towards Doug's pad. It was a two-minute walk, and she saw Cheryl stepping out of the SUV when she got there. The escort exuded sexiness as always, her hair and makeup done well, the red tube top and short black skirt showing off plenty of her long, beautiful body. Doug was in for a treat, Angela thought as she hid behind a car, not wanting Cheryl to spot her. Then she sat tight. The text arrived five minutes later. She went up the stairs to the apartment and waited a few seconds to confirm no one was behind the door before quietly opening it and stepping inside. He lived alone, but she was surprised at how well he had maintained the place. She heard faint sounds from behind the closed bedroom door. It sounded like Cheryl talking. Doug was probably too busy enjoying himself. Angela located Cheryl's purse and the key sitting next to it. She pocketed the key and left.

In a couple of minutes, she was inside the Escalade. Unlike Mark's car, this one smelled pleasant. Soothing lavender. It still had that new car feel to it. She didn't find anything interesting in the first two rows of seats. She had barely stepped into the rear when her phone buzzed. It was Doug. This was unexpected. She answered, quite certain this meant trouble.

"You better get the key back here quick. Like right now," he whispered, the fear in his voice crystal clear.

"What happened? I thought you had her for the hour?"

"I ... I kinda jumped the gun. The session is over," he replied, sounding a little embarrassed.

"Unbelievable!"

"Hey, it's been a while, you know. And she's so hot. Now, get here quick before she's out of the restroom."

"I need more time. Keep her busy in the bedroom. I don't care how you do it," said Angela firmly.

"But how ..."

"Just do it!"

She hung up and resumed her search. Soon she was smiling in satisfaction. In the rear lay four paintball guns and two large bags of paintballs. It couldn't be a coincidence. It must have been Cheryl. Most likely, Candy was the partner. Angela's phone buzzed again. A text from Doug.

"Bought you some more time. Cost me five hundred bucks for another pop."

Well done, Doug, thought Angela. The extra money was not her problem. She continued searching and found two black face masks. Perfect. Satisfied, she stepped out of the car, locked it and returned to the apartment. This time she could hear loud sounds from the bedroom, Cheryl moaning and screaming Doug's name. Angela shook her head in amusement as she put the key back in its place. Then she left. Now that she knew who was responsible, what was she going to do about it?

THE DIARY
APRIL 21

Maya and Meghna were all set to leave for their lunch date when they heard the doorbell. There was a man at the door. Vaguely familiar, Maya thought. He introduced himself as Jason Donovan, husband of Brenda Donovan. She recalled she had met him once at a company party when Brenda and she worked together. He had changed so much. At the time, he was stunning. In fact, Brenda's coworkers all teased her that she had lucked out, marrying a gorgeous movie star. But now he appeared pale and gaunt, with an unkempt look and dark circles under his eyes. She wondered whether it was due to Brenda's death.

"Oh yes, I remember. We have met before," remarked Maya as she welcomed him in.

"Yes, we have. Sorry if I am interrupting anything. Were you going somewhere?"

"Don't worry about it. Please do come in. I was so sorry to read about Brenda. She was an amazing woman."

"Yes, she was. She always spoke very highly of you."

"What can I do for you?"

"It's ... it's about her death. That's what I came here to talk about."

"Oh?"

"As you may have noticed, I haven't adapted well to her passing. Neither have the kids. The last few months have been rough. Finally, I thought, perhaps I was able to move on, or at least try to. So I started cleaning up her things, and I found her diary. She was very particular about it. I know I shouldn't have, but I couldn't resist reading it. The last few entries caught my attention."

"What were these entries about?"

"You see, she was always cheerful, but in the days before her death she was tense and stressed out. Like there was something weighing on her mind. She refused to discuss it with me. Said everything was alright. Just some nonsense at work. And then, then she was gone. Just like that."

Jason paused, a tragic expression on his face. His eyes were moist.

"How can I help, Jason?" Maya asked, feeling sympathetic towards him, but still curious about the diary.

"You know, all these months I wondered what happened to her. Every single day, I tried to make sense of it. There was a theory that she committed suicide. But I couldn't believe that. She would never do that. Even if she did, why go under a train? That's a ghastly way to die. Others said it was an accident. Yes, that could happen. But she was a careful woman. Then I came across these entries in her diary, and it started to make some sense. I still don't know what got her so upset, but I feel you may have the answers."

"Me? I don't understand."

He took out an elegant black diary with gold edges from his jacket pocket and flipped through it. Once he found the page he was looking for, he handed it to Maya.

"Read on, and you will see what I mean."

She started reading.

Jan 16

Exhausting day at work. And the children didn't make it easy. But I'm so excited to spend time with the girls tomorrow. Party!!!

Jan 17

It was an odd evening. Saw Maya in the parking lot. Can't believe she would do something like that. Was I mistaken?

Jan 18

Feeling miserable. Can't get it out of my mind. Jason has noticed but not sure whether I should tell him. Should I talk to Maya first?

Jan 19

They found Jay's body. In the same spot. Could it really be?

Jan 20

This is getting so difficult. I called Maya today but no answer. I know this may not be the right time. Maybe she is in mourning. Or maybe not. I don't know what to do.

Jan 21

I have to talk to someone. I can't take it anymore. No reply from Maya. I have to know the truth. I will talk to Jason tomorrow. He will know what to do. I shouldn't keep this from him any longer.

Maya's heart was pounding as she read the diary. Brenda had seen her dump the body. This was going to be tricky.

"I don't know what to say. I had no idea she saw me anywhere. We hadn't met in ages."

"I am sure she saw you do something. Something to do with your husband's death. And it drove her crazy. I just want to understand it all."

"But I never went anywhere near Sha Sha that night. She must have seen someone else and mistaken her for me."

"Perhaps. I was hoping you would be able to help me here."

"Sorry, I have not been of much help. Have you mentioned this to anyone else?"

"No, not yet."

"If you give me your number, I can call you in case I remember something."

"Sure. But we won't be around for a few days. I'm taking the kids to Brenda's parents' place to cheer them up. We'll be back next week."

"Okay. Have a fun trip. And take care, Jason."

Maya turned to Meghna with a concerned expression as soon as she had closed the door.

"What was that all about?"

Maya explained what she had read in the diary.

"Not very bright, is he?" remarked Meghna.

"No. But I think he knows."

"I doubt he suspects you. Otherwise he would not have come to you."

"Maybe not yet. But for how long? At some point the thought will occur to him. And we can't risk his telling anyone else."

Meghna was concerned and was quiet for a while. Then she said, "How about we do this."

Soon they had decided their next step.

LONESOME THREESOME
APRIL 27

Nine o'clock on a Friday night, and Shaun Jacobs sat alone at his desk, trying to wrap up some reports for his client. This was his last assignment before he went into retirement. Yes, retirement was finally here, what with the sizable payday he was to receive soon. He had worked long and hard over the years and had made considerable money, since he excelled at what he did. But it was not enough. Now, with this hefty payout, he would be home free. If not for the hitch he had run into, he would already have the dough. He could picture himself spending his days lazing on the white sands of the Bahamas, peering out at the clear, blue water, drink in hand. Evenings would be spent downing sumptuous steak dinners and more alcohol, to be followed up with divine bedtime action with the local beauties. Yes, that would be his life from here on. He had earned it.

He heard the main office door open. Odd. He didn't have any appointments. Perhaps a walk-in. But at this hour? Or had the cleaning lady come in early? The mystery was soon solved when two women entered his room. These were familiar, though unexpected, faces. They were wearing thick black overcoats and disarming smiles. He wondered what they were doing there.

"Ladies, this is a surprise. What brings you here tonight?"

"We are here to give you what you want," said the first one in a salacious tone.

Did she mean what he thought she meant? If that was the case, this would be like living out one of his fantasies. Both of them at once. Sure enough, before he knew it, they dropped their coats to reveal nothing but sexy, naked forms. Shaun felt his excitement grow as they started walking towards him. They licked their lips suggestively and moved their hands over their bodies. The first one stopped in front of his desk, while the second one came around and planted a full, wet one on his lips. By this point he didn't care about the reports. His hands were feeling their way around the curves. The second woman turned away, but not before showing him she was teasing and would be back.

Shaun turned his attention to the first woman, who by now was putting on an enjoyable show for him. He watched in delight, oblivious to the second woman closing in on him. In an instant, she had struck him on the head with the bust she had picked up from the shelf behind him. It was heavy, and the blow hard enough that he didn't stand a chance. He plopped to the desk, quite dead, with blood oozing from his head. Drops of blood had splattered all over. The advantage of wearing nothing was that the women were able to wipe it off themselves without leaving any evidence on their clothes. They exchanged glances, thrilled that they had pulled it off. It had turned out to be a lot easier than they had expected. They had overestimated this man. It didn't take much sexual bait to snag him.

They fished out gloves from their coat pockets and put them on. Then they proceeded to wipe down the bust and other objects they had touched. It was time to search. Twenty minutes later, they had located the envelope. They donned their overcoats and exited the office with their loot, leaving Shaun all alone, and permanently retired.

FIGURES IN THE DARK
APRIL 28

It was quiet on Elm Street in San Jose as the time inched past 2:00 a.m. A few dimly lit streetlamps provided scant illumination. One could be quite confident that most of the residents were comfortably asleep. But there was some movement. Anyone awake at that ungodly hour might have noticed the two figures dressed in black glide through the darkness. The figures stopped in front of Jason Donovan's home and tried the door. It was locked. Undeterred, they went around to the back of the house. They lucked out on the rear entrance. The tools could have stayed home. It was not easy keeping the doors secure in a house with little kids.

Before entering, they prayed there was no alarm system. Seconds later, their luck held, and they were inside, neighborhood peace intact. At this point they could have been forgiven the temptation to purchase some lottery tickets.

They turned on their pocket flashlights, just enough light so they could see, but not so bright that anyone outside the house could detect it. As per their plan, they started with the master bedroom. They searched meticulously. Closets, drawers, shelves, inside clothes, but an hour later they were still without success.

They moved on to the other bedrooms. This wasn't fruitful either. It was a cool night, but thoughts of failure were making them sweat. The living room and kitchen turned up empty too.

5:00 a.m. They didn't have much time left. It would be light soon, and they didn't want to risk being seen. What if they were unable to find it? They tried to stay calm and considered where else they could search. And then it struck them. There was one place they had not checked. They rushed to the master bedroom and pulled the mattress off the frame. There they saw what looked like the object of their desire. A quick check confirmed it. Triumphant at last, they walked out of the house, gripping the prize securely.

A NEW BODY
APRIL 28

Angela woke up feeling refreshed. It was the morning after a romantic and passionate date with Kyle. A satisfied smile crossed her lips as she turned her gaze to him lying next to her. She debated whether to rouse him for another encounter under the covers, but decided to let him sleep in a bit longer. She put on some clothes and walked over to the kitchen, following the trail of garments they had hastily shed the night before. That memory made her smile again. They had been dating for a few weeks now, and the relationship was flourishing. As she stood by the refrigerator, considering what to whip up for breakfast, her phone broke into song. It was Cynthia. A body had been found, and she would have to investigate. She sighed as she hung up. No more Kyle this weekend. Next thing she knew, she was trapped in a bear hug. He had crept up behind her and had wrapped his arms around her tight. A comforting warmth spread through her body. Before she knew it, they were kissing and groping each other. She tried to resist the urge at first, the corpse weighing on her mind, but then she caved. Just this once, work could take a back seat. After all, she had a life too.

Thirty minutes later, Angela picked herself up off the floor, face glowing with satisfaction. Kyle had outdone himself this time. It had been so worth it. Too bad she didn't have time for seconds.

ANGELA PARKED her car and walked over to the taped-off area. She spotted Officer Spencer at the door. Unlike the Jay Sharma crime scene, this one did not have any gawkers. Some passers-by did stop for a glimpse, wondering what had happened, but only momentarily. The simple reason being there wasn't anything to see. All the action was inside.

Paul emerged from his car and joined Angela.

"Awesome start to the weekend, right?" he quipped.

"Tell me about it. Hey, isn't this place familiar?"

"Yeah, we have been here before. Could it be ...?" he trailed off as they crossed the crime scene tape.

"Yep," she replied, pointing to the door that said, *Shaun Jacobs Private Investigator.*

They greeted Spencer and walked past him into the office and the familiar site of the messy little room, with the same worn desk and chairs. There was still a faint, musty odor, which had been overpowered by the scent of murder. The main difference in the room was that there was no creepy Shaun Jacobs grinning in his chair. There was only a dead Shaun Jacobs, with his head resting sideways on the desk and a mass of dried blood on that head. As before, the bust was on the shelf behind him, but this time the pristine white was marred by blotches of red. Angela suspected this was the murder weapon. Besides that, there was blood splattered all around him. Shawna from Forensics was already at the scene. She turned to them to report what she had learned so far.

"Happy Saturday morning, guys. Today's special is blunt force trauma. As you may have guessed, he got knocked out cold with that bust. Sometime between eight and ten last night is my estimate. I didn't find any prints on the weapon, but I did find a lot of partials on both sides of the desk. Probably from him and his clients."

"No signs of a struggle?" asked Angela.

"No. He must have been seated at his desk comfortably when it happened. His fingernails are clean. No defense wounds either."

"So it is likely he knew the attacker. Whoever did it had to walk over to that shelf behind him to pick up the bust."

"Well, we don't know if that's where the bust was originally. I found it on the desk and placed it on the shelf after my inspection. Before I bag it with the other evidence."

"It was on there the last time I saw it," replied Angela, as she examined the shelf.

"You've been here before?"

"Yes, a few weeks ago. For that Jay Sharma case. Look here. There's a layer of dust all around, except in this one spot. Quite likely, this is where it stood before the killer picked it up."

"You're right. The bust is a bit dusty too."

"Is it as heavy as it looks?" Angela asked. She could tell from the damage to Shaun's head that the impact had been forceful.

"Heavy enough that the killer didn't need a lot of strength to do that. He was seated when it happened, so gravity helped too."

"I see. Who found the body?"

"The cleaning lady came in early this morning."

"The cleaning lady? Did I hear that right?"

"Yep. Hard to believe this place has ever been cleaned, but apparently she came by once every two weeks."

"I would never have guessed that. Where is she now?"

"They took her to the hospital."

"The hospital? Was she hurt too?"

"No. It was too much of a shock for her. Thankfully, she was able to call 911. By the time we got here, she was in bad shape."

"I see. I guess the interview with her will have to wait."

Angela and Paul donned their gloves and surveyed the crime scene. Angela scanned the floor but didn't find anything unusual.

She checked his computer. It was locked. The desk was disorganized enough that it was not easy to tell whether anything was out of place. She opened the drawers, but all she could see was his diary, more documents and some stationery items. Like any other office drawer. She found it odd that the drawers were unlocked. She recalled Shaun had used a key to retrieve the diary when they had interviewed him. Had he been careless enough to leave them unlocked this time? Or did the killer do it? She bagged the diary and all the documents as evidence. She would have to review these for clues.

Since it was a small room, it didn't take long to complete the inspection. Angela moved on to Shaun's body next. The front pockets of his jeans produced a white handkerchief and a bunch of keys. She surmised these were for his car, his home and the office itself. She tried one which looked like it would fit the drawers. It did fit. His rear pocket contained his wallet. It had the usual mix of driver's license, credit cards, membership cards, and a little cash. Search complete, she decided to step outside and talk to Spencer.

"What could be the motive? It doesn't seem like a burglary. Everything appears to be intact. Something personal, perhaps? Maybe some pissed-off client or someone who got into trouble because of Jacobs' investigation?" Paul asked Angela on the way out.

"Possible."

"I didn't see any surveillance cameras around here. Don't you think it's strange a PI doesn't have any at his office? These days most businesses have something of the sort."

"Most retail businesses, yes. Worries about theft. But there's nothing to steal here. Perhaps that's why he never bothered."

"But the kind of business he's in, he must have made a lot of enemies. I guess he thought he could handle it."

"Yeah. Cameras would have made our job easier. Let's canvass the neighborhood after we talk to Spencer."

They found Spencer chatting with a short, slim woman. Angela estimated she was in her early fifties.

"Ah, Angela. This is Dana. She owns the nail spa next door," he said as soon as he spotted Angela.

"You're the detective? This nice officer here tells me there was some trouble in there last night?"

"Yes. Late last night. Why do you ask?" replied Angela, not wanting to divulge too much. She hated inquisitive bystanders.

"Well, the thing is, I was closing up shop, and I saw these two women go in there."

"What time was this?"

"Around nine p.m. I see all sorts of people go in and out of there all the time. It was kinda late, but I figured they must be his clients. Or his friends."

"What did they look like?"

"They were tall. Seemed blonde."

"Seemed?"

"They wore caps, so their hair was mostly covered. And it was dark. That light's been out a long time. Idiots haven't bothered fixing it," replied Dana, pointing at the streetlamp overhead. "Where do our tax dollars go?"

"Anything else?" continued Angela, sidestepping the discussion about government ineptitude.

"Oh yeah. It was odd. They both had on long, black overcoats. I mean, who wears overcoats this time of year? Heck, it hit the nineties yesterday."

"Interesting. Did you get a look at their faces?"

"Nope," Dana replied with a shrug, throwing a dejected look at the broken lamp again. "I mean, I wouldn't be able to recognize them, if that's what you're asking."

Angela nodded.

"So, what happened in there?" asked Dana as she leaned forward, wide-eyed.

Since she had been a good witness and had imparted some useful information, Angela decided to tell her. Maybe that would spur some more inputs.

"Shaun Jacobs, the PI who worked there, was murdered."

"Oh," Dana gasped. "Shaun's dead? To think I spoke to him just before he croaked."

That was an odd term to use, thought Angela. Dana had probably watched too many old mysteries.

"You talked to him last night? What time was this?"

"A little bit before I closed. I would say around eight thirty. He bummed a smoke off me. Still the same old Shaun. He was more interested in peeking down my blouse than in the Marlboro I gave him. Can't blame him though, it's quite a view," replied Dana, looking pleased with herself.

"You knew him well?"

"Not really. I mean, we chatted a bit every now and then when business was slow, but nothing more than the weather and the like. Wasn't my type. Though he did help me with my ex. Well, he wasn't my ex at the time. Shaun got me some juicy pics of my dear hubby fooling around with his girlfriend. Helped me get rid of that piece of shit. Now I have the whole place to myself ..."

"What did you talk about last night?" Angela cut in before Dana droned on further.

"Nothing in particular. Just idle chitchat as always. He was only in here a couple of minutes."

"And he seemed okay?"

"Yes."

"Thank you for the information, Dana. We'll need your contact info in case we have more questions."

"Sure, dear."

Once Dana had disappeared into the spa, Paul said, "Looks like she saw the killers."

"It's possible. Too bad we don't know what time those women left."

The detectives spent the next hour canvassing the neighborhood with nothing to show for it. Most of the adjoining businesses had closed early the previous evening. Two of the restaurants had been open, but the employees didn't have anything to report. They had been busy working indoors. Angela decided to get back to the station to log the evidence and write up the initial reports. The next step would be to locate the next of kin.

A TEARDROP FELL from Angela's eye and landed on Don's smiling face. She wiped it off and stared at the picture, taken at her high school graduation. Angela standing between her parents, bursting with joy. She had felt so secure with those pillars of strength next to her. She turned the page of the album. Angela in a t-shirt and jeans, her father in uniform, playfully placing his police hat on her head. This time she dried the tears before they could drop. Refreshing those memories of her father always made her emotional, but tonight she was overwhelmed. Looking at the upright cop before her, she felt guilty. She had crossed the line with her paintball adventures. Don would not approve. She closed the album and returned it to the shelf. To live up to his lofty standards, she would have to rein in these impulses. As she got into bed and turned off the light, she whispered.

"I won't let you down again, Dad."

BLACKMAIL
MAY 5

Maya and Meghna were in bed, enjoying another lazy weekend morning, when Maya's phone lit up. She saw "Unknown" flashing and wanted to ignore it as usual, but she decided to answer. It was a woman.

"Is this Maya?"

"Yes, who is this?"

"It's about the photographs. Are you ready with the money?"

"Which photographs?" asked Maya, a sinking feeling building up inside her.

"You know what I'm talking about. About Jay's murder. The agreement was for one million."

Maya froze. She had assumed the threat had been averted. But this new development brought the fear flooding back. She put the phone on speaker so Meghna knew what was going on.

"Who is this?"

"Does it matter? What's important is that we have the photographs, so you better pay up quick."

"We don't have the money. We need at least a week."

"Three days. That's all you get. I'll call again with the details."

Those were the last words she heard before the line went dead. The women exchanged worried looks.

"So he wasn't working alone," remarked Meghna. "That would explain how he managed to disappear and place the pics in our car."

"Another mystery. Who is this woman? His wife?"

"Perhaps."

"We don't have much choice here. We need to pay up."

"Yes, let's get started on that. But give me some time. This needs some deep thinking."

Maya could tell from her face that Meghna was not going to cave in so easily. A scheme was cooking.

A CLUE

MAY 7

Angela sighed in frustration. She had given the Shaun Jacobs murder a lot of thought and effort, but she had hit a wall. The diary and documents had some juicy details about his cases, but nothing that threw any light on his death. There wasn't much to go on, and she was clueless about who could have done it. She had interviewed the cleaning lady but hadn't learned anything more than what had been discovered at the crime scene. With the news hitting the papers, she had hoped she would get some leads from people calling in. But so far, there had been no productive calls. Even the search for Shawn's next of kin had drawn a blank. His parents had passed away a long time ago. He had no siblings, no children, and he had never married. From what she could tell, he didn't have any close friends either.

So when her phone sang, she decided to take the call. It was not like she had anything better to do anyway. Once they were done exchanging pleasantries, Margaret explained why she had called.

"I read the news about that detective, Shaun Jacobs. I think I may have had a vision about him."

"Can you tell me about it?" urged Angela with bated breath. Perhaps this would be the break she needed.

"I saw a man's head resting on a worn desk, turned to the side. It had been bashed in. There was blood all over. Some on the desk as well. There was an earring next to him."

"An earring? On the desk?" she asked in surprise. They hadn't found any jewelry. Could the cleaning lady have stolen it?

"Yes. It was one of those modern style drop earrings. Three layers, the first one had the initial 'R', the second one had a dragon, and the third one had the initial 'C'. The background was pink, the text and image were all in black, and the borders were all gold. Does it match what you found?"

"Interesting. Everything matches, except for the earring. We didn't find any. Are you sure about this?"

"Yes, absolutely. I saw this one a couple of weeks ago, but I remember it distinctly. Especially, since I loved the design."

"Thanks, Margaret. I will search the crime scene again. I don't know how we could have missed something that obvious."

"There's something more I want to tell you," continued Margaret, sounding a bit hesitant.

"What is it?"

"It's just that Shaun and I dated a long time back. It's so weird, him dead like this."

This was an interesting development, thought Angela.

"Oh, I am so sorry. I didn't know you were close."

"Don't worry about it. Nothing of the sort. We hadn't met in years. But I bumped into him on a hike a few weeks ago. We hooked up. Terrible mistake. He was still the same douchebag he always was."

"You hooked up? What about Arthur?"

"Oh, we broke up. Funny, I didn't realize that was Shaun's head when I had my vision. I had such an up-close view of it when I was in bed with him," chuckled Margaret. "Good way to do him in, though. Bash his funny little head."

"Where were you that night?" asked Angela, growing a little suspicious.

"Me? Oh, I was out painting the town red with my friend. Red ... red ... bad choice of word. Now it's reminding me of all that red blood on his head. How do you do it, Angela? How do you see all this gruesome stuff and go on with your life? Oh, and you know what? After I got back that night, I saw some suspicious characters loitering outside my neighbor's house."

Something about the exchange disturbed Angela. Did Margaret kill Shaun? Or was she just a bit off-kilter today? It reminded her of Paul's comments about crazy Margaret. And about Arthur's story. She ignored the question and comment and thanked her again. Then she hung up and told Paul about the vision. She decided not to tell him about the rest of the conversation yet. As expected, he rolled his eyes and went back to what he had been doing before the interruption. Angela would have to search for the earring by herself.

A few minutes later, she was at the crime scene again. It was still taped off. It was like she had last seen it, except that the body was no longer present. Yet, she sensed his presence, and it sent a shudder through her. He had been creepy enough alive, and now it was like he was haunting her in death. She slipped on gloves and scanned the desk and everywhere around it, but she did not spot the earring. On the way, she had called Shawna and Spencer and confirmed that no such article had been found. Then she peeked under the desk. At first, she didn't see anything, but soon her flashlight caught a glint of something. She extended her arm underneath to fish it out. To her surprise, it was the earring Margaret had described. Now she felt guilty about suspecting the cleaning lady. Could it belong to the killer? It was highly likely. It had some spots of what appeared to be blood. Dana had mentioned seeing two women enter around the time of the murder. This could belong to one of them. It must have fallen on the desk at some point. It could have ended up under the desk when the culprit cleaned up. She would ask Shawna to test whether the blood on it was Shaun's. As Angela scrutinized the earring, she realized it looked familiar. Where had she seen it before?

This discovery made her wonder what else they had missed.

Bagging it as evidence, she continued her search. She completed a sweep under the desk, but didn't find anything interesting, other than a couple of dust-encrusted pens which she guessed had fallen there before she was born. Then she proceeded to check the drawers again. There was nothing of note in there either. Except the last one, which was empty, but there was something odd about it. A little prodding indicated that it had a false bottom. Soon she had figured it out. A tiny chamber in the drawer revealed itself. There wasn't much in there, besides a photograph and a fragment of paper, possibly from a sticky note. The fragment said "$500,00." The picture shocked her. She saw two naked women in bed, lost in sexual frenzy. It wasn't the act or the nudity that shocked her. Not even the gender of the participants. What shocked her was the fact that she knew them, and she could not have imagined them involved in anything like this. The implications of this finding made her head spin.

BACK AT THE STATION, Angela relayed her findings to Paul. He was stunned. He hadn't expected Margaret's vision to amount to anything. Perhaps this would turn him into a believer. Or not.

"Maybe Margaret did it," he began. "I mean, Dana did say she saw two women enter. Margaret could be one of them. I feel she has something to do with these deaths somehow. How else can she have all the details? And you think the earring is familiar. You sure you didn't see it on her?"

"No, not her style at all. And if she did it, why draw attention to it? We have to find out who it belongs to. It will come to me. Soon, I hope. Now, Maya and Meghna are more likely suspects because of the photograph. The two-women story fits too."

"Except that the women were blonde."

"Dana wasn't sure about that. Besides, it's quite easy to put on a blonde wig to throw off suspicion. These are smart cookies we are dealing with. Don't underestimate them."

"That's true. You're right. The photograph is very incriminating. Makes me wonder how long it's been going on. They didn't indicate anything of the sort the last time we spoke to them."

"Quite likely, Shaun never stopped spying on them, contrary to what he told us. He used the pic to blackmail them, and they killed him. Though I don't understand why they left it there. Maybe they didn't see it because it was in the hidden chamber? I always had a feeling they were capable of murder, especially Meghna. Even with Jay's case I was quite confident she was involved somehow. We should question them right away."

ANGELA LEARNED that Maya and Meghna were living together at Meghna's in Milpitas. It was late, so the detectives decided to meet them there, once they were back from work. They received a cold welcome from Meghna, but Maya was friendly. However, Angela could sense that they were nervous. She hoped it would make them slip up and reveal the truth.

"What brings you here this time?" asked Maya.

Angela pulled out the photograph and held it up for them. She wanted to see their reaction. Genuine shock, followed by embarrassment.

"Where ... where did you find this?"

"Have you seen it before?"

"Yes. Oh, this is so embarrassing," replied Maya, her face turning a deeper red.

"We're sorry for putting you through this. We understand this is personal, but it is important for our investigation. Where have you seen it?"

"A few weeks ago, we were blackmailed by some guy. He had a stash of such pics, and he threatened to make them public if we did not pay up."

"Do you know who it was?"

"No. He instructed us to drop off the money at the specified location. The pics would be delivered to us later. We destroyed them as soon as we received them. Never saw the man."

"And this pic was among the ones you got?"

"Yes. He assured us there were no more copies, but clearly he lied."

"How much did you pay?"

"Five hundred thousand dollars."

That explained the amount Angela had seen on the Post-it fragment.

"That's a lot of money. You did pay up?"

"Of course, we did. Why else would he give us the pics?"

"Perhaps you decided not to. Instead, you killed him and stole the pics. But you didn't search well enough, and you missed this one."

"What are you talking about? We did pay him, and we didn't kill anyone. What gives you the right to come around here every few months accusing us of murdering someone?"

"Why didn't you come to us? The police can help in cases of blackmail."

"He warned us not to go to the cops. Besides, this is so embarrassing. We were not comfortable sharing this with anyone."

The answer was convincing enough for Angela.

"We found this pic in the office of Shaun Jacobs. A private investigator. He was murdered on the evening of April twenty-seventh. Where were you two that night?"

"Oh. So you think he was the blackmailer? Well, we didn't have anything to do with his murder. But we are glad someone took out the trash."

"That doesn't answer my question. Where were you that night?"

"We were right here, wrapping up some important personal stuff."

"Can anyone confirm that?"

"No. Only the two of us. As always, you can check our phone records. We were here the whole time."

"That doesn't tell us much. You could have left your phones at home. Let me tell you one thing. We have a witness who saw two women enter Shaun's office around the time of the murder. You have strong motive and no alibi."

"And I am telling you we never stepped out of the house. It could have been any two women. Like I said, we already received the pics. Why would we bother killing him?"

"Any proof that you paid up? Even if you did pay up, it's possible he continued to blackmail you with this pic. You decided enough was enough and ended up murdering him."

"We didn't do it. You can verify from our bank records that we withdrew five hundred thousand dollars in cash. But I agree, there is no way to prove that we paid him. Unless you search his belongings. He must have stashed it somewhere."

"Any contact with him after that?"

"No, nothing," Meghna lied.

Angela realized she wasn't going to get much more out of them. She would have to investigate and find the evidence she needed. But she was still curious about this close relationship between these women, who until recently claimed to be sometime-friends who were not in contact anymore.

"How long have you two been together?"

"A few months now."

"How did this happen? I thought you weren't in touch."

"I did tell you we were friendly. Yes, we had not been in touch for a while, but a short while after Jay's death Meghna called me to express her sympathies. We decided to meet up. It rekindled the friendship, and soon we realized we were in love," replied Maya.

It sounded quite convincing, but Angela still had her doubts. Seeing them together reminded her of the autonomous car theory, and how she had suspected Meghna was involved in Jay's murder with help from someone. Had she made a mistake by arresting Candy? Was Maya that accomplice? She knew she had to get to the bottom of this, but she was done with the questions for now.

THEY WALKED BACK to the car in silence. Once inside, they pondered their next move.

"Do you believe them?" asked Paul.

"I never do. Something about it isn't right. I will check on those phone records. We need some solid evidence. I think we should keep them under watch."

"What good is that going to do? They've already committed the crime."

"I have a feeling this is not over yet. They'll slip up at some point, and when they do, we'd better get them."

BACK AT THE STATION, the detectives discovered that victim number five had been found dead, in what Shibata jokingly referred to as the "Jack the Stripper" case. It was an appropriate title, given that they were chasing a serial killer who stripped his victims after killing them. Angela, however, did not find it funny. It was another of those sexist and demeaning jokes Shibata liked to crack. He wasn't shy about sharing intimate details about his visits to various strip clubs, and she was sure he had used the "stripper" term because it was a turn-on for him.

Victim number five was seventy-five-year-old Alan Boyd. He lived with his daughter and granddaughter. His daughter had discovered the body when she got back from her daughter's swim class. The murder had followed the pattern. He was found naked, with an empty syringe in his hand. The Taser and the poison were the same as with the previous victims. Once again, the killer had done a clean job, leaving no clues. Once again, the killer must have surveyed the house and its occupants to find an apt time to catch the victim alone. As with the previous murders, the victim must have known his assailant, since there was no sign of forced entry. As with the previous murders, Angela was positive they would be unable to find anyone Alan knew who would want to kill him. Once again, she wondered how long this would continue. When would they catch a break?

PLAYING HOOKY

MAY 9

The doorbell sounded as soon as Angela stepped out of the shower. She wondered who it was as she donned her robe. She was already running late for work and didn't want any further delays. It was Kyle, sporting a wide grin.

"Surprise!"

"Kyle! What are you doing here?"

"We're driving down to Carmel. You have been working too hard. You need a break."

"But it's Wednesday. Don't you have work to do? I know I have a ton of stuff to wrap up."

"Well, I called in sick, and I suggest you do too."

"I can't. I have an investigation to run."

"Oh, come on. One day away is not going to hurt anything."

Angela protested, but soon Kyle had convinced her, and they were on their way. It was a beautiful, sunny day, and it would be a shame to waste it working. First stop was in the charming downtown. They strolled down the main thoroughfare, checking out the dainty little stores and continuing on towards the beach. Angela looked forward to dipping her toes in the water. That was the most she would do, since she knew it would be chilly. She would relax on the sand while taking in the beautiful view, with the ocean and coastline in the distance. She was beginning to unwind as they continued down the street, hand in hand. Work was a distant memory. She was glad Kyle had planned this trip. His spontaneity was one of the things she loved about him.

Suddenly, she stopped in front of a bookstore. Something in the display window had caught her eye. It was a blowup of Candy's book with her beautiful, gleaming face on the cover. Angela had no idea it was out. She was curious. They entered the store, with Angela heading straight for the New Releases section. She scanned the description, and realized it was indeed about the recent events in Candy's life, leading up to the Lumiotech case. There was no way she could resist reading it.

While she waited in the checkout line, she examined the cover again. Candy had always struck her as an attractive woman, but here she was even more gorgeous. Styling, makeup, and the right photographer could do wonders. It reminded her of the Escorts Forever page, but the provocative images there contrasted with the demure face on this cover. As she studied the visage, she remembered something. This is where she had seen that earring. Candy had been wearing it during one of their meetings. It was a lovely set, and the unique design had lodged in her memory. She dropped the book and ran over to Kyle.

"We have to go back. Now!"

"Why? What happened?"

"Something's come up."

"But we only just got here!" he protested.

The disappointment on his face was apparent. Angela apologized, but insisted it was important. She knew it wasn't fair to Kyle, but this was a significant break in the case. It could not wait another day. They drove back in silence, with the only pause coming when she called Paul to report her latest finding. They would have to question Candy right away.

ANGELA MET Paul outside Candy's apartment. He was two knocks into his three-knock routine when the door opened to reveal the familiar face, with a glass of wine in hand. The scorn on the face was familiar too.

"You again! You do remember you already have me on trial, right?" shrieked Candy.

"This is a different case. Sad to say, you're a suspect again," replied Angela as she stepped inside, not waiting for an invitation.

"You have got to be kidding me."

"I wish I was."

"What did I ever do to you? Why are you out to mess up my life?"

"Trust me, it's nothing personal. I would gladly leave you alone if you stopped knocking off people."

"I told you. I didn't kill anybody! You know how fucked up my life is? I am out of money paying legal bills. Heck, if it weren't for Cheryl, I couldn't even post bail. I would still be rotting in jail. And I hardly have any income. Everyone thinks I'm a killer, so my regulars don't want to risk it, and any potentials are scared away. The few clients I do get come out of curiosity and are lowballers, offering nowhere near the thousand bucks an hour I made before. And now this."

"You sure you're out of money? I saw your book. Congratulations. That should have you rolling in dough."

"It helps a bit. But Francis Dern costs a lot more. Did you read it?"

"Not yet, but I will," replied Angela as Candy sipped her wine.

"Kinda early for that, no?" said Paul, pointing to the glass.

"Aren't you the judgemental one. It's five o'clock. I would say not. Besides, red wine is good for you."

"Yeah, that's what they all say."

"So. What is it this time? You mentioned some case. Let's get it over with."

Angela showed her a picture of the earring.

"Recognize this?"

"Oh. Did you find my earring? I have searched all over for it."

"So it is yours?"

"It's got to be. It's a custom design. There are only two sets. Cheryl, remember her? She made these, one for her and one for me. To celebrate our friendship. She is so talented. She does jewelry design on the side."

"So that's what the letters stand for? R for Rebecca and C for Cheryl?"

"Wow, you aren't as dumb as I thought you were. Yes, of course," replied Candy in a mocking tone.

"You'd better watch your tongue!"

"Or else what? You'll lock me up again even though I am innocent? Where did you find it?"

"Right next to a guy with his head bashed in."

Candy's face turned pale, just for a split-second before she recovered.

"What do you mean?" She downed the rest of her glass in one shot.

"You know Shaun Jacobs?"

"That private investigator? You mean he's dead?!" Candy's mouth opened in complete shock.

Quite a performance, thought Angela.

"Yes, that's the one. How do you know him?"

"He's a client. Actually, he was Cheryl's client. She introduced him to me when I was going through a rough patch. To help me financially."

"You saw him often?"

"Yeah. A few times."

"Where did you meet?"

"Various motels. But the last time was at his office."

"His office? When was this?"

"A few days ago. I don't remember the exact date."

"So you are telling me you did it in his office?"

"Yeah. He wanted some excitement. Doing it on the desk with the chance some client could walk in at any time. That must be when I lost the earring."

"Where were you on the evening of April twenty-seventh?"

"Here we go again. So you found my earring in his office. That's why you think I did it? Seriously? Any excuse to get me. What did I ever do to you?"

"There's no need to get dramatic. Answer the question."

"I need some more wine."

Candy got up and poured herself another glass. She emptied it in one large gulp, then started to pour one more, but stopped. She placed the glass on the counter and walked back, looking quite relaxed.

"What was the question again?"

"April twenty-seventh. Where were you that evening?"

"That was Friday? Yeah, I remember. Cheryl and me were at the movies."

"Which show?"

"Oh, it was the eight o'clock show at Shoreline. The Avengers movie."

Angela pondered over that for a moment. Cheryl was the only one who could vouch for Candy. But she knew Cheryl was not a reliable witness when it came to Candy. Besides, two women had been seen entering Shaun's office. Candy and Cheryl fit the bill. She didn't think Candy could have managed it alone. But the earring would not be enough to convict. Angela needed some solid evidence.

"Can you prove it?"

"You can ask Cheryl."

"We don't trust Cheryl. We don't trust you either."

"Oh yeah, not surprising at all. Let me check my purse. I might still have the stubs."

A couple of minutes later, she was back with the ticket stubs and a smug countenance. She handed the stubs to Angela and returned to her seat. That still didn't prove anything. They could have left the show early. Or purchased the tickets and not gone at all.

Angela couldn't resist it any longer. She realized she had to get it out of her system. The smug expression only egged her on further. She asked the question she had been dying to ask, but she asked it casually enough.

"You like paintball, Candy?"

"Huh?" replied Candy, now sporting a deer-in-the-headlights look.

It was just the effect Angela wanted. Though she could tell from Paul's confused expression that she had some explaining to do later. She was relieved he let her continue.

"You love paintball, don't you? You and Cheryl. Both of you."

"I don't know what you mean," replied Candy with a little more confidence, but her face betrayed her thoughts.

"Driving around Sunnyvale, following evening joggers, shooting at houses. Sounds like a lot of fun, doesn't it?"

Candy didn't reply.

"Did you shoot, or did you drive?" It was time for some directness.

"I ... I shot. Cheryl doesn't let anyone else drive her car."

By now, all the color had drained from Candy's face.

"Thank you for your honesty. Probably the only time you haven't lied to me. Why did you do it?"

"I was angry at you. I wanted to get back at you somehow. But it was Cheryl's idea."

"You could have said no."

"Yes, I could have. What are you going to do now?"

"I don't know yet. But soon I will. Wait and see," replied Angela in a cool, even tone which carried an edge of menace.

The fear on Candy's face was priceless. It was all Angela needed.

CONFUSION

MAY 10

Angela got in to work with a splitting headache and bloodshot eyes. After questioning Candy, she had entered the nearest bookstore to buy her memoir. She had stayed up late to finish it. The lack of sleep was showing. Paul noticed it too.

"Rough night?"

"Kinda. I couldn't resist reading Candy's book. Quite the page-turner. Made my blood boil. You know she makes all detectives sound like bumbling fools? That bitch!"

"Whoa, whoa. Calm down. I have never seen you this angry before. That's her way of getting back at us. Just ignore it."

"Trust me, I'm trying. What worries me is, with Lumiotech she went free. In the book she presents herself as this unfortunate woman from a small town, beaten by circumstances every step of the way. It's not her fault that she does what she does for a living. And she got framed for a crime she did not commit. It was pure luck and her awesome attorney who helped her go free. Anyone reading this will be swayed in her favor. It could impact our case. What if she goes free for Jay's murder as well?"

"That's a possibility. I can see why they rushed it out. The mastermind Francis Dern at work. Not to mention, the publishers realized they can make a lot of money off it while she's in the lime-light again. Not much we can do about it. The important thing now is the Shaun Jacobs case. Did she do it?"

"We have to gather more info. I have asked for her and Cheryl's phone records."

"What would be their motive for killing him? He was a lucrative client."

"Well, we know what a twisted guy he was. Maybe he made her do something she didn't want to do, and she snapped."

"As far as motive goes, Maya and Meghna are more likely candidates."

"That's true. Let's hope our investigation bears fruit."

"By the way, what was all that about paintball? I didn't get a chance to ask. She looked like she had seen a ghost."

Angela filled him in on all the details.

"Wow! You never cease to amaze me. So, what are you going to do now?"

"Nothing."

"Nothing?"

"That spooked look is everything. She is going to spend every day from here on fearing the moment when I will do something to get back at her. That's good enough for me."

"Evil! What about Cheryl? You going to terrify her as well?"

"I don't think that will be necessary. I bet Candy called her and told her everything the moment we left. Cheryl must be spooked too."

"Awesome!"

THE THEFT

MAY 11

"I just had a very interesting conversation," said Cynthia Crowley as soon as she reached Paul's desk. He was with Angela, case discussions in full swing. Both detectives turned to her, waiting for what she was going to reveal.

Cynthia continued. "Do you remember that woman who was found dead on the Caltrain tracks some months ago? Brenda Donovan."

"Vaguely. Wasn't it ruled an accident?" replied Paul.

"Yes. Well, her husband, Jason, was here today. He told me she maintained a meticulous diary, and she had some interesting observations around January seventeenth, a few days before her death."

"You mean something about the Jay Sharma case?" Angela asked as she sat up straight.

"Yes. She was at Sha Sha that night, and she thought she saw Maya doing something strange. From her entries, it seems it had something to do with Jay's murder. The whole thing stressed her out."

"Where is the diary? Can we take a look?"

"Now, that's the problem. That's what brought him here. The

family was out of town for a few days, and when they returned, he discovered it was missing."

"Someone stole it?" asked Angela, wide-eyed.

"Not just someone. Jason claims it could only have been one person."

"Who?"

"Maya Sharma. She is the only one who knew about it."

"Interesting. But why did he tell her in the first place?"

"Good question. It was not a smart move. But according to him, the diary did not directly implicate her in the murder. It indicated she was involved in something that distressed his wife. And he knew how much Brenda admired and respected Maya, so he didn't think she would have done anything wrong. He went there to find out if Maya knew what his wife had seen. But now that the diary is gone, he's sure she had something to do with it."

"The Donovans live in San Jose, right?" asked Angela.

"Yes."

"Did he report the theft to SJPD?"

"He did. But as you well know, SJPD is even more understaffed than us. No one showed up to investigate. They told him to file an FIR online."

"Oh. Do we know when it was stolen?"

"The family was gone for a few days. It could have been anytime during that period."

"And they're on Elm St?"

"I'm not sure. We'll have to look it up. Why do you ask?"

"I spoke to Margaret Lane the other day. She lives next-door to the Donovans. She mentioned she saw some suspicious characters lurking around their house the night of April twenty-seventh. Quite possible that's when the diary was stolen."

"Interesting. What else did she say?"

"Well, I didn't think much about it at the time. If I remember correctly, she said it was around two a.m. that she saw them. Two figures dressed in black. She called the cops, but no one showed up."

"You sure she saw something, or was this another one of her 'visions'?" It was Paul at his sarcastic best.

"Hmm ... I would have thought SJPD would at least send someone for a live incident," remarked Cynthia, ignoring him. She didn't give much credence to the "vision" talk either, but she didn't feel she could completely ignore Margaret.

"Precisely why I think she's making it all up. I bet she didn't call anyone," he continued.

"Well, Friday nights can get busy. Maybe that's why no one came."

"It can't be a coincidence that two women in black were seen at Shaun Jacobs' office, and a while later two figures in black were seen at the Donovans. Might be the same duo in both cases. Which makes me think Maya and Meghna were involved," added Angela.

"Or Margaret. It's interesting how she conveniently sees a vision about Shaun, and also happens to live next door to the Donovans. And she magically happens to see some suspicious figures there," Paul continued with his conspiracy theory.

"Paul, why would she care about the diary? There is nothing in it about her."

"Don't underestimate her, Angela. Under that calm demeanor is a shrewd woman who knows how to manipulate. By stealing it, she puts Maya under suspicion."

"Good point. But how did she find out about the diary? Jason only told Maya."

"I don't know. Just saying, let's not rule her out as a suspect. And I just had another idea while thinking about the Jacobs case."

"What's that?"

"You know how some people commit crimes, like killing people, and when questioned they say they hear voices telling them to do stuff?"

"Yes."

"Let's believe for a second that she does see these visions. But she views it as a directive from God, advising her what to do. Then she follows through on the vision by killing."

"That sounds crazy."

"What if she murdered Shaun? She tells us there was an earring on the desk. No one found it."

"But I did find the earring. Under the desk."

"Right. What if she planted it there? To incriminate Candy. The 'vision' was an excuse to get us to search."

"Then she could have left it on the desk. Why go to the trouble of putting it under the desk and risk it not being found?"

"Hmm. I don't know. But it's something to think about."

"Perhaps."

A CASE CLOSES
MAY 16

Angela walked into work and was surprised to see a lively atmosphere. People were huddled together, laughing and chatting, quite a contrast to the glum faces she was used to seeing in the homicide department. Wilson and Shibata were sporting generous smiles and seemed to be sharing a joke with Paul. Even Cynthia had joined in the festivities. As soon as Paul spotted Angela, he walked over, his face bursting with delight.

"Told you!"

"What?" she asked with a puzzled expression.

"Told you she's a loon going around killing people."

"Who? Margaret?"

"Yep. We got her this time."

"Who did she kill?"

"Jack the Stripper. She's the one."

"I don't believe this. She confessed?"

"Not yet. But we have strong evidence for at least one of the murders. This is where you come in, Cinderella," added Shibata as he joined Paul.

"What do you mean?" asked Angela.

"She says she will only talk to you. We need your help to interrogate her and get the confession."

"Why me?"

"I don't know. You'll have to ask her yourself."

Over the next hour, Wilson and Shibata filled her in on the case details. They had been clueless after the first few deaths, but they had lucked out on the last one. The victim's surveillance camera had caught Margaret entering and leaving the house around the time of the murder. They had searched her house and had found a notepad with the names and addresses of all the victims. They also discovered a Taser, several syringes, packs of cocaine and some vapes. It was all they had needed to arrest her.

Angela still couldn't believe Margaret could have done something like this. She stepped into the interrogation room and saw the suspect seated, a picture of serenity. It was odd seeing her in this setting. They had always met in Margaret's home, which was spacious, well-lit and beautifully decorated. But this was a small, cold room with a single light hanging above the table. It was designed to break down all but the toughest of criminals.

Margaret smiled as Angela sat across from her. Angela managed to force a smile back. It was an awkward situation for her, and she knew it would be difficult to keep it professional. But she had a job to do.

"Margaret, did you really ...," she began, then hesitated.

"Did I kill them all?" Margaret replied calmly.

"Yes."

"Well, I did do it."

"Can you tell me in detail? I need it for the records."

"Sure. I killed them all. Adam Newman, John Robbins, Miguel Santoro, Ted Brown, Alan Boyd."

"Why?"

"They are all men I have dated in the past. And they all dumped me once they found out about my visions. None of them could handle it. They thought I was crazy. Jerks, all of them. You know how difficult it has been for me? I always believed in being truthful in my relationships. But I would tell my dates about it, and they would all walk away. Then I started hiding it. But that wouldn't last long. They would find out at some point. It was so frustrating."

"I understand your pain, but killing them? That's too extreme. I don't think anyone deserves that."

"That's what I told myself all these years. But a few months back something snapped in me. I don't know why. Maybe it was because I retired and had too much time on my hands. Maybe it was because Arthur dumped me. Or maybe I am getting old and my mind's failing me. These thoughts started consuming me. I felt like I had to avenge myself. Avenge my humiliation. I checked online, and most of these guys had gone on and married, had kids, even grandkids. Living normal, happy lives while I was alone all my life. It made me so angry. You won't understand how terrible it is to go through life all alone."

"Margaret, I know the single life."

"Yes, but you are still young. You'll have a different perspective thirty years from now."

"But it's never too late. You might still have found love."

"Nothing that would last. Eventually the next one would find out too and leave like the others. Besides, once I tasted blood, it was difficult to stop. It is quite thrilling."

"You think murdering innocent people is thrilling?" Angela couldn't believe what she had heard.

"It is. Not just the killing. The planning and preparation. Watching them. You should try it sometime."

"You are crazy!"

"Yeah, that's what they all say. You know, if I had the physical strength, I would have strangled them. Slowly up the pressure on their necks and watch the life drain away."

"How did you commit all these murders?" continued Angela, trying hard to ignore that last statement. Was this woman really so sick? How had she not seen that?

"It was so easy. Getting their names and addresses was a piece of cake. The wonders of modern technology. Then I thought, how should I do it? That's where your case helped. I read about the Taser and the poison-laced syringe and concluded it would work for me. Getting the coke was quite an experience. I mean, I smoke pot occasionally, so I know how to get my hands on that, but this was so different. But I managed to figure it out. Next thing was to catch them alone. I watched their places for days until I found a suitable time. I would show up at their door, introduce myself and, luckily, they all remembered me. For a moment, I would wonder whether I should spare them. They were all kinda nice in that they let me in. Trusting fools. Once inside, I zapped them and injected the poison. It was painful to watch, but so satisfying once they stopped struggling. Gave me a sense of achievement. Then I took off their clothes, rearranged the body and the syringe and walked away."

"I'm curious. Why did you strip them? And what is the significance of the arrangement?"

"It was like a signature. I figured I should have some fun while I was at it. And it helped with my visions. I didn't know what they would be wearing when I showed up. So it was easy to say I saw some man with no clothes in my vision."

"So you don't get visions? You make it all up?"

"No, no, dear. I do get them. I told you that before. But for these murders I made it all up. It was a fun thing to do, you know? People hardly ever believed my true visions, so this was my way of getting back at them. I know I am going to kill someone, so I say a few days prior that I saw a dead man with no clothes on. If they had ever listened, they might have been able to prevent some of these deaths."

"Margaret, you know your visions aren't much to go on. Given the limited information, even the best detectives couldn't tell who is going to die."

"I guess you're right. But still, why mock me? It's mean."

"I agree, it's mean. But why did you report only two visions? You killed five men."

"Oh, I figured it would be too much if I reported them all. I didn't want anyone to suspect me. And here's the thing. For the first one I wasn't all that confident. I had never done anything like that before. What if I failed? So I decided to play it safe. Once the first one went smoothly, I grew more confident."

"Do you have more guys on your hit list?"

"Oh yes. There's another five. You must have seen the list in my notes. Too bad I couldn't finish what I started. I got a little too cocky and ended up a careless old fool. I am sure with a bit of research I would have found that pesky camera."

Suddenly, a horrifying thought occurred to Angela. It wasn't pertinent to the case, but she couldn't resist.

"Margaret, when we first met you said my father left you because of your visions. Did you ... did you kill him too?"

It was Margaret's turn to be horrified. "Oh no, my dear! I genuinely adored your dad. He was my one true love. I could never hurt him. Like I told you, all this only started recently."

"How about Jay Sharma? Did you murder him?"

"No, certainly not! I didn't even know the guy. Besides, I thought you already had your killer."

"What about the diary? Did you steal it from Brenda's home?"

"What diary? I don't know anything about a diary. Is that what those people were doing that night? Stealing a diary?"

"Quite possibly, yes."

"What was so important about it?"

"I am sorry, I can't tell you."

"Oh, well."

"And Shaun Jacobs? You dated him. Did you kill him too?"

"No. Though he would have made my list eventually. Too bad someone else got to him before me."

Angela mulled over everything Margaret had told her. It was clear the woman was nuts. She was relieved her father had ended it with Margaret. But what made him do it? Was it the visions? Or was it something more? Had he sensed the evil lurking inside this woman?

"Are you thinking about Don? About why he left me?"

"What, you're a mind reader now?" asked Angela in amazement.

Margaret laughed. "Nah. But I wish I had that superpower. It was a lucky guess. He had his doubts once he learned about my visions, but he was patient with me. What I am about to tell you ... I kept this from you earlier. I have confessed so much now, might as well tell you this too."

Angela leaned forward in anticipation.

"Diane was a good friend to Don. It was a platonic relationship, but I was jealous of her. I wanted him all to myself. So I did a horrible thing. You will hate me after you hear this. That is, if you don't already."

"What did you do?"

"The three of us were at Yosemite one weekend, hiking one of the trails. I forget which one. At one point the trail narrowed. Don was leading, followed by Diane, and then me. I saw my chance and tried to push her off the edge. But she was stronger than I expected. He caught me before I could get her off her feet. That's when it ended between us."

"You tried to kill my mother! You sick, sick woman!" It was all Angela could take. She stormed out of the room, tears welling up in her eyes. As she walked past Shibata, she blurted, "You have your confession. Nail that bitch!"

MONEY, MONEY, MONEY
MAY 19

Meghna was exhausted. She had been walking in the dark for hours now, unable to find a way out. The idea of a nighttime hike to see the supermoon had sounded exciting, and she had enjoyed it for the most part. Until a few moments of inattention had separated her from the group and had left her lost. It did not help that the clouds were obscuring the moon frequently, depriving her of much light to navigate. That's when she noticed a faint glow in the distance. She moved towards it and was surprised to see a tall tower in the middle of the wilderness. The light was coming from the top. It reminded her of Coit Tower in San Francisco.

Meghna headed for it and entered. The interior was empty, except for a spiral staircase which appeared to go to the apex. Like a moth to the flame, she was attracted to the illumination and started climbing the stairs. She fought her way through the exhaustion and ascended steadily. As she rounded the last curve, the moon was obscured again. At the same time, the light at the top went out, leaving her in complete darkness. It took her a second to react, but it was too late. She missed a step and lost her balance, plunging towards the ground and to certain death.

The impact shook Meghna awake, and she was relieved to be alive. The firm sureness of her bed was comforting. It was the same nightmare again. She wondered, what did it mean?

PUTTING TOGETHER one million dollars in cash was never easy. Having paid out another half million so recently made it even more difficult. Maya and Meghna were lucky the blackmailer had been willing to negotiate and had given them more time. Now it was time to pay up. They were ready, with the money all packed up in a bag. As instructed by the woman, they would be dropping it off at Valley Fair Mall. The pics would arrive by the end of the day. Maya hoped this would conclude this bad chapter in their lives.

They entered the mall at 1:00 p.m. sharp and melted into the throngs of shoppers. It made sense that the blackmailer had selected this location. It would be nearly impossible to trace anyone here. Maya dropped the bag in the precise spot near the Gap store and left, resisting the temptation to turn around.

Two minutes later two pairs of legs walked over, picked up the loot and blended into the crowds. Neither the women, nor the blackmailers, knew they were being watched. Soon the woman watching from the second level made a call to her boss, reporting that the transaction had been completed.

MAYA AND MEGHNA got into the car and waited. Meghna was determined not to let the blackmailer get away this time. She had placed one of the Vroom mini-GPS tags at the bottom of the bag. The plan was to find out who was blackmailing them and get even. She couldn't stomach the fact that someone had not only violated her privacy, but would also get away with all her life savings. No, that was unacceptable.

The tracker began moving, taking the ramp to 880-N. She followed as it exited onto First Street. Up ahead she spotted an SUV and wondered whether the blackmailer was in it. It turned into the parking lot of a run-down motel just off the exit. The tracker halted as well, and it indicated the same location. By now she was convinced that the blackmailer was in the SUV. She saw two figures get out. One of them was holding the bag. Her heart started pounding. So there were two of them. She hoped no one else was involved. Maya and Meghna could take on two. More would be a problem.

The blackmailers made their way to the second level and into room number twenty-two. Meghna parked and waited a few minutes. She saw one of them exit the room and leave the lot on foot. This was their best chance. It would be much easier to overpower their opponents one at a time. Meghna raced up the stairs, with Maya close behind, cautiously looking around for any signs that the one who had left was returning. Waiting outside the door for a minute, she took a few deep breaths to calm herself. She took out her Glock 19 and got it into position. The hope was that it would not be necessary, but she figured having one would help their cause. Procuring it had been easy.

Meghna knocked on the door. She heard a faint voice inside saying something she couldn't catch. She knocked again. This time the door opened to reveal a familiar face. The jaw dropped. In turn, Maya and Meghna were shocked too. Candy reacted first and tried to close the door, but Maya was too quick for her and forced her way through. She pushed Candy hard, causing her to fall onto the bed, while Meghna pointed the gun at her. Maya took a moment to let it all sink in. So Candy was the one blackmailing them. She knew it was two women, but she had been unable to recognize them, what with the baseball caps worn low over the face.

Candy was still reeling as she asked, "How did you ...? We were sure no one followed us."

"Never mind that. Where's the money? And the photographs."

Candy pointed to the TV. Maya saw the bag sitting on the floor right below it. She checked the drawer and found an envelope. It had ten pictures, any one of which would have gotten them hanged for Jay's murder.

"Is this all?"

"Yes."

"How do we know there are no other copies?"

"You have to trust me. There aren't."

"We were promised the same for the previous set of photos. But the cops found another copy."

"Oh. I don't know anything about that. That was all Shaun."

"Shaun Jacobs? Was that the man we dealt with previously?"

"Yes. He's the one who took all the pics. He was the one black-mailing you."

"We heard he was murdered. Did you kill him?"

Silence.

"Who's the other woman?"

"Cheryl."

"She coming back soon?"

"In a few minutes. She's picking up some food and champagne. We were going to celebrate."

By now Candy had tears in her eyes. Her get-rich-quick dream was going up in flames. And she had a gun pointed at her. By someone very much capable of taking a life.

THE KILL
MAY 19

As Meghna stood there with the gun pointed at Candy, her heart raced. Adrenaline was rushing through her body. She pictured what it would be like to pull the trigger and see her target's face explode. Her mind strayed, bringing up memories of times she had felt such fear and excitement. Jay's face appeared before her, the precise moment she had plunged the syringe into him. Then her thoughts leapt to a time farther away, when she was ten. The first time she had taken a life.

A BEAUTIFUL SUMMER day in Mumbai, the city where she had spent her entire life before moving to California. It was her first day in a new place, her family having moved to the suburbs. Meghna, excited, out hunting for new friends, ignored all the girls and their boring games. She found a group of boys playing cricket and got included after persisting against their initial reluctance.

A short while later she took the crease, aware that some of them were snickering. But not for long. She whacked the first ball for a four, and the next two for sixes, leaving everyone, including the star bowler, dumbstruck. The last shot landed far out of sight. A search party left to retrieve the ball, while the rest of the boys congratulated her, impressed by what she had done. Who didn't love a winner?

When the group didn't return, they were concerned. A lost ball meant the game was over for the day, so it was essential that they locate it. They walked over to find the others and were met with an interesting sight. The boys stood in a small garden, with the ball visible in the grass. On top of it sat a massive, revolting lizard. No one dared move forward, much to Meghna's amusement.

On seeing her smile, the star bowler challenged her to fetch the ball. Before long, the others joined in, making nasty comments about her being too girly to do it. She knew this was just a cover for their fears and embarrassment. But she shrugged her shoulders, stepped up to it and picked up the lizard. She heard the amazed gasps going around. Under normal circumstances she would have thrown the reptile away and returned with the prize. But the taunts and the goading got to her. She felt like she still had something to prove to these guys. She twisted the lizard's neck until it snapped, and the blood oozed out. There was a stunned silence. She threw the two pieces into the onlookers, watching as they instantly dispersed with horrified screams. It was oddly satisfying, even though she knew she would never be allowed into their games again. Perhaps she was better off without such lousy friends anyway.

MEGHNA'S MIND returned to the weapon in her hand. Now she felt rage, rage against Candy for messing with her life. She wanted to pump bullets into her and watch her bleed. It was a relief she had not loaded the gun.

Now that they had the money and the photographs, they decided to leave. Maya turned around to see Cheryl standing in the doorway. Cheryl moved before Maya had a chance to warn Meghna. The

Glock flew out of Meghna's hand as Cheryl lunged at her. Meghna was caught by surprise, but she did not lose her balance. Muscle memory kicked in from the umpteen judo lessons she had taken as a child. She managed to throw her attacker to the floor and make a dash for the gun.

In the meantime, Candy took advantage of this opportunity and attacked Maya. The women were wrestling on the ground when Meghna whacked Candy on the head with the pistol butt. Candy fell back in pain, blood oozing from her head. By now Cheryl was back on her feet, but before she could move, Meghna pointed the gun at her. She hoped Cheryl wouldn't call her bluff. Things would get tricky if they figured out it wasn't loaded. Maya and Meghna escaped while they still had the upper hand. Cheryl went a few steps forward to give pursuit, but decided it was more important to tend to Candy. The cash and the pics were gone, their hopes of riches and revenge smashed in an instant.

PURSUIT

MAY 19

Angela hung up. She had been waiting for this update. Their team at Valley Fair had spotted Maya and Meghna making the drop and the blackmailers picking up the money. This confirmed Angela's hunch that the extortion had not ended with Shaun Jacobs' death. But now the question was, with Shaun dead, who were these new players? And was this duo responsible for his murder? Her mind was full of these thoughts when her phone crooned again. The team had followed the blackmailers to a motel in San Jose. Time to get on the ground. The phone rang again as she drove off with Paul. It was news she hadn't expected.

"Maya and Meghna are there too?" he asked, just as confused as she was.

"Yes. They must have tailed them too. Now they're making their way up to the room."

"Shaun blackmails them. We find him dead. Now these women blackmail them, and they follow the women. You think they're on a revenge spree, knocking off anyone who shakes them down?"

"If that's the case we'd better get there quick. I don't want another murder. Not on my watch. Then again, we could let things play out and catch Maya and Meghna in the act."

"Option two sounds good. I don't care about extortionist scum. Should we ask the team to hold them?"

"No. Let them leave. We know where to find them. I want the team to focus on the blackmailers."

By the time the detectives arrived, Maya and Meghna had made their getaway. They synced with their team in the parking lot. The blackmailers were still in the room. Angela and Paul went up the stairs. Angela didn't have to knock, since the door was open a crack. She pushed it to reveal Cheryl sitting on the bed, tending to a sobbing Candy who had blood trickling down her head. From the looks of it, this was a nasty surprise for the escorts. Angela was a bit surprised herself. She had suspected Candy of murders but had not considered her as a blackmailer.

"What happened here?" she asked, hoping she would get a straight answer.

"Nothing. Rebecca fell and hurt her head."

Angela sighed. They would not make it easy.

"And how did she fall? Maya and Meghna have anything to do with it?"

She could tell the comment had hit home. She hoped, now that Cheryl knew that Angela knew something, she would tell the truth.

"Yes, they attacked us. They even had a gun. We thought we were going to die," replied Cheryl with a hint of drama.

Smart touch there, thought Angela. Playing the victim card.

"And why would they attack you?"

"I don't know. They just showed up here. Total surprise, really."

"So it has nothing to do with the fact that you were blackmailing them?"

Cheryl realized the jig was up. No point lying about the black-mail. But how much more did the detectives know?

"Alright, yes. We were. We had pictures that would ruin them."

"What was in these pictures?"

"Proof that they killed Jay Sharma."

"What?!" Angela did not see this coming. She was quite certain these would be the same nude pics as before. But if there was evidence Maya and Meghna had murdered Jay, it would help solve that case. It would also mean she had been on the right track about Meghna at one time. The question still remained about who killed Shaun.

"How did you get these pics? I assume you didn't take them yourselves, or you would have presented them when Candy was arrested," asked Paul.

"We found them."

"Where?"

Cheryl hesitated. Candy sat in silence, her hands shaking.

"Where did you find them, damn it?! You steal them from Shaun Jacobs?"

"Oh, Cheryl. They know," said Candy in panic.

"Shut up, Rebecca!" replied Cheryl. "Don't listen to her," she continued, turning to the detectives. "That head wound is making her delirious."

"Candy, tell us how you got the pics." He turned his attention to Candy.

"Don't tell them anything, Rebecca!" Cheryl cut in, the panic in her voice increasing.

"We took them from his office," Candy replied, ignoring Cheryl's pleas.

"And he let you take them?"

"He had to. Dead men can't do much." Candy started to break out into laughter. Yes, she was getting delirious.

"Damn you, Rebecca! After everything I did for you!" Cheryl was furious now. "Don't listen to her. Can't you see she's badly injured? She has no clue what she's saying. We should get her to the hospital."

"How did Shaun die, Candy?" asked Paul in a gentle tone. They were getting close.

"Oh, Cheryl whacked him on the head," she giggled. "You should have seen his face. That twisted pervert. Drooling over our bodies. And then she did it. It was awesome."

A wave of excitement ran through Angela. Candy had given them what they needed for Shaun's investigation. But she needed to know about Jay Sharma.

"Thanks so much, Candy. Now tell us. Where are those pics showing Jay's murder?"

"They took them. With the money. Our million dollars." Candy started sobbing again.

The detectives left their team to complete the formalities of arresting the women and taking them into custody. They had to get to Maya and Meghna. Fast.

Fifteen minutes later, they were at the Milpitas home, hoping they weren't too late. Maya welcomed them with a surprised expression. As Angela walked towards the living room, she saw Meghna standing by the mantel, sporting a mysterious smile. Angela soon realized why. The fireplace was on. Next to it was the bag of money. On top of that was an empty envelope, big enough for a few photographs.

"Where are the photographs?" she asked.

"Take a guess." Meghna's smile grew wider as her gaze turned to the fire.

Angela's body tensed. There was nothing left to save. She had lost once again.

"You destroyed evidence!" raged Paul.

"Evidence of what? Those pics would have humiliated us. This was our only choice. Nothing illegal about it."

"Those pics showed you two killing Jay and disposing of the body."

"What? I don't believe this. You are still on that crazy theory? These were pics like the one you had the other day."

"That's not what Candy told us."

"Surely you don't trust that woman? You know she murdered him. Isn't that why you arrested her? And now that her blackmail attempt has failed miserably, she is trying to malign us to save herself."

"They told us you threatened them with a gun. And you assaulted Candy."

"I did have one. But it was not loaded. I needed some insurance. We didn't want any violence, but that other woman attacked us. We had to defend ourselves."

"Is this where you destroyed Brenda's diary too?" Paul tried a different tack.

"I'm not sure what you mean. Jason took the diary back with him," replied Maya, her face oozing innocence.

"You know exactly what I mean. What did you do with it after you stole it?"

"We didn't steal it. What would be the point?"

"It was proof that Brenda saw you dispose of Jay's body."

"It didn't say anything of the sort. What Brenda saw, I don't know. But I can assure you, it wasn't me and Jay. Candy killed Shaun. Candy killed Jay. Quite likely, she stole the diary too. It's as simple as that. Just do your damn job and make sure she gets what she deserves."

Angela didn't know what else to say. Yet again, she had no proof about Maya's and Meghna's involvement in Jay's murder. She was certain these women had done it, but there was nothing to nail them for it. What was worse, she didn't have much against Candy and Cheryl either. Blackmail, yes. But evidence for Shaun's murder, none. Sure, Candy had confessed to them in the motel room, but it was because of her mental state at that moment. Angela knew that once Candy had some time to think about it, she would deny everything. Without her confession, they had nothing. All that hard work, and they ended up with nothing. It was frustrating. All of a sudden, Angela felt weak. She was finding it difficult to handle this setback. Two cases, and both concluded in failure. And she was so close. She walked out of the house, shoulders hunched and head bent low.

DEAD ENDS

MAY 21

As expected, Candy denied knowing anything about Shaun Jacobs' death. Cheryl, likewise. Their phone records showed they were at Century Shoreline Theatre in Mountain View the night of the murder. The question remained about how they had obtained the photographs from Shaun. The simple response from Candy was that she had extracted them during the office session after getting him drunk. There wasn't much Angela could do with that. But there was one useful thing she had learned. Brenda's death was not an accident. Shaun had murdered her. Angela didn't have any proof, and had her doubts about trusting Candy, but she didn't see any reason why she would lie about this. There was nothing to gain. It did help provide some closure to Jason and his family.

The investigation into the theft of the diary didn't reveal anything either. SJPD did not find any interesting prints at the Donovan residence, and there was no evidence of a break-in. Except for Margaret, none of the other neighbors had noticed any unusual activity that night.

All their major investigations had reached a dead end. Exhausted, the detectives decided to take a break.

"What's your plan for the evening?" Paul asked Angela as they stepped out of the building.

"Well, I have an annoyed boyfriend to tend to. I think I'll surprise him by driving him to Carmel tonight. We'll stay there a couple of days, or at least until his mood lightens. I owe him that much."

"Yeah, pamper him good."

"Oh, I'm sure he will be the one who will be pampering me once we get there." She winked as she strode off towards her car.

Paul got into his car, dreading his commute back to Mountain House. He yearned for a sweetheart to tend to, too. Like his cases, his personal life had hit a dead end.

ANGELA HOPPED into the shower as soon as she got home. She was excited about her plan. Kyle would be so surprised to see her at his door, and even more surprised when she whisked him away for the romantic getaway.

She was still drying off when her phone buzzed. It was Shawna, sounding exhilarated.

"Angela, you have got to see this."

"See what?"

"Remember the bust at Shaun Jacobs' office? We were working with it for blood samples and fingerprints. One of the techs noticed there was something odd about the eyes. It's not something you can detect unless you inspect it up close. He probed further and discovered there's a video camera in there. One of those tiny spy cams. Greg from computer forensics helped check on it. Turns out it has built-in memory where all the videos get stored. We found some from the night Shaun was murdered."

"Where are you?" asked Angela, pumped up about the case again.

"At work."

"See you in fifteen."

Kyle could wait.

IT TOOK THIRTY MINUTES, but Angela was finally sitting in a room with Shawna and Greg, eyes glued to the screen. Her progress to the Santa Clara County Crime Lab in San Jose had been stalled by the usual evening commuter traffic. The recording for April 27 was playing. The video was high-resolution, impressive for such a tiny camera, thought Angela.

"Let's move it to nine p.m.," she requested.

Greg dragged it forward. It showed Shaun seated at his desk, busy typing. A minute later the door opened, and two women walked in. There was no doubt about their identities. Angela watched it all the way through until Cheryl grabbed the bust and brought it down on Shaun's head. This was it! This was what she needed! Ecstatic, she hugged Shawna and Greg. Candy and Cheryl were done for.

"We may have some more goodies for you," said Shawna, with a twinkle in her eye.

"What more could you give me?"

"We're not sure yet, but it's promising. At the bottom of the bust we found a small panel. It covers a little storage area. Inside that were a few SD and microSD cards. They're encrypted, but Greg is working on cracking that. This might be where Shaun backed up all his important documents, including photographs."

"So it's possible it has those pictures of Maya and Meghna?"

"Yes."

"I'll keep my fingers crossed. Good work, both of you."

THE CONFESSION
MAY 22

Angela sat across from Candy in the interrogation room, playing the video from Shaun's office. She studied her, saw her expression change from one of extreme cockiness to fear. It was important to convince Candy that she was done for and extract a formal confession out of her. While the video was strong evidence, it could be dicey in court. Angela wanted to ensure they had an airtight case.

As the bust made contact with Shaun's head, Candy pushed her chair back and threw up. Angela had not expected such an extreme reaction. But she was happy to see it. This meant she had broken her. Angela handed her some tissues to wipe her face and got down to business.

"Killing him was Cheryl's idea. I told her about the pictures and thought we could steal them. But she said it was too risky. Shaun would find out and make us suffer. He had to go."

"And you agreed?"

"At first I didn't want to. I was scared, you see. I mean, I was on trial twice for crimes I didn't commit. With my luck, I was sure I would get caught. But she convinced me it was necessary. She reminded me about all those times that bastard abused me. And I thought, yeah, I need some revenge."

"What happened next?"

"We started planning. Most important was the alibi. We kept it simple. Cheryl bought tickets for consecutive nights. We saw the same show the previous night, so we could answer any questions about the movie. On that night, we drove separately to the theater and left my car in the parking lot with both our phones in it. If they tracked our phones, it would look like we were at the theatre when he was killed. Then we went to his office in Cheryl's car. We parked a little farther from the entrance, in case someone noted which cars were around when he died. You know the rest. I wish we had checked for cameras."

"Don't beat yourself up about it. You couldn't have found this one."

"But I was careless about the earring. I didn't realize when it fell. And I only noticed it missing the next morning. I was worried, so I drove there to look for it, but by then the body had been discovered."

Angela pressed Candy to talk about everything that happened inside the office. Candy obliged. Now Angela had the entire confession. A couple of hours later, she had one from Cheryl as well.

THE SEARCH
MAY 23

Angela's heart skipped a beat when she saw who was calling her. It was Greg. She grabbed the phone, anticipation building up. He asked her to come over and review what he had found. She was there in record time.

"So, there were five cards in there. We have been able to decrypt three so far. The remaining two have us stumped, but we're working on those. He was smart enough to use a different key for each card. The first two are a backup of all the videos from the bust. Nothing interesting there, I presume. You already have the video you need. The third one is full of photos. I haven't had a chance to review it, but you are welcome to."

Angela accepted the offer and sat down. She hoped she would find what she was looking for. The pictures were not organized in folders or named in any intuitive way. Shaun's digital world was as messy as his office. A saving grace was that the dates on the files varied widely, and she assumed those indicated when they were taken. She sorted them by date and began searching for January 17 of that year. But she didn't find anything. Disappointed, she wondered whether they were in one of the other two cards. Or what if Shaun had been true to his word and had deleted the copies? That would be a bummer.

Angela decided to take a break. Fifteen minutes later, she was back with a cup of coffee. A couple of sips refreshed her, and she started browsing the disk again. Curious, she clicked on a few pics at random. They were of people she didn't know. Soon she hit the first one with a familiar face in it. It was Jay. He was standing with his right arm around a gorgeous woman and leaning in for a kiss. She felt disgusted watching him cheat and hurried to the next pic. Some pics later, she saw him again. He was with another woman this time, but the situation couldn't have been more different. His hand was moving across her face, striking it hard. The woman's face showed how much it hurt, but in spite of the pained expression, Angela could tell this was Meghna. This must have been the day Meghna had confronted him, the day Shaun had entertained himself instead of helping a woman in distress. Angela felt rage bubble up inside her, and for a moment the thought crossed her mind that Jay had got what he deserved. She could see what had driven Maya and Meghna to murder him. Perhaps it wasn't too bad that they had gotten away with it.

Angela closed the window and leaned back in the chair, stretching her body to relieve the tightness building up in her neck and shoulders. She pondered her next move. The pics she wanted were not there. She would have to wait for the other cards to be decrypted. But then the dedicated professional in her woke up. Whatever Jay's faults, and whatever justification there may have been for what the women had done, they had broken the law and deserved to bear the consequences.

Angela opened the window again and scrolled through the dates. This time she noticed there were a few pics dated January 1, 1970. She had enough of a technical background to know this was a special date in the computer world. Clocks on most systems used it as day zero when tracking time. If some of the files had this date, it likely meant that the date was not set on whatever system these pictures originated. Or it was a glitch. She did a quick count. There were ten such pics. She opened one at random and froze. There it was. Meghna and Jay in a car. Meghna with a syringe in hand. The money shot. Angela rushed through the remaining nine. It was enough to follow the key sequence of events that occurred that night. With this evidence, Maya and Meghna didn't stand a chance.

GOODBYE

JULY 25

Paul was done for the day. He stood up and stretched, still sore from his workout that morning. He had found his motivation and had been hitting the gym with a vengeance. The belly was gone, and he had packed on some muscle, reminding him of his glory days as a college football star. Before leaving, he stopped by Angela's desk. She seemed busy, attention focused on her screen.

"You stare any harder and the monitor will confess," he laughed.

Angela smiled back. "Just wrapping up the report."

Maya and Meghna were in jail, their bail request denied. Candy and Cheryl were in, too. Francis Dern had finally run out of miracles.

"You look so content. You managed to get those women."

"More relieved than anything. For a while there I thought I had failed. I hope all goes well in court. Anyway, what's up?"

"They're showing *The Philadelphia Story* at Stanford Theatre this weekend. Want to join me? No murders, I promise. Good, clean entertainment. And you get charmed by Cary Grant and James Stewart."

"And who's going to charm you?"

"Katherine Hepburn this time. Might be the last time we can catch a movie together."

"What do you mean?"

"I'm moving back to Wichita."

"Oh! Why?"

"You know I never fit in here. It's like a different country. Besides, you have awful football teams."

"True. Our teams suck," Angela replied with a laugh. "Maybe if you gave it more time?"

"Well, the real reason is, Brigette called a few weeks ago. She broke it off with the other guy. Said she missed me. Realized she'd made a mistake. We want to give it another shot."

"That's wonderful. When do you leave?"

"Next week."

"So soon? And you're just telling me now?"

"Yeah, sorry about that. I didn't know how to tell you. You are probably the only reason I would have stayed."

"Aw, that's sweet. What do you plan to do there? Back on the force?"

"Not sure yet, but that's what I would like to do."

"You will be missed, Paul."

"I'll miss you too. You can always call me, you know."

She nodded. If he had observed closely, he would have noticed the misty eyes.

"So, how about that movie?"

"Let's do it."

"Awesome! Good night, Angela."

"Good night, Paul."

THE END

Thank you for reading!

If you enjoyed this book, please leave a review.
Reviews help more readers find me and my work, so a positive review
can be very helpful and is appreciated.

To learn more about me and my work, visit my website, https://www.
vineetvermaauthor.com/ or my Facebook page, https://www.
facebook.com/VineetVermaAuthor/. You can also sign up for my
newsletter to receive the latest updates, details about my writing, and
other interesting tidbits.

Curious about what Paul does next? Check out my short
story, *The Stick*, on Amazon.

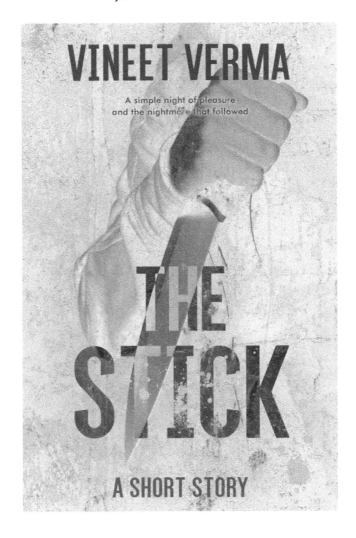

CPSIA information can be obtained
at www.ICGtesting.com
Printed in the USA
FSHW010920200221
78789FS